Dangerous

Alycia Linwood

Copyright © 2011 by Alycia Linwood

First Printing, 2013

Cover Stock Images Copyright: ©Depositphotos.com

ISBN-13: 978-1491092378
ISBN-10: 1491092378

Dedicated to my dear friend, Gray, who has been my greatest support.

Chapter 1

Magic has always existed in every part of our planet. No one knows when and how people acquired it. There are many legends and stories about it, but it's hard to tell if any of them contain some truth.

The best known is the story of God of Magic, who came to our planet many years ago and gave every human being control over one of the four main elements: fire, water, air, or earth. The magic ability was supposed to help people and make their lives easier, or at least that was what God of Magic wanted.

People were very grateful for God's generous gift and agreed to follow the only rule he gave them. And that was the rule that elements shouldn't mix. Ever.

Ah, how I wish it had stayed like that, but no. People had to be people and ignore the rule.

A few hundred years ago, people were still worshipping God of Magic, and they were carefully choosing the person to start a family with. But the world began to change; people discovered science and some stopped believing in God of Magic, claiming that all the stories they were told had been invented. According to them, magic is just in our nature, a part of our genetic code.

But science wasn't the only reason people stopped following the rule. The difference between the rich and poor was growing, and people had trouble finding the right partner, because the social status became as important as an element when it came to choosing a person to spend the rest of your life with. As a result, only a few people could have gotten married, and that made the rest of the population really unhappy.

No matter what their reasons were, people started having families with those who had different elements. But they didn't expect there would be horrible consequences. The children whose parents had a different element inherited only one of the elements, but much weaker than the original one.

By further mixing the already weakened elements, children who didn't have any kind of an element were born. Not having an element isn't exactly the worst thing in the world; the worst is the disease that was created in the process. Apparently, some kind of a genetic mistake occurred in a few cases, and because of it, people who didn't have an element wanted to have one really badly, which turned them into cold-blooded murderers.

Today known as magic disease carriers, they have the urge to kill someone with an element to get it for themselves. Of course, once they start killing and feel the joy of an element in them, they can't stop. And because an element can't stay in their system for long, they have to kill again.

When the first cases of magic disease appeared, they caused panic all over the world. But that was nothing compared to what happened when it was discovered that magic disease is contagious. People were so afraid of getting the disease that they decided that anyone who showed the symptoms should be killed.

At that time, many people were killed simply because someone had accused them of having the disease. There almost wasn't any way to prove you didn't have the disease, except to show your own magic ability, which was a problem for those with a weak or nonexistent *element. Luckily, those days are behind us, and there are special laws and police today to take care of the 'magic disease carriers' problem.*

But thirteen years ago, even special police couldn't do much to avoid a big incident when it was discovered that one of the richest and most influential families actually had the disease. Mr. Liandre, like every great businessman, managed to hide all the murders he and his wife had committed over the years. Maybe they would have never been discovered if he hadn't made a mistake and killed a member of another famous family.

Even though the special police was sent to take care of that matter, people were too outraged to let it go and went to burn down Mr. Liandre's house. I don't remember much of it, though, but it must have been horrible. Today, no one really wants to remember or mention that incident, and it's better like that.

There are still many questions left about magic disease, and scientists are trying to find a cure or simply find out more about the disease. Just a few years ago, it was discovered that the disease could actually be transmitted only by sexual contact. It couldn't even be transmitted by blood, which puzzled the scientists a lot. Well, I guess magic disease simply doesn't have any logic.

My best friend Paula is determined to change things. She has always wanted to become a scientist and discover a cure for magic disease. For that reason, she decided to take Biology and Genetics at the University of Magic. Yeah, it's the same university I'm going to, just I didn't choose anything as complicated as that, so with obligatory Magic Studies, I picked History and Geography.

I've always loved history and tradition. Actually, my family is in one third of the population that still has a pure element. I wouldn't have gotten into the University of Magic if it weren't so. The university only accepts the best, and I'm proud that Paula and I are among them.

I developed my family's element, fire, when I was sixteen. Yeah, it was a bit later than usual, but I had never really been afraid I wouldn't develop it. Paula got her element, air, like three years before me, even though she is six months younger, but she was being nice about it and didn't show off with it in front of me.

Of course, we don't really know much about using our elements because that is what the university is for. I really hope to learn more than just setting something on fire. Like I've said before, I strongly believe in keeping elements pure and enjoying in them...

"Ms. Milanez?" I heard my professor's voice and realized he must have asked me something, and I hadn't responded. Great, I was always so lost in my thoughts.

"Um, yes?" It was my first week at the university and the professor already knew my name. But that wasn't strange since he probably knew my father or had heard of my family. My father was more than generous when it came to giving donations to the university.

"Answer the question, miss," he said. Yeah, I would totally answer it if I knew what it was about. Too bad Magic Studies consisted of a theoretical and practical part, and we were stuck with theory. Would they ever let us do something with the damn magic?

"I don't know," I said.

"The question or the answer?" The professor raised his eyebrows at me expectantly, and the whole class was watching me in silence. Oh, just perfect.

"The answer." I thought it was better to say I didn't know the answer than admit I hadn't been paying attention.

"You don't know what happens to a person with the magic ability when one gets magic disease?" He glared at me incredulously. Oh, crap. Of course I knew. Everyone knew that one.

"Sorry, I forgot," I lied and flashed him a smile, hoping he'd let it go.

"Well, Ms. Milanez, it can be a serious problem if you truly don't know," he said. Some students started giggling, and I frowned. What the hell? Why was he making such a big deal out of it? But I still couldn't just let it go.

"Are you implying that I'm lying?" I asked.

"Of course not." The corners of his mouth turned up, and he looked around the classroom for the next victim. I so hated that guy.

"Miss Arnolds? Perhaps you could enlighten your friend," he said, looking at Paula. I had to count to ten to stop myself from getting up, walking out of the class, or setting him on fire. He could have said anything else he wanted, and it wouldn't have bothered me, but asking my best friend… No, this guy totally had something against me.

"Someone who gets magic disease loses their element," Paula said. "The disease destroys it completely."

"Correct!" he said, giving me a meaningful look. Seriously, he was driving me crazy, and I didn't understand what the hell magic disease had to do with this class. He finally let it go, and I went back to my thoughts, even though I knew I shouldn't.

I wanted to think happy thoughts, but I couldn't stop thinking about the stupid magic disease question. I was glad that at least Paula had ended up looking like the smart one, because she really was a genius. She would undoubtedly discover something important connected with magic disease someday.

I didn't know if it was worth it to research magic disease. Many people didn't have an element already, but some were so scared of the disease that they had decided to abandon their element. Yeah, giving up your element was actually possible. So everyone who wanted to do it could simply avoid using the element when it first appeared and let a year pass. And just like that, the element was gone. I had no idea how people managed to do it, because the desire to use an element for the first time was really strong.

Of course, thinking that soon there wouldn't be anyone with the magic ability was crazy, but it still worried me sometimes.

"Ria! Come on!" Paula's voice brought me back to the present. I realized the class was over. Wow, that was truly a relief. I was on my feet in an instant.

"Let's go!" I smiled at Paula, who was watching me carefully with her blue-green eyes.

"What were you thinking about?" Paula asked as we were walking down the hallway.

"What?"

"In class... You seemed to be completely in another place."

"Oh, that." I waved my hand. "The class was too boring, that's all."

"I know! I can't wait until we get to the practical part." Her full lips curved upward.

"Yeah. I wish we could just skip this." I yawned. Really, I could have lived without that class. We were just about to enter the lunchroom when I saw a guy. Okay, not just a guy, but a super extra hot and cute guy. He had such gorgeous wavy brown hair, which was cut short, and I wanted really badly to run my fingers through it. His eyes seemed to be the warmest green I'd ever seen, and the green sweater he was wearing fit almost perfectly with them.

He wasn't much taller than me, and his skin was a bit paler than mine. Oh, he was just perfect. I really wished I could go up to him and say something, but I knew I'd be too nervous. Suddenly Paula caught my arm to stop me and turned in the hot guy's direction. My heart nearly stopped.

"Hey!" Paula smiled at the guy, and I froze. No way. There was no way she could know him. But that was Paula; always charming and friendly.

"Hey, Paula!" He grinned, showing his perfectly white teeth. I couldn't believe he knew her! And he seemed genuinely happy to see her. Of course, which guy wouldn't be? She was tall, slim, had long curly blonde hair, and her eyes were a beautiful mix of blue and green. I was just an average-looking girl with my long straight dark brown hair and dark brown eyes.

"This is my best friend, Ria," Paula said, and the guy's eyes turned to me. He flashed me a smile, and I felt warmth coming into my cheeks.

"Ria, this is Michael," she said. Michael offered me his hand and I took it, hoping that I could at least shake hands with him without fainting or doing something equally embarrassing. I had no idea why I was feeling like that.

"Nice to meet you, Ria," he said.

"You, too." I managed to smile and look more or less

normal, even though my heart was doing a happy dance inside my chest.

"Oh, Ria, I forgot my book! I'll be right back," Paula said, her eyes twinkling, and went down the hallway. I stared after her, wondering if she had really left the book, or if it was so obvious that I liked Michael. But even if it were, she still shouldn't have made such a silly excuse.

"So, how do you like it here?" he asked.

"It's fine, I guess." I shrugged. "Hard to tell after a few days. You're not the first year, are you?" I was totally guessing that since I figured I would have seen him before if he were.

"Nope, second actually." A smile touched his lips.

Now I was wondering how the hell Paula had met this guy, and, more importantly, where I had been then. "Oh, good. Did you pass all the exams from the first year? I really hope it isn't anything hard."

"Yeah, I did," he said. "Passing Literature and History was easy since the program was very interesting. Magic Studies are definitely the hardest thing to pass, even though it doesn't seem so at first."

Yay, History! We had something in common. But hey, passing all the exams and studying Literature and History proved that he wasn't just hot; he was smart too. "It's the professor, isn't it?" I asked. "I bet he doesn't let anyone pass because he's a frustrated old freak."

"The Magic Studies professor? Actually, he's one of the best professors ever." His face was serious. Oops, I'd totally screwed this up, hadn't I?

"Really?" Warmth crept up my face. "Maybe I just got a wrong first impression."

He laughed, and I didn't understand why.

"Don't worry, many students hate him, but that doesn't mean he's a bad guy," he said.

"Yeah, right." How can someone who had embarrassed me in front of everyone be a good guy? Ah, whatever, it didn't really matter.

"What's your element?" He tilted his head.

"Fire."

Something changed in his eyes, but his face remained smiling and happy. "Oh, nice."

"And yours?"

"Water," he said, and I froze. No, it couldn't be. I had thought he was perfect… That we could have something… But no, we weren't meant to be… at all.

"Oh." I couldn't say nice like he had. I just couldn't. Paula came back right at that moment, and I was grateful.

"What happened?" Paula eyed us carefully, all her cheerfulness gone. I looked at Michael and realized that he wasn't smiling anymore either.

"Nothing," Michael and I said at the same time. I even managed a small smile.

"Ooookay." A smile spread across Paula's face again. "Let's go to lunch!"

The three of us were sitting at the table, eating something that I wasn't really sure was food. My pizza had a strange taste to it, but I was hungry. Paula was talking most of the time, and Michael sometimes nodded or smiled, just like me. I'd had no idea that the revelation that Michael and I had different elements would affect me so much, but it did. It was weird to feel like that about a total stranger.

"…and then he asked me the same question," Paula said, and Michael laughed. It took me a moment to realize she was talking about what had happened today in class. I couldn't believe her!

"Ah, so that's why you hate him!" Michael said. "I completely understand you now."

"Really?" I rolled my eyes, but he looked serious. Paula just winked at me when Michael wasn't looking. She totally had some weird plan going on in her head, but I didn't understand what it was.

"Do you know Michael's element is water?" I turned to Paula, expecting some kind of a reaction, but nothing happened.

"Yup, I do. It's awesome, right?"

I was really surprised by her answer and even more curious about her plan. "When did you guys meet?" I asked.

"A year ago," she said, and I stared at her in surprise.

"How?"

"On the Internet." Amusement crept into her eyes. "Well, we hadn't realized at first that I was going to go to this university, too, but we figured it out like two weeks ago."

"Wait, you met him on the Internet?" I raised an eyebrow. "Isn't that, like… dangerous?"

"Yes, it is." Michael chuckled. "I'm a total maniac who wants to kill you and your friend. Be afraid!"

We all laughed. It was really hard to think of him as a maniac, especially when he was being so sweet and funny. Suddenly I felt as if someone was watching me, and I looked around. I saw some guy looking straight at me, and I involuntarily shivered. There seemed to be something so cold about him... and I realized what it was. His eyes. I had a feeling like a wolf was watching me, because his eyes were a pale blue or gray color – it was hard to tell from the distance.

He was actually sitting on the table, and he was dressed in dark blue jeans and a black shirt. His short messy hair was almost blacker than the shirt, and I was suddenly glad I hadn't run into him in the dark. The three guys around him were talking about something, but he didn't pay any attention to them. He was staring right at me, and then he smiled. I gasped and averted my gaze. Paula and Michael both looked in the direction of the guy, and Michael frowned.

"Who is that?" I whispered to him because he obviously knew the guy.

"Adrian Liandre."

"Liandre?" I frowned. "The Liandre?"

"Yes," he said quietly, "the son of the most famous magic disease carriers."

"But it can't be!" My mouth went slack. "Wasn't he supposed to be... I don't know... dead?"

"Only his parents were killed, not him," Michael said.

"But it's a hundred percent sure he has the disease! Why is he here? He's dangerous!" I tried really hard to keep my voice as low as possible, even though I wanted to yell.

"He hasn't done anything yet, and he's here because they believe they can keep an eye on him easier. Besides, his guardian works here," Michael said.

"Huh, so they are basically waiting for him to kill

someone here?" I rolled my eyes. "That's so awesome. Really."

"It's strange you haven't seen him before. He should be in your Magic Studies class," Michael said. "He's in the first year again because he failed everything."

"Oh come on! That's not fair!" I was getting really angry and starting to think about calling my father and telling him about this. But I didn't want to do it. Especially because it had been my father who had told me I would learn here that I couldn't always get and do whatever I wanted. Besides, he had probably known it all along.

"Yeah, it's stupid that he has to take the theoretical part of Magic Studies. It's useless because he doesn't have an element." Michael was actually clenching his fists.

I realized that Paula wasn't saying anything, so I looked in her direction. She was staring at Adrian with an almost fascinated expression on her face. Okay, I could admit that the guy wasn't bad-looking at all, but he was still creepy as hell.

"Paula," I said, but she didn't hear me. "Paula!"

"What?" She looked at me as if she saw me for the first time. I waved my hands in front of her face.

"Who's absent-minded now?" I smiled at her.

"Oh, sorry. I was just thinking how I could use him for my research…"

My eyes widened. "Are you insane? Even if he would help you, which I doubt, no one here would let you do the research."

"I know." A look of disappointment appeared on her face. I felt compelled to tell her she could do her research or whatever she wanted, but I kept my mouth shut.

Instead, I glanced at Adrian. He wasn't looking in our direction because a man who looked like a professor was approaching him.

"That's Alan," Michael said, pointing at the man. "I forgot his last name because he wants us all to call him by his first name. You go to him if you have problems or if you do something wrong. Oh, and he was there when Adrian's parents were killed, and he's actually Adrian's guardian."

"Aaah, so if Adrian kills me, I go haunt that man. Cool," I said. We all burst into laughter.

When I looked back at Adrian, he rolled his eyes at something that Alan was saying to him and then got up, took his things, and they walked out of the room together. I noticed some girls were watching Adrian with adoring eyes – something I completely couldn't understand – and when he was gone, they were giggling.

"Why are they acting like that?" I frowned at the girls. "I have a feeling like I'm stuck in high school again."

"Yeah, well, this is not a normal university." Michael smiled, then his face became serious again. "You'll have to get used to the fact that Adrian is quite a celebrity here. Girls obviously love danger."

"Yeah, they can't wait to get killed or get the disease." I rolled my eyes. "Well, let them try. Maybe we'll get rid of him sooner."

Michael just offered me a smile, and Paula didn't look very approving of my comment. I just shrugged and continued to eat my already cold pizza.

Chapter 2

I was sitting on the bed in Paula's room, waiting for her to collect all the books and notebooks that she needed for class. Mine were already in my black leather bag, which I had thrown on the orange round carpet as soon as I had come in. I was a bit disappointed that we were having Magic Studies again, but at least I got to go with Paula.

Last week had been really crazy, even without the big revelation about the magic disease carrier at the university. I hadn't seen him since that day, and I was glad, but something told me that he'd be in today's class. I simply wasn't feeling lucky.

"Have you talked to someone about changing your room?" Paula asked as she stuffed the books into her blue backpack.

I shook my head. "I wasn't sure who to ask. Besides, I don't feel like doing anything today."

I still hadn't gotten used to living at the university. It was weird not to be in my old room in my parents' house. We had our own rooms here, and they were pretty big and nice, but the one I got was on the completely opposite part of the building from Paula's, and um, Michael's too.

"Talk to Alan. He'll help you," she said.

"Alan? Adrian's guardian?" My eyebrows shot upward.

"Sure! Don't look at him as Adrian's guardian, because he's not just that. I've already spoken to him. He's quite nice."

"You actually spoke to him?"

"Yes, this morning. I wanted to ask him something about my research."

"And?" I wondered if she had really asked Alan about something as delicate as the magic disease research. But I guessed she couldn't have asked him that directly anyway.

"Well, I asked him if I could use the laboratory sometimes for homework tasks," she said. "I told him I might want to test some theories and things that we'd be learning about, too."

"Wow, you never fail to impress me! And he believed you?" I laughed.

"Sure. He said he would ask my professor about it, and maybe if I proved to be a great student and really interested in learning more, they might allow me to use the laboratory outside class." She couldn't help but smile.

"That's awesome!" I went to hug her.

"Oh, we're going to be late! Come on!" she said after a few moments. I let go of her and picked up my bag, thinking about Alan. Maybe I should go talk to him… or maybe not.

Paula and I made it to the classroom just in time. My *favorite* professor still wasn't there, and tension left my shoulders, because at least I wouldn't be getting any of his lovely comments about coming late. I didn't know why I assumed he would do such a thing.

But I didn't even need the annoying professor to make my day worse. My nightmare was here. Adrian Liandre was sitting on one of the desks near the window and obviously flirting with some blonde girl.

She was smiling so sweetly and innocently at him that it was making me sick. Seriously, what was wrong with this girl? Wasn't she afraid the disease could choose this very moment to show and she would be the first in danger? I found an empty seat as far away from him as I could, and exactly at that moment, the professor stormed in. Oh yeah, this was going to be a loooong day.

Adrian jumped off the desk and casually slid into his chair. Of course, he didn't miss the chance to smile at the blonde, who was sitting two desks away from him. Damn, I felt as if I were in some kind of a twisted soap opera.

The class was boring... again. I didn't care what Michael had said about the professor not being so bad because he was wrong. But every time I thought about Michael... Well, that was another story. I still thought he was insanely hot, even though he couldn't really be my romantic interest. And despite everything, I still hoped to see him again and find out more about him.

"Ms. Milanez?" I heard the professor's voice and cursed everyone and everything in my mind at that moment. This so couldn't be happening again.

"Yes?" I said, bracing myself for another catastrophe.

"Could you set the paper in this bowl on fire, please?"

"What?" I was completely taken aback.

"If I remember correctly, your element is fire. So, could you, please, set the paper on fire for the demonstration?" He placed the bowl with the paper on my desk.

"Um, okay," I said, concentrating on that part inside of me that contained my element. It was hard to explain how I was doing it, but I felt warmth all over me and focused on the bowl with the paper. A few seconds later, reddish flames were coming out of the bowl, and it made me smile.

Everyone in the classroom was looking at me curiously. I guess I would be looking at someone else using their element too, because there was simply something special about an element being used around you. I had felt this strange tingling sensation before when Paula had been demonstrating her powers in front of me.

I looked up from the flames I had made, and the professor continued talking about something connected with fire. I was still slightly smiling, proud that I hadn't embarrassed myself again. But my smile faded as I saw Adrian staring at the flames from across the room. There was an awkward grimace on his face, as if he were barely containing himself… and then his eyes met mine.

I was completely sure at that moment that the look in his eyes made me feel colder than I would have felt if someone had thrown icy water over me. I wanted to look away, but I couldn't. He didn't smile at me this time; he just angrily pressed his lips together.

I didn't know what to do, and I guess I panicked. It must have shown on my face because the professor was addressing Adrian next.

"Mr. Liandre, is there a problem?"

"No," Adrian said through his teeth and finally looked away from me. A huge wave of relief washed over me, and I could finally relax in my chair. But I was still feeling as if icy cold fingers were pinching my skin. I wanted to get out of the classroom as soon as I could, and that was what I did when the professor told us we could go. I didn't even wait for Paula.

"Ria!" Paula was calling my name, but I didn't want to stop walking. At least not until I was safe in my room and out of Adrian's sight.

"Ria! What's wrong with you?" Paula yelled as she closed the door of my room. Good. I was feeling much better here, sitting on my bed. Paula was looking at me for a long moment, expecting an answer or maybe even an apology.

"That was... scary," I finally said, and she sat on the bed next to me, putting her hand on mine. I looked at her, and some kind of a realization flashed through her eyes.

"Oh, I'm so sorry," she suddenly said. "Adrian scared you, didn't he?"

"A bit." I nodded. "He was looking at me as if I had taken something valuable from him... and he would kill me for it."

"You're overreacting." Her lips curved into a smile. "But I'm starting to see your point about that professor being an asshole."

"What?" I gaped at her. Was I really overreacting? And why was she talking about the professor now? That didn't make sense.

"Yup, I can see it now. What he did to Adrian was simply mean."

I blinked at her. I had no idea what the hell she was talking about. "Mean to *Adrian*?"

"Yeah. Everyone knows that people with magic disease have it much harder to control themselves around elements that are being used. And they let Adrian take the theoretical part of Magic Studies simply because elements aren't supposed to be used during it. Don't you get what the professor has done?" There was a hint of anger in her voice. "And he chose to demonstrate only fire, aware of the fact that Adrian hates it."

"So, you're saying that the professor tried to provoke Adrian to … What? Get him to attack someone?" Or maybe he'd wanted to provoke Adrian to kill *me*. But I didn't want to say that in front of Paula because it sounded very silly and egoistic.

"Yes, well… I believe he was trying to get him to lose control. Maybe he doesn't want him in his class."

"How do you know Adrian hates fire?" I watched her carefully, wondering whether there was something more than just her research that made her so interested in that monster.

"They burned his house… and his parents in front of him!" Tears formed in her eyes.

"So? They totally deserved it," I said. "Besides, they didn't set them on fire to kill them. They were already dead, right?"

"Yes, but…" She took a deep breath. "It was still cruel! And Adrian had to watch that. How can you be so cold-hearted?"

"I'm not cold-hearted! I just can't feel pity for someone who is going to turn into a killer soon. He inherited all of his parents' money and has a nice life. I wonder if he gets girls into his bed with that story. Don't tell me you're falling under his charm, too."

"I'm not!" She crossed her arms.

I just smiled.

"I'm not!" She raised her voice. "But I'm going to ask him to help me with my research."

"You're crazy. He's not going to help you."

"Why not? I might find a cure for the disease," she said. "He'll want to help me."

"All right, maybe he will. But not for free."

"What does that mean?" She frowned.

"It means that he might help you if you sleep with him."

Her face paled and she looked disgusted. "I would never do that."

"I know," I said. "That's why I'm sure you won't get him to help you."

"You really think some girls slept with him?" she asked after a moment of silence.

"Yes, I do." And yes, I did think that. Girls seemed to be very fascinated with him, and since everyone kept saying you could get the disease only during unprotected sex, they had probably figured they weren't in danger if they used a condom. Yeah, they were *really* smart.

"I'm still going to ask him," she said quietly. "Maybe he's not who you think he is."

Who *I* think? She clearly had a different opinion about him, but I didn't want to push it. Soon enough she'd see what kind of a bastard he was. I was sure of it. "Will you come to the library with me?" I wanted to change the subject really badly. "I need some books for my homework."

"Um, I can't. Sorry. I need to do something," she said. "But I'm sure Michael would go with you if you asked him nicely."

"Whoa, whoa, slow down." I raised my hands. "If I didn't know better, I would say you are trying to set me up with him."

"Come on! I know you like him." She laughed.

"But I can't be with him!"

"Why not? You can't have a good time because of the element thing?" Amusement gleamed in her eyes. "You could still date him, you know. It's not as if you have to marry him or anything."

"Then I don't see the point in it." I sighed.

"Oh, come on! You dated, like, five guys already, and you didn't get married to any of them, so where was the point in that?"

"But their element was fire actually, and I believed at some point that we were going to be forever," I said. "This would be... I don't know... useless."

"Yeah, yeah, whatever you say. But I still think you should go with him to the library, even just as friends. He's really awesome."

"Why don't you date him then if he's so awesome?" I teased.

"Because he's totally not my type." She laughed.

"Oh, and black-haired dangerous guys are exactly your type?"

"No!"

"I wouldn't agree with you."

"Hey, it's not funny!"

"Nope, it isn't funny at all," I said, jumping off the bed and grabbing my pillow. Paula realized what I was doing and she was on her feet in an instant, grabbing another pillow. It was time for a really awesome pillow fight!

"Someone's going to kill us!" Paula laughed as we sat down on the bed again, completely breathless. There were feathers all over the room, and of course, my pillows were completely unusable.

"No one's going to find out," I said, taking a feather out of Paula's hair. "Unless we go outside looking as if we had been on a chicken farm."

We both laughed, and I was wondering why the hell we still had feather pillows when there were better materials. But then we wouldn't be able to have so much fun with them.

"Oh, come on! You need new pillows and you'll have to explain what happened to your old ones," she said.

"I'm not going to tell anything to anyone. I know where they keep the pillows. I'll just throw this somewhere and steal new ones."

"Wow, the perfect crime." Paula laughed. "But I have to go now."

"Heey! Don't tell me you're going to leave me with all this mess." I grabbed her arm as she was getting up from the bed, but she just grinned at me.

"Fine! I'm going to find someone else to help me." I crossed my arms in fake indignation. She waved at me from the door and left. I looked around the room once again and sighed. I had soooo many things to do, and no, I wasn't brave enough to go ask someone to help me with the mess, especially not Michael.

It took me almost an hour to clean up all the feathers, and I was sure there were still some left under the bed. Yeah, running all over a huge room with half-ripped pillows hadn't been such a good idea after all.

But cleaning up wasn't the worst part; stealing new pillows was. When I finally found courage to leave my room and go pillow hunting, I almost bumped into Michael. My heart got stuck somewhere in my throat at the moment I looked up into his green eyes. Damn, he was just beyond gorgeous.

"Going somewhere?" He smiled at me.

"Um, yeah," I said, trying to look casual and failing.

"You're blushing," he teased. "Will you tell me what you're up to? Because I'm sure you're up to something."

"Hey!" The corners of my lips went upward. "Well… If I tell you, you'll have to help me."

"Really?" He raised his eyebrows. "Is it dangerous?"

"Very."

"Oh, then I'm in."

"Great!" I was ecstatic. "Oh, and don't laugh when I tell you what we're going to do."

He just eyed me suspiciously, and for a moment, I was thinking about inventing something more interesting to do, but I couldn't come up with anything.

"We need to steal some pillows from the storeroom," I said, immediately feeling stupid.

"Steal some pillows?" I thought he was going to start laughing like crazy, but he didn't.

"Yeah. I need new ones."

"And what happened to your old ones?" he asked. "Something so bad that you can't simply ask for new ones?"

"Um yeah, something like that. But not really bad. It was more like... childish."

"Aaah," he said, "then it must have been so much fun that people here wouldn't understand."

"Pillow fight with Paula," I whispered into his ear. He immediately started to laugh.

"Yeah, Alan and the others so wouldn't understand that," he said, still smiling.

"Great, let's go get some pillows!" I said, and we went down the hallway.

Actually, it turned out to be really easy to get new pillows because there was no one really *guarding* the storeroom, and there was no one in the hallway since at this time most people were in class, the library, or outside.

But we still grabbed the pillows and ran like crazy down the hallway, afraid that someone might show up. When we reached my room, we were breathless and still high on adrenaline. It was funny how such a trivial thing had brought the hottest guy ever into my room.

For a moment, the irrational part of my brain was telling me to get closer to him, maybe even kiss him and then blame the moment. And I would have done it... if I were in a movie or something. In a movie, Michael would have kissed me back and we would realize how we loved each other forever. Unfortunately for me, my life wasn't a movie. While I was busy thinking, Michael had moved away from the door and was now sitting on my bed.

"I see you were careful enough to keep the pillow covers safe." He chuckled.

"Yeah." I flushed. "Didn't want to rip that, too."

"Well, this was fun. Anything else you need?"

"Um." I hesitated. "There is this one thing... But I don't want to bother you."

"I'd say it wouldn't bother me, but I can't since I don't know what it is." His green eyes shined like two emeralds.

"It's my History homework, actually," I said and immediately felt bad. What could he be thinking about me? Probably that I was just using him.

"Oh, sure. I can help you with that."

"Um, forget it. It doesn't matter. I can do it on my own."

He got up, looking simply devastatingly handsome in his blue jeans and a light blue shirt, and came closer to me. "It's okay. I was heading to the library when you showed up anyway, so we could just go there now, and I can show you where to find the right books. I know my way around here better than you do, okay?"

"All right." His kindness brought a smile to my face, and as we were leaving the room, I wondered if he really was so perfect or some sick part of my mind made him look like that to me so I would fall in impossible love. Oh well, I had all the time in the world, or more like a few years, to find out.

Chapter 3

I was sitting in the library, chatting with Michael and checking out some of the books, when I saw Paula standing at the door. She looked… horrible. Tears were streaming freely down her face, and I immediately got up, glancing at Michael. He just nodded at me in understanding, and I hurried over to Paula before anyone else could see her.

I was glad that people were mostly busy with their books; we so didn't need others to bother us. I just took Paula's shaking hand and led her to my room since it was closer than hers was.

"What happened?" I asked when we were sitting on the bed.

"I… I asked him…" she whispered, "and he… he…"

Suddenly I had a moment of realization; she had asked Adrian to help her with her research. He had probably refused just as I had expected.

"Oh, Paula." I hugged her. "Adrian is an asshole and we all know it. But why are you crying? You can do your research without him. It's not the end of the world."

"He… he said I was stupid." She hiccuped. "…and that he didn't care about my research anyway, but that he would help… if I… gave him what he wanted…"

"That son of a bitch! I'm going to kill him!" I said, trying to get up, but Paula wouldn't let go of me. I was beyond pissed. No one made my friends cry. No one.

"No," she cried. "No, don't! I was stupid to think he would just…"

"No! This isn't about you! It's him!" I was yelling and I didn't care if someone could hear it outside.

"No, I was wrong to go to him just like that and ask such a huge favor," she said, and I was glad that she had at least stopped crying, but her weird way of thinking completely puzzled me.

"Oh, that's it! You stay here and I'm going to deal with…" I was saying as someone knocked on the door and opened it before I said it was okay. Huh, that was so not nice.

"Is everything all right?" Alan asked. Oh, perfect, Adrian's guardian was here. I opened my mouth to say what Adrian had done to Paula, but she was faster.

"Everything's fine," she said.

"Are you sure?" His brow was drawn in concern. "Have you been crying?"

"Um, I'm fine, really. It's just… I had an argument with my boyfriend." She actually smiled a little.

"Since when is…" I started to say, but Paula actually put her hand over my mouth and removed it a moment later, but it was enough to stop me from speaking. Alan frowned, but probably decided we were just crazy girls.

"Well, if you need to talk, you know where to find me." Alan's lips spread into a smile. I glared at him because that was just plain weird. I knew he was supposed to be like some kind of a counselor, but to discuss students' relationships… That was just too weird.

Paula nodded and thanked him. I hoped he would leave, because I was prepared to go out and hunt down Adrian. Even set him on fire. Yeah, I wasn't really rational when I was mad.

"Oh, Ms. Milanez," Alan said, "I need you to come down to my office so we can talk about something."

"Um, all right," I said, even though I had no idea what the hell he wanted to talk about. Maybe he wanted to talk about Paula, or maybe that asshole of a professor had said something about me. The first one was much more likely, because the professor had seemed just fine with me today.

"Now," he added, and I frowned. Oh, come on! I had better things to do! But I couldn't use 'I have to kill someone first' as an excuse, so I just got up.

"Are you going to be okay?" I asked Paula. She gave me a small smile, and then I had no other choice but to follow Alan.

Alan's office was very small and almost claustrophobic. There was just a desk, which was taking up most of the space, Alan's black leather chair behind it, and two red ones in front of it. The walls were completely white and plain, and I was surprised there wasn't even the university's crest. Damn, this room was creepy.

"So, Ms. Milanez... May I call you Ria?" He looked at me expectantly.

"Um, sure." I wasn't really happy about it, but I assumed it would be awkward for me to call him by his first name if he couldn't call me by mine.

"Great! Ria, I want to talk to you about something that happened during the Magic Studies class."

Ah, I had so known that! He was eyeing me carefully, probably expecting me to start talking, but I kept my mouth shut. Instead, I decided to look at him more closely too.

I noticed that his hair was mostly dark brown, with a few strikes of gray showing. His brown eyes looked warm and kind, but there was also something else in them that I couldn't identify. And he definitely didn't fit in with the other professors and university staff because he was dressed in dark jeans and a light blue shirt, which was just too casual.

"I would like to know if it's true that your professor asked you to use your element in class," he said after he realized I wasn't going to say anything. I was surprised for a second that he wanted to know about that and not about something else. Or maybe this was just what he had thought of as a good start.

"Yeah, I was asked to demonstrate my element in class," I said.

"So it's true." He sighed in disappointment. I didn't know what to think. Had someone tried to accuse me of using my element without permission?

"And I thought he was lying to me," Alan said, and I knew he was thinking of Adrian. It was about Adrian, not me. Phew.

"Well, that's all I wanted to know, actually." A smile appeared on his lips. "Maybe you have something to ask me."

No matter how much I wanted to get out of this tiny space and go back to check on Paula, I decided that I did have questions. "Could you, please, help me with something?"

"Maybe," he said. "What is it?"

"Um, Paula is really depressed right now after everything that happened with her boyfriend, so I'm trying to find something to cheer her up. And since she really loves biology and doing research, I was thinking maybe you could give her permission to use the lab today or tomorrow."

Alan just looked at me for a moment, and I was wondering if he had somehow realized Paula didn't have a boyfriend. But it was her story anyway, and getting the lab to herself would certainly make her forget that idiot. Maybe Adrian's guardian could fix the damage Adrian had done.

"That's a good idea," he said. "She already asked me to give her access to the lab outside class, and that will have to wait. But a few hours there today couldn't hurt, I suppose."

"That would be awesome!" I grinned.

"Okay." He reached for something inside the pocket of his jeans. "No one uses the lab today, so I can give you the key. But you have to return it to me before eight this evening and make sure I don't regret it, all right?"

"Yes, thank you." I took the key from him. Damn, this was good.

"Paula! You'll never guess what I got!" I said when I was back in my room and found her still sitting on my bed. She looked up at me in surprise, and I waved the key in front of her.

"What's that?"

"Lab key!" I flashed her a smile. Her face lit up, but a moment later, she was eyeing me suspiciously.

"What? I thought you'd be happy."

"I am. But how did you get it?"

"Well, I didn't steal it," I said proudly. "Alan gave it to me for you. You can have the lab until eight as long as you're not doing anything dangerous."

"Really?" She was almost jumping up and down in childlike delight. "How did you do that?"

"Well, sweetie, he was worried about the depression you are going through because of *your boyfriend*." I laughed. "Even though I'm still not sure how Adrian came to be your boyfriend."

"Shit! Tell me you didn't say Adrian was my…" she said, panicking.

"No! Of course not! I'm just kidding. I know you invented that because you didn't have anything else to say. No one can find out what kind of research you are planning to do. I'm not stupid."

"Right." She hugged me. "Thank you! Thank you so much!"

"Hey, that's what friends are for." I gave her the key. "Enjoy your time in the lab!"

"Thanks, but I don't know where to start now." She sighed. "I wanted to take a look into Adrian's DNA, which I don't have."

"Oh, I'll get you his DNA… on my hand. After I punch him in the face."

"Ria!" she said disapprovingly.

"What? I'm still mad at him for making you cry."

"Just let it go." She glanced at her watch. "Oh, I have to go! The lab is waiting, but I guess I'll have to try to sneak into Adrian's room first."

"What?" I gaped at her. "What the hell are you talking about?"

"I need his DNA, and there's plenty of it in his room. I just need to make sure he's away and get some."

"Oh no, you're so not doing that!" That was a bad idea because I knew how nervous she would be, and if someone saw her, or he returned… I didn't even want to imagine that.

"But I have to!" she insisted.

"Ah, what the hell." I groaned. "You go to the lab, and I'll go to Adrian's room."

"No, you've already done enough. I can't ask this of you."

"I'm doing it," I said determinedly. "It would be pointless if you got in trouble, and then they wouldn't let you use the lab at all."

"All right," she said after considering it for a few moments. "I'm going to the lab, but if you can't get the DNA, it's fine. I'll find another way to start, okay?"

"Okay."

She smiled and went for the door. Damn, what had I gotten myself into?

"Wait!" I said, and she turned around, looking at me. "How am I supposed to get into his room without the key?"

"Oh, he never locks his room."

I wanted to ask her how the hell she knew that, but I figured I probably didn't want to know. "Um, okay," I said, and then she was gone.

Fifteen minutes had passed before I finally decided to leave my room and go near Adrian's. I was shaking a bit and my heart was thudding very loudly. I might have felt brave when I'd been angry, but that had passed out of my system already. Besides, thinking and talking about something was much different from actually doing it.

I was standing in front of the door, wondering whether Adrian was inside. I had no other way to check but to knock. I figured that if he opened the door, I'd just attack him because of what he had done to Paula. That was a completely reasonable thing to do, at least for me.

I took a deep breath and knocked really hard. It was a miracle the door hadn't opened by itself. After a few moments of waiting, I realized he probably wasn't there. I looked around, and when I was sure no one was in the hallway to see me, I slowly turned the knob.

It was dark in the room, and I felt as if I were going into a forest filled with monsters. I wondered what happened to the windows... if he actually had them. Somehow, it wouldn't surprise me if he were living in a room turned into a cave. There were high possibilities that there was a light switch somewhere on the wall to my left, but I didn't dare to turn the lights on. Instead, I just kept going forward, leaving the door a bit open so I could find it when it was time to leave.

Now that I was sure Adrian wasn't here, I finally relaxed, thinking hard how to find something with his DNA. I walked farther into the room and bumped into something. The slight pain in my leg told me that it was probably a desk or a bedpost. I felt around for something, but there was only a flat wooden surface. Great, he wasn't keeping anything on his desk. Not even books or notebooks. Oh, I'd almost forgotten; he didn't care about studying.

I was trying to move away from the desk and reach the bed when I felt movement behind my back. Letting out a startled gasp, I looked in the direction of the door and saw that it looked just like I had left it. I waited for a moment, completely still, not even breathing. I had probably imagined it all.

Just as I turned around, I had a strong feeling someone was observing me in the darkness. I felt like a trapped animal in a predator's lair. But I was sure it was just my mind playing with me. Surely, no one could have been so quiet to…

Someone grabbed me from behind into a tight embrace. A scream got stuck in my throat, and I shivered. It took me a moment to start thinking clearly again through all the fear I felt. Adrian must have returned.

"I know who you are," he whispered, sniffing my hair. Oh, shit. Even if I wanted to, I couldn't move. He was too strong. And if I tried to set him on fire, I'd probably get burned too. My feeling of a trapped animal returned, except this time I pictured a wolf as the predator.

What I didn't understand was how he knew who I was in this darkness. Maybe he thought I was some girl he was supposed to meet. I thought his confusion might be my chance to escape, so I tried to squirm out of his embrace.

"Don't... do that... Ria," he said, and I froze. How the fuck did he know? I was sure I had to escape as soon as possible, so I tried to kick him. But he was too close; close enough that I could smell his cologne, which was a mix of pine, musk, and some other tree scents that I couldn't quite identify.

"I know it's you. I got a good taste of your element in class," he purred into my ear, and I felt something cold pressing against my neck. Oh, shit! He had a knife! I didn't even have time to think how interesting it was that he could not only tell which element someone had, but also make a distinction between them. People with elements couldn't do any of that.

I finally found my voice, and said, "Let go of me."

"But why would I do such a thing? You came to me."

No, I hadn't. But I didn't know what to say.

"I know this game very well," he said. "There are always a few girls who accept the bet."

"The bet?" I jerked my head back. What was he talking about? I didn't really care, but if he kept talking, maybe I could use the distraction and get free.

"Don't try to deny it. They dared you to come here and try to kiss me," he said softly, "and you accepted."

Huh? Girls really did that? They were sooooo dumb. Oh, wait. Did he expect me to… kiss him? Ewww! Now I *really* had to get away. But the only way to get out seemed to be by playing his game. Besides, I didn't have a better excuse to explain why I had come to his room.

"Um, yeah," I said. He spun me around, putting both of his arms tightly around my waist. I couldn't see his face in the darkness, but I realized I had my hands pressed to his chest. And damn, I could feel some nice muscles under his shirt, but that wasn't the point. The point was that I could actually move my hands.

"Will you kiss me?" I said, trying to sound at least a bit sensual, but I failed. There was too much fear in my voice. I only managed to raise my hand and touch his face.

At that moment, I realized that the cold thing was no longer pressed against my neck and that it probably hadn't been a knife at all. I had no time to think what the hell it could have been, so I ran my fingers through his soft hair and suddenly pulled with all my strength.

He cursed, and his grip on me loosened. I pushed him aside with all my strength and ran for the door. I didn't stop running until I reached the lab.

Paula looked at me with wide eyes, and I, still breathless from running, showed her the lock of Adrian's hair I had managed to pull out.

"What did you do?" She gaped at me.

"I got his DNA." I smiled stupidly. "And now he's probably going to kill me."

She ran her fingers through her hair, speechless. I took a seat in one of the chairs and started telling her everything that had happened. I was in some serious trouble and I had no idea how to handle it.

Chapter 4

I was still sitting in the lab, watching Paula work. I might be scared of Adrian coming after me, but I didn't want Paula to miss her chance to do experiments. And according to the time on my phone, we had only two hours until the time when we were supposed to return the key to Alan.

"Damn," she said, breaking the silence.

I looked up at her in surprise. "What?"

"I can't find anything unusual!" She rubbed the back of her neck. I just shrugged, because this was totally not my thing. I probably couldn't even tell what she was looking at.

"Um, and there's supposed to be something unusual?" I said, half-expecting that she wouldn't answer.

"Yes! He isn't supposed to have an element, right? So, why the hell can't I see that damn gene missing?"

"Because it's not missing?" I said, and she actually looked up from the microscope and rolled her eyes at me.

"But that's not possible. It says in the book…" She stopped in the middle of the sentence and frowned. "Unless every disease case is different… or maybe because

Adrian hasn't shown the signs of the disease yet. But I'm sure he doesn't have an element, so…"

"But Adrian showed signs of the disease. He could actually feel my element. And we can't do that."

"Oh, right," she said. "But I can't find a book that contains a comparison of someone who has the DNA like one of us does, someone who doesn't have an element at all, and living magic disease carriers."

"Well, someone has probably done it in some part of the world. But it's not as if they are planning to share that knowledge with us. You know that this thing is still kind of a taboo. And maybe there's nothing to be compared since every case is different."

"Huh, maybe." She sighed. "But there has to be a reason why people who decided not to use their element simply gave up on it without consequences and people with magic disease are different."

"Don't you think they would have discovered it already if it were simple?"

"Yeah, but…" She sat down, a look of disappointment on her face. Crap, I didn't want to make her feel miserable again.

"Look, I'm sure you're going to figure out something," I said. "Just keep his DNA, because I don't feel like getting it again."

"Yeah, my first idea was wrong, but it's just the beginning."

"Great!" I grinned. "Now that we've solved that, can we go for my last coffee?"

"Last coffee?" She looked at me, her brows drawn together.

"Yeah, did you forget that Adrian is going to kill me? I sent my dad a message to get me out of here if he can't get Adrian to leave."

"What? Are you insane?" Paula yelled at me. "You can't leave! And neither can Adrian! Besides, he's not going to kill you! I thought you were joking when you said it the first time."

"You thought I was joking?" I glared at her. "I pulled some of his hair out! And if you add that to the fact that he's a murderer…"

"Ria, are you listening to yourself?" She came over to me, looking at me with her big eyes that looked completely blue under this light.

"Yeah, I am. But are you listening to me?"

"He's not a murderer! You can't blame him for having the disease!" She clenched her jaw.

"Fine, he hasn't killed anyone yet… as far as we know. You know what his parents did. For all I know, Alan could be covering up the killings for him. Hell, maybe it would even explain why you can't find the difference in the DNA."

Her body went rigid as she considered everything I had said. "Sometimes I think you have a heart made of stone," she finally said.

"Yeah, heard it already, and oh sorry, I forgot. Poor little innocent boy tragically lost his parents thirteen years ago and he has the disease he totally didn't deserve! Let's all cry for him, kiss him, and make it all better," I said cynically. "Maybe even help him kill someone or spread the disease so he can get through all that suffering. Damn it,

Paula, I have already told you, he has and does anything he wants. There's no need to feel sorry for him!"

She pressed her lips together, turned her back to me, and walked out of the lab. Great, just fucking great.

My phone rang just as I was going out of the lab. It was my dad. Oh, goodie.

"Hey, Dad," I said, walking to the end of the hallway because it was less likely for someone to overhear me there.

"Ria, honey! I got your message. What happened?" He sounded worried. "I'd have called Alan immediately, but I had to know the details first. Tell me. Are you hurt?"

"Um no, I'm fine." Damn, I hadn't thought about what I was going to say when I sent that message. So dumb and so typical of me. Could I tell my father that I'd gone into a boy's room? Adrian Liandre's room of all? And pulled out some of his hair for my best friend's illegal experiment? Yeah… right.

"Honey, are you sure?"

"Yeah, actually… about this whole thing…" I said. "I kind of invented it because I miss you and Mom."

I could deal with Adrian Liandre by myself. Letting him intimidate me had probably been a big mistake, and yeah, I simply felt brave when he wasn't around. Just the usual.

"Oh, Ria." My father sighed. "I know you miss us, and we miss you, too. But we can't come to see you this weekend. Maybe your brother could…"

"No!" I nearly yelled. I didn't want to see my brother. Hell, I didn't even want to hear about him. He was twelve years older than me and we never got along.

Besides, he was always away from home for school or something.

"Okay, okay," he said. "Do you need anything? I can send you whatever you want."

"No, I don't need anything. Sorry I bothered you."

"Are you sure you don't need anything?" he persisted. Okay, when he wanted to talk, maybe I could ask something smart for a change.

"Um, do you think someone will find a cure for magic disease?" I said, wondering why I had never discussed this with him.

"Why do you ask such a silly question? Those people don't deserve to live! The last thing we need is for someone to spend money and time on finding a cure when we can simply wipe them all out. Too bad the government changed the law! Anyone who doesn't have an element doesn't deserve to live."

He actually had a point. And even though I didn't really mind people who didn't care about their element, they were still putting us all in danger. I didn't want to die because some morons had decided to mix their elements and created a murderer in the process. But still, I supported Paula because she was my best friend, and if she wanted to find a cure, then why not? I didn't really care that our parents were against it.

"Just wondering," I said. "Because of Adrian being here and everything."

"Don't worry, honey. If that bastard shows any sign of the disease, no matter how small, you call me, and he's gone," he said, and I believed him.

"Sure, but I don't think it'll be that easy to get rid of Adrian…" I turned around and nearly dropped my phone. Adrian was standing just a few inches away from me, looking grim. Oh, come on! My life was turning into some stupid horror movie!

"I have to go. Call you later." I ended the call and slid the phone into my jeans pocket.

"Ah, so that's your plan." He smiled bitterly, taking a step forward, so he ended up almost touching me. I didn't back away or try to run. I didn't even feel scared because I was still angry that he'd appeared here and overheard my conversation, which had seemed practically impossible to happen.

"What the fuck are you doing here?" I said, putting all of my anger into that sentence.

"Don't tell me you're mad at *me* for discovering your dirty little plan?"

I made a mistake of looking into his gray-blue eyes. At that moment, all of my anger disappeared, and I backed away from him, my back hitting the wall. I was suddenly feeling cold as if I had walked out into the coldest winter day.

"Stay away from me," I whispered shakily.

He smiled and leaned on the wall next to me. "Really? And what about your plan to get rid of me?" He reached for me, and I closed my eyes. "Do you think I can just forget that?"

When I opened my eyes again, I saw him playing with a lock of my hair. My heart was thudding loudly in my chest, but I refused to simply run away from him or make everything worse by setting some part of him on fire. I had to get over the fear somehow.

"What? Did the cat get your tongue?"

"Fuck off," I said.

"Listen, bitch, I'm going to get your element one day," he whispered into my ear.

"Get away from her!" someone yelled, and I recognized Michael's voice.

Adrian rolled his eyes and stepped away from me. I looked up at Michael and suddenly felt much better. And damn, he looked really hot when he was angry. His soft brown hair was flying around his face and his green eyes were blazing. For a second I thought he might be an angel of revenge, ready to jump on Adrian and make him pay for what he had done to me.

"Aaah, here comes Prince Charming," Adrian said sarcastically.

"Ria, are you okay?" Michael gave me a concerned look, and I felt warmth well up inside of me. Adrian gave me a nervous look. Wait; was the warmth I felt inside me connected to my element too?

"Well, I'll leave you two lovers alone," Adrian said, walking away, but then he stopped and looked back at us. "Be careful, Michael. She's dangerous."

"Don't you ever come near her again!" Michael yelled after him.

"Yeah, yeah," Adrian said dismissively and left. Michael rushed to my side, taking my hands and looking at me carefully.

"Did he hurt you?" he said, his voice full of worry.

"No, he just... he was just being an asshole."

"Typical." Michael rolled his eyes. "But if he ever comes near you again…"

"Don't." I flashed him a smile. I didn't want to talk about Adrian. Michael looked at me in surprise, but then he realized what I meant and smiled back at me.

"Would you like to go for a coffee? And maybe explain to me how you got yourself into this," he said.

"Sure, why not?" I nodded, and we went down the hallway.

Michael and I were sitting as far away from the other tables as we could. This café wasn't really one of my favorites, but it was the nearest one to the university; we hadn't wanted to go to one of the university's cafés because they were usually overcrowded and without any privacy.

"So, what did Adrian want from you?" Michael asked, and I noticed a certain hostility in his voice.

"Let's just say I pissed him off, but I don't want to talk about him. Don't tell me you're obsessed with him, too."

"No." Michael curled his lip in disgust. "How could you even say such a thing?"

"Fine then." I chuckled. "Now tell me, can you do something fun with your element?"

"Sure."

"Show me."

"We aren't supposed to…"

"I know." I leaned forward. "And I don't care. Show me something." The university's policy about not using our elements in public until we graduated was silly anyway.

He gave me a skeptical look, then, after making sure no one was watching us, he concentrated on the glass of water in front of him. I felt that strange tingling sensation around me even stronger than before because Michael was sitting so close to me.

Suddenly, the water slowly rose until it was floating above the glass, still preserving its shape. The water was perfectly still for a moment, and then it parted and formed the shape of a heart.

"Wow," I whispered, afraid that any movement would destroy the beauty in front of me. Then the water moved again and formed a rose. I stared at it, wondering why we weren't allowed to do this all the time. The rose was as perfect as if it had been made out of ice, but since it was still water, it had a feeling of life and warmth to it, which ice could never have. I felt compelled to touch it, to feel the power in it.

Michael was smiling at me, and then the rose dissolved into hundreds of shiny drops and fell back into the glass. I kept staring at the spot where it had been, but there was nothing but air.

"Do you like it?" he asked.

"Yes, it's… it's amazing. When did you learn that?"

"Last week, actually."

"You learned all that in one week?" I said in disbelief.

"Of course not." Amusement flickered in his eyes. "It took more than that. But they decided to teach us the final steps last week."

"Damn! That means I have to wait one more year to learn the cool stuff!" I pouted.

"Yes, but it's worth the wait."

"True."

"Are you going to the party this weekend?" Michael gave me a curious look.

"Um, what party?" I actually couldn't believe I didn't know about a party! It seemed completely impossible.

"Great!" Happiness registered in Michael's voice, and I looked at him in surprise. "Would you like to go with me?"

"What?" Yeah, it was extremely stupid to say that when I should have totally screamed *yes* to him. But I couldn't accept anything just because he was hot. Or maybe I could?

"It's a *secret* party for sophomores, and since you don't know about it… it means no one has asked you to come. So, would you like to go with me?" He smiled so sweetly that my heart melted.

"Sure," I said. "But why is it secret?"

"I don't know. Probably to make it seem more special." He shrugged. "Anyway, it's different from other parties because you can get in only if you're a sophomore or accompanied by someone who is."

"Ah, okay then. So, it's this weekend?"

"Yeah, on Saturday."

"Is that like… a date?" I looked at him hopefully.

"Um, I guess it is."

"Does it bother you, you know, the fact that we have different elements?"

He hesitated for a moment, and then his green eyes met mine. "No," he said and meant it. "And you?"

"No, not really." I knew I was risking it, but I really, really liked him. Besides, it was just dating, not getting married or planning a family. But why in hell did it feel as if this were an important decision in my life?

After my coffee with Michael, I went straight to Paula's room. I didn't care if she was still mad at me for what I had said about Adrian; we were best friends and that was more important than any stupid quarrel. I knocked on the door and didn't have to wait long for her to open it.

"Oh, great! You're here!" She grabbed me by the arm and pulled me inside. I looked at her in surprise because I had at least expected her to be a bit angry.

"Am I… missing something?" I said, and she smiled coyly.

"Yes! Some guy approached me in the hallway. He kind of asked me to go to a party with him."

"Wow." I couldn't wait to hear all about the guy. "Who?"

"Oh, you probably don't know him." She waved her hand. "He's some weird geek. Not attractive at all. But I was so impressed that he dared to ask me that I actually told him I was going to think about it! Can you believe it?"

"Um, actually no. So, what kind of a party is it?"

"I'm not sure I can tell you. Well, it's a secret party for sophomores."

"You have to go to that party!" I said, excited that she could come with me.

"Why?"

"Because Michael invited me! And I can't go without you!"

"Michael invited you? Oh, that's so awesome!" She came closer to hug me.

"Well, you can wait until someone better invites you. I know they would all like to go with you."

She suddenly stopped smiling. "It doesn't matter who invites me. The only one I would like to invite me already has a date." She sighed.

"Tell me you're not talking about that bastard."

She rolled her eyes at me. "I like him. And I believe everyone deserves a chance to show who they really are. You can't judge people without knowing what's inside."

I frowned. "Oh, I think I know very well who he is. You keep thinking you'll find an angel inside of the devil's body, but trust me; there can't be anything good about that guy. Who's his date anyway? Probably some slutty blonde."

"You know nothing about him. Well, neither do I, but I would like to." Her eyes softened. "And he actually asked Ariadne to go with him."

"Um, who the hell is Ariadne?" I was sure I'd never heard about the girl before.

"She's that shy redhead who's really sweet and intelligent. I talked to her during lunch, remember?"

No, I didn't remember her at all. She had to be one of those plain faces that are easy to forget.

"And he actually noticed her?" I asked, but then I realized what the whole thing was about. "Oh, poor girl. That bastard is going for shy and innocent girls so he can get what he wants! Don't you see it? Those girls will do anything he asks just because someone as good-looking as him noticed them!"

"You're so prejudiced! It doesn't always have to be like that!"

"Okay, okay. Whatever," I said. "But you have to go!"

"Sure, sure. I'll go. I wouldn't want to miss you and Michael getting close." She grinned.

"Hey! I don't want you there to stare at us! I want you to have fun, too. But I need my best friend there in case something bad happens."

"Something bad? Like spilling a drink over your dress?" She laughed.

"Yeah, something like that." I smiled. "So, what are you going to wear?"

"Me? You're the one who has to take Michael's breath away."

We spent the rest of the day planning our outfits, which was even more fun than I had thought it would be.

Chapter 5

When Saturday finally came, I was so excited that my hands were shaking while I was putting on my dress. After changing my mind more than a thousand times, I finally decided to wear a dark blue cocktail dress. Paula agreed it looked good on me, and it was still very comfortable. I also decided to wear my favorite black shoes, and Paula helped me put my hair up.

She chose to wear a long dark green dress, which went perfectly with her eyes. I managed to convince her not to straighten her hair. I really loved her curls and wished many times that I had curly hair just like hers. And she liked my straight hair more. But no matter what we did with our hair, mine would never stay curly and hers would never stay completely straight. We had actually laughed about that many times.

The party was being held in a house near the university. Someone had rented the house just for that occasion. But I didn't really care where we were going; I only wanted to be around Michael. He came to my room so we could go together, and I almost fainted when I saw him. He was wearing dark blue jeans and a white shirt, and his hair seemed so soft and shiny that I thought he could easily take part in some shampoo commercial. The smile he flashed me was completely breathtaking.

"Wow, you look... beautiful," he said, and I blushed. His presence was enough to warm the whole room.

"Thanks."

He took my hand, and we walked out. Paula and her companion met us in the hallway. I couldn't help but stare at the guy. He had really short brown hair, green eyes, and a huge nose. He was also wearing a hideous check shirt and was a bit red in the face, probably because Paula looked like an angel next to him. Oh God, what had I made my friend do!

The four of us walked together to the party, and I was actually impressed when I saw how nice the house was. There were many people inside, and the music was very loud. One room, which was completely empty of furniture, had been turned into a dance floor. Two smaller rooms were full of drinks and food, and another one had been turned into some kind of a chatting room, with many armchairs and cushions, where the music wasn't so loud and people could actually talk and hear each other.

While we were checking out the place, I saw *the monster* in the company of a plain looking red-haired girl, who had to be Ariadne. The poor girl was laughing nervously at something he was saying to her, and she already looked pretty drunk. I couldn't really blame her because Adrian looked just fine in his black shirt, which was unbuttoned a bit, and dark gray jeans. But when he looked up at me, I immediately felt cold in a room that couldn't get any warmer.

I was really glad when Michael took me to the dance floor, because as soon as we started dancing, the world around us stopped existing. I let the rhythm of the song take me over, and I enjoyed being in Michael's arms. It turned out that he was a great dancer too.

I don't know for how long we'd been dancing when I spotted Paula in the corner of the room, looking bored and desperate. She wasn't dancing, and the weird guy was nowhere to be seen, so I figured she must have come here to escape from him. I couldn't just ignore that.

"Michael," I yelled, "I'm going for some drinks. Could you go dance with Paula?"

He looked at me in surprise, glanced at Paula, and then just nodded. I really hoped he could cheer her up a bit, because he was her friend too. I knew that if I went there to talk to her, she would feel even worse.

I found my way to the room with drinks, pushing away several very drunk guys who tried to get hold of my arm. Just as I was taking two beer bottles, I felt someone's presence behind me, and then someone's arms were around my waist.

"Ria," Adrian breathed into my ear, and I turned around, almost hitting him in the head with the bottle. He managed to dodge it by very little, and he was smiling at me.

"Get the fuck away from me." I raised the bottle in my hand to emphasize the point. That didn't even faze him.

"Now, now, don't be so mad."

"Where's your date?" I couldn't see Ariadne anywhere nearby. I secretly hoped the girl had gotten scared and run away from him. And yeah, I would really love to rub that in his face.

"In the bathroom, throwing up." He flashed me a smile.

I couldn't help but laugh. "Ah, and why aren't you there holding her hair or something?"

"Because there are plenty of girls left here to seduce."

I frowned at him and wished Paula had heard this.

"Then why are you wasting your time with me?" I asked. "Or has no one else fallen for your charm, so you're so desperate that you came to me?"

"You'd love that, wouldn't you?" He reached for my arm, and I moved away.

"You're such a jerk." I tried to get past him, but he stepped right in front of me.

"I saw your beautiful blonde friend here. I bet I can get her to dance with me."

"She has a date," I said, even though I had no idea where that guy was. But Adrian didn't need to know that.

"That freak? Oh, please. She'll forget about him as soon as I appear in front of her."

"Did you forget that you insulted her when she asked you for your help?"

"I'm sure she's forgotten about that," he said. "And if she hasn't, she will. Trust me."

"Don't you dare go near her," I said through my teeth, anger taking over me.

"Oh, I'm really sorry, but I won't stop until she ends up in my bed." He smiled.

"That won't happen."

"Who's gonna stop me? You? Your daddy?" He laughed.

"She will," I said.

"We'll see," he said and turned around to leave. I was already shaking from anger, warmth welling up inside of me. I really wanted to set him on fire. He suddenly turned around, looking tense.

"Don't," he said, breathing heavily as if he'd been running. I stared at him, realizing that my element was truly bothering him. I'd used my element to make the room warmer instead of setting something on fire, and I knew it must have been circling in the whole room. That had to be driving him crazy.

Suddenly he crossed the distance between us and grabbed me by the shoulders. I froze. All the warmth inside of me was gone as soon as his hands touched my skin. And I had no idea how that had happened.

"Do that again and I'll kill you, you stupid bitch," he said.

"Then don't come near me."

"Well, I just wanted to let you know about my plan so you can suffer knowing that your friend won't trust you anymore," he said. "It's a fair payback for you plotting to get rid of me. She'll be mine."

"I'll tell her about this. She'll believe me," I said, even though I wasn't really sure. Could this asshole really ruin our friendship? I hoped not.

"No, she won't." He laughed.

He let go of me and went out of the room. I stood there for a moment, unsure about what had happened the moment he'd touched me. I knew the warmth was all mine, but from where had all that cold come? I realized I was still holding the beer bottles in my hands, and when I lifted them, I saw thin ice around them, which just began melting. How the hell had that happened? As I was trying to think through all of that, Michael appeared in front of me.

"What took you so long? We were already getting worried," he said.

I handed him the bottle and tried to smile. I didn't want this to ruin the night. "I wanted Paula to cheer up. I thought you'd dance longer."

"She didn't really want to dance with me." He grimaced. "She thought it was weird, so we just talked."

"Oh, that's just fine." I opened the bottle and took a good swig of my beer. I was really getting tired of my creepy encounters with Adrian.

Michael and I returned to the dance floor and danced for some time. I was just starting to relax when I noticed Paula was dancing with Adrian. She was smiling like never before. Oh, shit. So he had managed to charm her after all. I wasn't surprised, actually. But I didn't feel like going over to them and making a scene, because that as hell wouldn't help.

"I need another beer," I said and pulled Michael away from there. A few beers later, we were in some corner, chatting and laughing. I had no idea what we were talking about or why we laughed, but in one moment we looked at each other and everything was forgotten. His green eyes were shining like diamonds in the light, and I reached out to touch the soft skin of his face with my fingertips.

He took my hand and kissed it. I think I smiled for a second before his soft lips touched mine in a gentle kiss. I must have kept my eyes closed, because I remember only his warm kisses and his arms around my waist.

Chapter 6

Someone's rough touch woke me up the next morning. Or at least I thought it was morning. I didn't want to open my eyes because my eyelids felt so heavy, just like the rest of my body. There was also this horrible throbbing inside my head.

"Ria, wake up!" I heard Paula's voice. I briefly opened my eyes.

"Why?" I groaned, putting my hands on my head.

"Well, it's 3 p.m." A hint of a smile appeared on her lips. "You're going to miss lunch."

"Three? Oh, shit!" I didn't move. "I feel horrible."

"Well, you look horrible, too," she said. "And you need a shower."

"Thank you." I finally managed to open my eyes completely. She looked great as usual. Actually, maybe even better than that. "Why are you so cheerful?"

"Oh, I'm just… happy." She grinned. "I had a really great time last night."

"You did?" I was surprised for a second, then I remembered seeing her dance with Adrian.

"Yeah." When she didn't say anything else, I got a bit worried.

"Tell me you didn't sleep with Adrian," I said.

Her eyes widened, and then she frowned. "Hey! Are you insane?"

"Phew. I was just worried. That's all," I said. "I'm glad he didn't get you drunk like he did with Ariadne."

"Oh, please. He didn't get Ariadne drunk. She got drunk because she was nervous or something."

"Ah, so how did he explain the fact that he'd left his date and come after you?"

"He said he'd realized they had nothing in common, so they had agreed to part." She tilted her head back.

"Yeah, right. Till your unwillingness to sleep with him parts you." I rolled my eyes.

"Look, he's a nice guy. He even apologized for refusing to help me that day, and he looked really sincere. I would appreciate it if you didn't talk about him like that, because he asked me out on a date."

"Paula! He told me himself that he was just going to seduce you!" I felt the headache getting stronger.

"You're lying." She gave me a slow, disbelieving shake of the head. "I know you hate him, but that doesn't mean you have to invent things like that about him! I talked to him! I know he's nice!"

I stared at her for a moment, trying to think. Obviously, there was nothing I could say to make her see reason. I guessed I had to let her learn the hard way or risk losing her as my best friend. "All right, if you say so," I said. "But don't let him make you do anything you don't want."

"Of course I won't."

I sighed.

"Well, I'll leave you now to get dressed and everything." She offered me a smile. "Oh, and there's aspirin on the desk if you need it."

"Oh, thank you, hun!" I said, and she left, smiling as if she were the happiest girl in the world. *Damn you, Adrian, damn you!*

I waited until Monday to see Michael because I didn't want him to see me with a hangover. We had lunch together, exchanging a kiss or two. Paula actually said we were disgusting at some point, but we just laughed at it. Her face, however, completely lightened up when Adrian walked into the room.

He hopped onto the table where he usually sat with his *friends*, who for some unknown reason weren't there this time. Paula followed him with a longing look in her eyes.

"Hey, you're drooling!" I said.

"No, I'm not." She frowned at me. Then Adrian looked in our direction and made a movement with his hand for her to join him. I thought I was going to be sick.

"You're not going to go to him like some stupid puppy, are you?" I asked, but she was already getting up. "Paula!"

She didn't listen. She simply walked over to him and let him put his arms around her. Michael lightly touched my hand.

"Let it go," he said. "He won't be able to hide for long that he's a complete jerk. She'll see it soon."

"You think?" I looked into his deep green eyes, which became a bit darker as he spoke.

"Yes, I'm sure of it," he said. It was actually so easy to believe him that it surprised me. But he was right; Paula wasn't stupid. I was sure that in a few days she would be totally over Adrian.

But days had passed and Paula was still with Adrian. They were now officially dating, just like Michael and I were. Because of romantic dates and all the work that had to be done for the university, I didn't see Paula as often as I'd used to. And even when we were together, we just talked about anything else that didn't include our boyfriends. It was weird, actually.

While my relationship with Paula was getting worse, Michael and I were doing great. We spent all the time we could together, and I actually found out a lot of things about him. He told me about his Russian ancestors, his favorite things and pastimes, his childhood, and many other things. I particularly enjoyed the story about his aunt, who had run away with her boyfriend and gotten married even though he had a different element from her. Of course, her act had been a big humiliation for the family and she had been disowned, but she still lived happily with her husband and their adopted children.

I really enjoyed spending my time with Michael and I somehow started to see myself married to him. The only problem was that my parents had informed me that they might come to visit me soon. I wasn't planning to tell them about my relationship with Michael, not if I could help it. But still, some part of me believed that when they did find out, they would accept it because they loved me so much. I really hoped I was right.

One day, I walked into the girls' restroom and saw Paula fixing her make-up. I hadn't truly seen her in days, only during classes and in the hallway a few times, but we'd never had a chance to talk. I was getting really sick of this situation. I knew she was as busy as me, but Adrian took up all of her free time and she had none left for me.

"Paula?" I said, and she smiled at me. "Did you pass the exam?"

"Oh, yes!" she said cheerfully. I had known that already, but I didn't want her to run away from me again.

"That's great." I waited for one girl to get out of the restroom. I didn't need witnesses, especially not when Paula and Adrian had become one of the most popular couples here. I wondered how the news hadn't gotten to Paula's parents. "Listen, now that you passed the exam, would you like us to have a girls' night? You know, like we used to have before…"

"Um, that would be nice, but I have to ask…"

"Don't tell me you have to ask your boyfriend for permission." I tilted my head. "I'm your best friend! It's not as if you're meeting some guy."

She looked at me for a moment. I couldn't believe what that bastard had done to my friend! He'd completely sucked her brain out!

"All right," she said after some time. It took me a moment to process what she had said. I'd half-expected her to refuse.

"Great!" I smiled. "Come to my room at eight. I'll be waiting."

"Sure," she said, fixing her hair. I walked out of the restroom to prevent myself from making a comment that would make her change her mind about our little party tonight. Just as I closed the door, I spotted Adrian in the hallway. He was leaning on the wall and watching people pass by, occasionally smiling at girls. I rolled my eyes. Why didn't Paula see it?

I realized he was waiting for Paula, and that scared the hell out of me. He hadn't been here when I entered, so he must have used his ability to find Paula by identifying her element. He could track anyone here at any time... Even spend some time with another girl, knowing for sure that Paula wouldn't find him. I didn't even want to think how he could use this ability when the disease showed its ugly face.

"You stupid, manipulative, controlling bastard," I said to Adrian as I got closer to him. I was feeling brave with all those people around us.

"Ah, Ria, always so sweet." His lips spread into a smile, and then he became serious in a second.

"You're really enjoying this, aren't you? But what if Paula's parents find out about your relationship?"

"If they find out, your parents will find out about you and Michael," he said coldly. "Actually, I'd love to see that happen. Would be fun."

I gritted my teeth to stop myself from saying anything else and walked away before Paula could see us and blame me for molesting her dear boyfriend.

Michael was waiting for me at the café near the university where we usually went. Just the sight of him sitting there made me smile, and I had to refrain myself from running up to him. Damn, it almost seemed as if I had to refrain myself from doing something all the time today.

"Hey, you're here!" Michael got up to give me a kiss.

"Guess what, Paula and I are having girls' night tonight," I said as we sat down.

"Wow, that's an achievement."

"Yeah. Did you know that the bastard can feel where she is all the time?"

"Really? He can do that?" Michael frowned. "Well, that sucks."

"Yeah. I can't believe she's become a completely different person because of him."

"Did I change you somehow and you haven't noticed?" He smiled playfully. "Am I turning you into a zombie?"

I laughed. "Sure, honey. I've never had to hide anything from my parents before."

"Oooh, you see, all guys eat their girlfriends' brains." He raised his hands up, imitating claws. We managed to stop laughing when the waitress brought me my coffee.

"What are we going to do about my parents? I really want to tell them," I said.

"Then do it."

"But it's not that easy! I don't know how they'll react." I chewed on my lip. "What if they force me to break up with you?"

"Then we'll have to meet in secret." He touched my hand.

"That could be fun." I laughed. "I'm going to tell them. I have to… Before someone else uses it against me."

"You mean before Adrian tells them?" He became deadly serious, watching me intently with his warm green eyes.

"Yes."

"I won't let him push you into something if you're not ready." Michael took both of my hands into his. "Listen to me, Ria, do this only if you feel you should. Don't do it because of him."

"It's not just him… it's me, too."

"Tell them. You know I'll be there for you no matter what."

"Okay," I said, getting the phone out of my pocket.

Michael frowned. "What are you doing?"

"I'm going to tell them," I said, knowing that it was now or never.

"Over the phone?"

"Yeah, better than being in front of them, trust me." I gave him a reassuring smile. "This way they'll have time to calm down before they get here."

"Okay, you know best," he said as I dialed the number. I chose to call my mom rather than my dad because it was more likely that she would have time to listen to me. The phone rang a few times, and I outstretched my left hand to Michael, hoping that his hold on me would help me to stay calm.

"Yes?" my mother finally answered. I took a deep breath.

"Hey, Mom," I said, trying to sound cheerful, but completely failed at it.

"Ria? Are you okay?"

Why the hell did my parents always assume something was wrong when I called? Oh, maybe because they called me in most cases, and I called only when I had a problem or needed more money. Right, that was it.

"Yeah, I'm... great," I said. "Mom, listen, I have to tell you something."

"Sure, honey. What is it?"

"I have a boyfriend."

"Oh, all right." I could hear the surprise in my mother's voice. She definitely hadn't expected me to say something like that.

"His name is Michael," I said. "Michael Teregov."

"Teregov?" she said, and I squeezed Michael's hand really hard, waiting for my mom to recognize the name.

"Yes, have you heard of his family?" There was silence on the other side of the line and then some typing. Was my mother searching the name online?

"I'm not sure, honey. The only Teregovs I've heard of are those whose element is water," she said. "And surely you can't be dating someone who..."

"Mom, I'm dating him. I know his element is water, but we get along great and I think we might have... a future together." My heart was beating like crazy.

"What? No, that's not possible. You can't have a future with that guy! Think about it, honey," she said angrily. "You can't throw away your family, your inheritance, your life... just because some good-looking guy made you believe you love him! He's not crazy to throw away his life either, so he must have been looking for an adventure and you fell for it."

I couldn't believe what my mother was saying. It almost seemed as if I had told her I was dating Adrian. Michael wasn't like that, and he would never do anything to hurt me, especially not try to get me into his bed and leave. But how could I convince my mother?

"Mom, Michael isn't like that! I'm not stupid. I know what it means for me, but didn't you tell me that love was the most important?"

"Yes, it is! But you should marry someone of your own element who you love, and to find him you have to date guys who are acceptable," she said.

"I'm not talking about marriage yet, but I want to try out all the options. I thought you'd support me no matter who I chose. Besides, I'm not the only child. Even if I choose to marry Michael one day, it won't harm the family tradition."

"Ria! You're out of your mind! That boy has completely confused you!" she yelled. "Your dad and I will come this weekend and we'll sort this out. Okay, honey?"

"Mom!" I was slightly lightheaded, but I realized my mother probably needed time. "Okay, we'll talk about it. Oh, and just so you know, Paula is dating Adrian Liandre."

"What?" I had to move the phone away from my ear. Yeah, it was mean of me to do that just so my mother would see there were worse things than me dating Michael. I regretted it as soon as it came out of my mouth, and I knew that it could hurt my best friend. I was completely sure my mother would call Paula's mother in a second. I just hoped Paula's mother was a lot more understanding than mine.

"Yeah, well, bye now," I said and ended the call.

"Paula will never forgive you for this," Michael said, and I frowned. I didn't need him to tell me that.

"You shouldn't have done that!" Michael's face reddened, his nostrils flaring.

"I know!" I snapped at him, getting up from the table and nearly spilling everything. I ran back to the university, not paying attention to Michael yelling my name. I had no idea what was wrong with me. Must be that time of the month.

I spent some time crying in my room and then I focused my attention on doing homework and studying. I finished just in time to prepare my room for the party, which also meant smuggling some beer bottles and clearing up my stuff so we could sit on the floor. Strangely enough, I didn't feel upset about what had happened anymore. But there was an unusual warmth spreading through my body. Could it be my element?

I heard a knock on the door and went to open it. Paula smiled at me as soon as she saw me. Damn, I'd missed her so much. I let her in, taking a box of chocolate cookies she brought with her, and closed the door.

"It's so hot in here," she said. Hot? I hadn't even noticed it. I placed the cookies on my desk and went to open the window. The cool breeze reached me, and I shivered. Had I accidentally warmed the room with my element? Oh well, I didn't have time to worry about it.

"So, how's everything going?" I asked as we sat down on my blue plush carpet. My parents had actually sent me the carpet since they knew I liked to sit on the floor, and they didn't want me to catch a cold or something.

"Exams are going great. Love life is going great. Experiments… not so well." She sighed.

"You still find time to do the experiments?" That was impressive. No one but Paula could manage all that. But then again, when she was studying, she actually concentrated on it, while I spent hours staring at the book and trying to memorize one stupid sentence.

"Sure." She flashed me a smile. "Adrian is helping me a lot."

I raised an eyebrow at that. Could Adrian actually be helping? That was hard to believe. I handed her the beer bottle that I'd just opened and went to grab the other one for myself.

"Okay, I'm going to promise you something," I said, and she looked at me expectantly. "I'm not going to say anything bad about Adrian in your presence if we can just be best friends like we used to."

"All right." She bobbed her head. "Does that mean we can talk about our boyfriends again? I'm dying to ask you something about Michael."

"Sure." I wondered why I always chose the wrong time to do things. I was almost sure Paula would never forgive me for what I had done, and this moment of our renewed friendship wouldn't last long.

"Did you sleep with him?"

"You're not asking me that!" I frowned and then laughed. "No, we figured it's too early for such a thing. Wait, don't tell me you and Adrian…"

"We did." She giggled. "You don't know what you're missing."

I stared at her and took a good swig of the beer. So she had slept with Adrian and he was still around. What the hell? I'd thought he'd move on when he got what he wanted. Was it possible that Paula had managed to steal the monster's heart? Somehow, I doubted it.

There had to be something else he wanted from her, or she just looked good on his arm in public. Or maybe I was just being an envious bitch. Well, not exactly envious of her being with Adrian, but envious of her because she was happy. She always seemed to have everything, but on the other hand, she could be thinking the same about me.

"Aren't you afraid of catching the disease?" I asked.

"No, we were very careful," she said. "I think I'm in love with him. But it worries me that I can't find anything in his DNA."

"What if you don't find a cure? What if no one else finds a cure? I hope you're not thinking of marrying him."

"I don't know what will happen. I just know I'm ready to spend my life with him no matter what if it turns out that we really love each other."

"Paula, you can't do that. I won't let you marry him. I bet your parents won't allow it either. Being with him now is one thing, but when the disease shows… he'll kill you." Tears appeared in my eyes. "I don't want him to hurt you."

"Heeey, don't worry about me. I haven't decided anything yet," she said. "It's not as if he proposed or anything."

"Yeah, but you're actually considering marrying him one day. You can't have a family with him."

"Aren't you considering marrying Michael, too?"

"Yeah, sometimes. But that's not the same. Michael's not going to turn into a murderer. And we can adopt children if we want." I realized how weird this sounded. I wasn't ready to marry or have kids and probably wouldn't be for some years. "Unless my parents forbid me to see him," I added. "Told my mom today. She was furious."

"Wait, you told your mom about Michael?" She stared at me in shock. Yeah, no one had seen that one coming, not even me. It had been a weird day, really.

"Yeah, I shouldn't have, but I did it." There was no point in crying over spilt milk, but if there were a way to turn back time, maybe I would have done things differently.

"Do you think they'll understand?" She looked genuinely worried. And it shouldn't have surprised me. She was a good friend. I was the one who was a bad friend here, and she kept reminding me of that without even knowing it.

"I don't know. I hope so." I sighed. "They're coming to see me."

"You're brave, you know?" She smiled, clearly trying to cheer me up. "I wouldn't have dared to tell my mom about Adrian. She only knows I have a boyfriend, but doesn't know who he is."

"What do you think will happen when your parents find out?" I asked.

"I don't know. They'll probably freak out. But I don't care." Her jaw was set, her chin high. "I'm not a kid anymore. They don't have a say about who I choose to be my boyfriend. And my grandma promised to help me if my parents start making trouble."

"So your grandma is the only one who knows?"

She nodded.

"You have a really cool grandma. Mine would… you don't want to know." I laughed, imagining my grandma's furious face. If I chose to marry Michael one day, I was sure she wouldn't want to see me again.

"Forget about it then," she said. "I didn't mean to upset you even more. And, please, stop doing that!"

"Doing what?" I frowned. I had no idea what she was talking about.

"Getting this room even warmer than it is." She waved her hands in front of her face to get cooler.

"But I'm not doing anything." I narrowed my eyes in confusion.

"Yes, you are. I can feel the tingling in the air."

"I'm not…" I started to say and then realized I really was using my element. How the hell had that happened again without me noticing?

"Sorry," I said, "it must be stress."

"No problem." She shrugged. "I can get some wind in here if you want."

"That would be great!" I said, and a few moments later felt the air moving around us. Of course, the familiar tingling sensation was there, and I smiled. Some of the papers that I had left on the floor near the bed were now flying around us, and I had to get up to catch them. Paula laughed.

"Isn't it better now?" she asked when she was done. Indeed, I felt much better immediately.

"It's great. So, is there anything I can do to help you with the research? Of course, you can pull Adrian's hair out all by yourself now."

We both laughed. Then she looked thoughtful for a moment.

"I don't think you can help me with this. I'm trying to get Adrian to find some of his parents' old medical files, but he refuses every time I ask," she said. "I understand that it's hard for him to go through his parents' old stuff, but there could be key info that could help us to cure the disease or keep it under control."

"Why do you think there's something useful in those files? You know exactly what Adrian's parents had been doing."

"Yeah, but I want to know when exactly the disease broke out for them," she said. "That could be helpful to Adrian. This way we can never know when…"

"Um, I don't think there are files about when the disease broke out," I interrupted her. "Even if those files had existed… They were probably destroyed already. It would have been a risk to keep them."

"I'm aware of that." She lowered her gaze. "But maybe there's something different in the early medical files that no one noticed at that time. Maybe the doctors didn't know what to look for."

"Well, Adrian won't give them to you, so it doesn't really matter, does it?" I was skeptical about her theory and didn't want her to get in danger just because someone found wrong files in her possession. It was good that Adrian hadn't given them to her.

"Maybe I can persuade him." She played with a lock of her shiny hair. No, I didn't want to know how she was planning to do that, so I just shook my head at her in disapproval.

"A little bird told me there was going to be a ball next weekend," she said.

"Huh, a ball?" I raised an eyebrow at her. "Do we need fancy dresses for that one?"

"Yeah, actually we do. We're celebrating I don't know how many years of our university, and they want it to be special."

"Are we going shopping?" I fluttered my eyelashes, making her laugh.

"Yup, we are." She nodded, and I went to hug her. I really missed doing these little things with her. We talked some more about anything that came to our minds. It seemed as if we had come together again after many years of separation. And I really enjoyed catching up with things that had been happening in her life.

Someone knocked on the door, and I had trouble getting up off the floor to go open it. I must have had a beer too many because the world was spinning around me for a moment. I nearly closed the door as soon as I saw Adrian standing there.

"What the hell do you want?" I asked.

"Her." He pointed at Paula, who was giggling behind my back.

"You found me again," she said.

"Of course I did." He flashed us a smile. "I always do."

Damn, there was something so wrong about this. Why couldn't Paula see it? I would freak out if Michael tried to control me like that. But she was just smiling and looking dreamily at him.

"You shouldn't have looked for her. She wasn't missing," I said bitterly. He'd managed to ruin my good mood solely by showing up.

"I'm sorry your boyfriend doesn't care where you are," he said, and I wanted to hit him in that arrogant face. Paula came to stand between us, planting a gentle kiss on Adrian's lips. His cold gray-blue eyes stared at me as he kissed her back. Damn, what was Paula doing with that jerk?

"You two will just have to get along better." She frowned. "I don't want my boyfriend and my best friend to hate each other."

"We'll try then," he said, smiling. "Anything for you, my love."

I wanted to throw up, and it wasn't because of the beer.

"Ria, please, will you try?" Paula pleaded. "For me? Please?"

"Okay," I finally said. If she wanted it so much, then I could do it. And yeah, the evil part of me hoped my mother had already contacted hers and told her about Adrian.

"Great!" Paula squealed in delight, hugging me. "Now Adrian and I have to go. I'm looking forward to our shopping spree!"

"Me too," I said. "Just don't bring your boyfriend with you. It's a 'girls only' thing."

"You won't mind, will you?" She looked up at him. Did she really need his permission for everything?

"Of course not," he said, and then they walked out of the room, acting as if they were on a honeymoon. I closed the door and suddenly the world went black.

Chapter 7

Water. I could feel water all over me, but I wasn't drowning. I wanted to touch it, to wrap myself in it, to drink it all up...

"Ria! Come on!" I heard someone's voice, but it seemed so distant, and I wanted to stay in the water. A few moments later, the image in front of my eyes began to dissolve, and I saw a shadow leaning over me.

"Ria, please, wake up."

I blinked and saw relief cross over Michael's face. He was holding a glass of water, trying to make me drink. I managed to take one gulp, but this water wasn't as amazing as I had imagined it, so I ended up coughing.

"What... what's going on?" I asked, looking around. I was lying on the floor in my room and Michael was the only one with me.

"I think you fainted." He helped me to get up and reach the bed. "I was worried when you didn't answer my calls, so I came here and found you lying on the floor."

He looked truly worried, and I tried my best to smile. "I'm fine, Michael. Really."

"I'll go get a doctor," he said, and I grabbed his arm before he could get away from the bed.

"No, don't. I just fainted. I guess I drank too much beer."

"Are you sure?" He gently placed his hand on my face.

"Yeah."

"All right." He pressed his lips together into a tight line. Well, I wasn't happy that I had fainted, but I didn't want to see a doctor. There was no reason to make a fuss about something as trivial as this.

"Will you stay with me?" I took his hand. His green eyes met mine, and I saw reluctance in them. Why didn't he want to stay with me? I almost asked him, but he must have read my question on my face because he answered it.

"You know that we're not permitted to spend the night in another student's room," he said, and I frowned.

"Oh, please. As if someone is going to check! We're not kids anymore!"

"True. But I would like to be in my room if Alan comes to look for me in the morning."

"Alan?" My eyebrows shot upward. I didn't really like Alan because he seemed to be too involved in everything.

"Yeah, he's trying to convince me to take on some additional classes. He says this is too easy for me." He smiled. Damn, I had a smart boyfriend.

"Will you do it?" I asked. "I'm pretty sure you could. And I bet it would look good on your resume one day."

"I don't know." He caressed my hair. "I haven't decided yet. But that would mean I'd have less time to spend with you."

His lips met mine in the sweetest kiss ever.

"Aww, that's so nice of you," I said. "And as much as I would like to spend all of my free time with you, I suggest you try. You can always quit later."

"I'm not a quitter like you," he teased.

"Hey!" I gave him a light punch in the shoulder. "I just quit ballet when I was little, and trust me, that wasn't my thing at all. Oh, and I quit cheerleaders because I thought it was stupid, and I…Okay, never mind."

"So how did the girls' night go?" he asked, and I told him a few things that I'd discussed with Paula. He promised he'd stay with me until I fell asleep. I think he kept his promise because when I woke up the next morning he wasn't there.

The rest of the week passed in a flash. I was glad that Paula and I had agreed to go shopping before my parents came to ruin my life. Yeah, I started to believe they would ruin everything because they had avoided any conversation about my relationship with Michael when they had contacted me. I had kind of hoped they would've called me the other day and told me they understood and that we didn't need to have special talks in person about it.

But no, that hadn't happened. Did they believe the problem would go away if they didn't talk about it? Did they expect me to tell them it had all been a joke when they got here? I had no idea and it drove me crazy, but I didn't want to ask anything because I was afraid I would make everything worse.

Paula came out of the changing room in a long white gown that looked almost like a wedding dress.

I frowned. "You're not going anywhere in that. I don't want Adrian to get ideas."

She smiled, twirling in front of the mirror, but then she went back inside to try another dress. I went through four fashion magazines and didn't see anything I liked. Damn, why was finding the perfect dress so difficult?

Paula was out in a gorgeous red gown, and the sight of her in it made me gasp. I really liked the way its ruffles alternated with the organza. And the whole skirt was made even prettier by silver embroidery and scattered sequins. The upper part of the dress was also embroidered and beaded to fit the rest, and its draped sweetheart neckline fitted Paula perfectly. The dress seemed to be made for her.

"Wow," I said.

"Should I ask them to attach the straps to it?" she asked, inspecting the dress carefully.

"No. It's perfect like this."

"Are you sure it won't slide down? I don't want to keep pulling my dress up the whole night."

I got up from the white couch I'd been sitting on and walked over to her to get a closer look. "It won't slide down. It fits you perfectly."

"Yeah, but what if…"

"No ifs," I said. "You found your dress."

"You think I should take it?"

"Yup. Actually, if you don't take it, I'm going to force you."

"All right," she said. "What about your dress? Anything good in that catalogue?"

"Nope." I sighed. "Nothing looks good enough."

"How about that green one over there?" She pointed in the direction of one dress. "It would fit with Michael's eyes."

"Yeah, it would. But I don't like it."

"Let me guess, you want something specific." She cocked her head.

I smiled. "You know me so well."

"Of course I do. I'm your best friend." She laughed. "Tell me."

"Water," I said. "I want something simple but beautiful... something blue... something like water."

"Blue, huh? Okay, we'll look for it. You're really trying to impress Michael, aren't you?"

"Impress? No, I want to leave him breathless." I grinned from ear to ear. Paula shook her head at me and went to change back into her clothes. After she bought the dress, we visited maybe six or seven different shops, but I didn't find anything. Just as I was about to give up on everything, I saw the dress I wanted.

It was a pale blue V-neck dress, which had a low back satin bodice and full organza skirt. The skirt looked simple, but there were tiny ruffles on it, which fitted perfectly to my idea of a watery effect. The bodice was covered with hundreds of small shining crystals, which reminded me of drops of water.

"I want this one," I said. Paula raised an eyebrow, clearly surprised. I supposed she had expected me to never find the right dress.

"It's pretty! Try it on." She took the dress from the hanger and pushed me toward the changing room. I needed some help to get into the dress because I was afraid I'd ruin something. I didn't want a single crystal to fall off, and the saleswoman assured me that wouldn't happen, but I was still afraid.

I couldn't help but smile when I saw myself in the mirror. It was just as I wanted it to be.

"You look great," Paula said. "Michael will approve."

"Thanks." Oh yeah, I was more than ready to rock Michael's world.

Chapter 8

Paula and I were just about to enter the university when my phone rang. I saw Michael's number on the screen and answered. "Hey, honey," I said cheerfully.

"Ria, you have to get here immediately." His voice was strained.

"What's wrong?"

"Your parents are here."

"Oh shit," I said. "I just got here. Where are they?"

"Um, we're all in your room."

"I'm coming." Fuck! My parents were waiting for me in my room with Michael! So they had met Michael before I could come up with a nice introduction. And now they knew Michael had a key to my room. Great. Just great.

"What's going on?" Paula asked.

"My parents are here." I hurried down the hallway.

"Oh, do you want me to come with you?" Paula yelled after me, sounding worried.

"No," I said. "I'll call you later, okay?"

"Okay!" I heard her yell a moment before I went around the corner. My hands were shaking, and I could hear my heartbeat ringing in my head when I finally reached my room. I waited for a moment and then turned the knob.

"Honey!" my dad said, obviously trying to make this situation less tense, but my mother just stood up, glaring at me, her lips pressed together tightly in a straight line.

"Hey," I said. I stopped in the middle of the room, not knowing what to do. I just smiled at Michael, not daring to go over to him and kiss him.

"Where have you been?" my mother asked.

"Shopping," I said.

"Shopping, huh?" she said, tossing her shoulder-length dark brown hair out of her face. "Well, I'm glad you finally appeared. I thought you'd leave your *boyfriend* alone."

The way she said the word boyfriend made me cringe, but it also made me brave enough to go sit next to Michael on the bed.

"I would never leave him alone," I said determinedly.

"What do you want, Ria?" she suddenly asked. "You have our attention now. So what is it that you want? More money? A new car?"

I stared at her in shock. I couldn't believe she thought I was dating Michael to get something! Surely enough, I had done some things they didn't approve of to get what I wanted when I was younger, but this wasn't something I'd play with.

"Dad, do you believe this, too?" I looked at him, but he just shrugged.

"I don't know, honey. Why don't you tell us?"

"All I want is that you accept Michael as my boyfriend."

"No! You're not going to ruin this family!" My mother's face was red with anger.

"Ruin the family? What the hell are you talking about?" My blood boiled. Michael touched my hand, and I looked at him in desperation. Then he interlaced his fingers with mine and just held on tightly. We could do this together. I knew we could.

"You're going against tradition. Our family's reputation will be ruined!" she said. "As soon as the press finds out, it will turn into a scandal! You can't do this to us. We've given you all you ever wanted. Please, think about it."

My mother's face turned from cold and angry to disappointed and sad. Even her eyes started to get teary. What the hell? I'd had no idea my mom could be such a great actress.

"Mom, you told me you didn't care about this whole reputation thing," I said, frustrated. But then I realized something; there had to be a reason why my mother had suddenly turned into an unknown person.

"What are you hiding from me?" I looked at both of my parents, who seemed to be startled for a second. I frowned. There was something horribly wrong here.

"Mom? Dad?" I said when I didn't get an answer.

"We need to talk in private," my mom said. I was completely puzzled, but Michael and my father were already going to the door. My mother came to sit next to me, and it seemed she was back to her normal self.

"Honey, you mustn't marry Michael," she said.

I looked up at her dark eyes. "I didn't say I was going to marry him."

"But you might," she said. "And that can't happen."

"Why?"

"Do you remember your great-grandpa?" she asked, straightening her long dark brown skirt. My great-grandpa had died when I was five, so I couldn't really say I remembered him much. He was more like a blurry image in my mind.

"Um, not so well," I admitted.

"Well, he was determined to keep the family's element pure, so he forbade his children to marry people who had other elements. Of course, he was afraid that his children wouldn't do the same with their children." Her voice was gentle now. "So he decided to do something about it."

"What does that have anything to do with me and Michael?" I asked. "No one can forbid us to marry if we want to. Not even you."

"I know. I wouldn't even try."

"Then what the hell was all this drama?" I was completely perplexed.

"It was… your father's idea… Obviously a bad one. We were afraid you'd secretly marry or do something as crazy as that. And we didn't want to tell you the truth about… your great-grandfather." She sighed.

I gaped at her. This was weird on so many levels that I didn't know what to say. So my parents weren't against my relationship? Huh? What had I missed? "Mom, I'm not following you. Are you telling me that you and Dad are okay with me being with Michael, but that my dead great-grandfather isn't?"

"We're okay with it if you truly love him. Of course, it's still early to say at the moment, and we would prefer that you choose someone of your own element… especially because you can't officially marry Michael, but you can live with him."

"I don't understand." And I really didn't. I considered pinching myself just to make sure I wasn't dreaming.

"Your great-grandfather made a deal with someone," she said. "We've been trying to find out who it was, but to no avail."

"What kind of a deal?" My voice was barely audible.

"Anyone who marries someone whose element is air, water, or earth will be killed," she said, and I nearly laughed.

"It's not funny, Ria!" Her lips curled, her eyes hard. "Do you remember your aunt Olivia?"

"Sure. She died in a car crash."

"No, her car was pushed off the road a day after she secretly married Bruno, a guy whose element was air. We found out about it after a lot of investigating, but it seems that the deal is still on," she said.

"Wait, someone killed Olivia because she married that guy?" I raised an eyebrow. "I just… I can't believe that. Who would have done it and why? Maybe it was just a coincidence. Maybe someone got confused and went after her car believing she was somebody else."

"I know. I thought that at first, too, but we found the mark," she said. "The same symbol that was on the document your great-grandfather had signed. Then we realized that something we had thought was over was still active."

"Okay, Mom, if you don't want me to be with Michael, just tell me. This whole thing you're saying belongs to a movie or a book." Really, if someone told you your great-grandfather made a deal so that someone kills off your family members who marry the wrong person, would you believe it? I don't think so. If you would, then you had a hell of a strange family.

"See, that's exactly why we tried the other way first." She took my hand. "I knew you wouldn't believe it, but it's true. Your great-grandfather gave a lot of money to that person and maybe did some other kind of a favor, because it was obviously enough that this continues even after his death and probably the death of that person, too."

I didn't know what to think. This did sound quite insane, but my great-grandfather hadn't been the nicest of people either. He'd certainly had enough money and power to do it, but who was crazy enough to keep honoring the deal after his death? I wished my mother had never told me this. I was almost sure I would have nightmares because of it.

"How many people died?" I asked.

My mother seemed to be thinking about it. "Four. It could be five, actually, but that happened a long time ago, and we can't prove it."

"And there are absolutely no clues about who it could be?"

"No. But we believe it's someone influential, or there would be no way to cover it all up."

"Okay, I'm not marrying Michael," I said. "Actually I'm not marrying anyone for some years."

"Well, like I said, we were afraid you'd get a crazy idea to run away and marry in Vegas," she said, "so we preferred to prevent it. We don't want to lose you, honey. Especially not because of some narrow-minded bastard."

I couldn't help but smile. My mom reached out to hug me.

"I'm glad we sorted this out. I really didn't want to start hating you." I grinned and then panicked as another thought came to me. "Did you tell Paula's mom about her daughter's boyfriend?"

"No," she said. "Is she really dating Adrian Liandre?"

"Yeah, but don't tell anyone." The tension left my shoulders. "She'll tell her parents when she's ready."

"Well, I'm not surprised. He's a handsome boy."

I raised an eyebrow at her. "Handsome? Maybe. But he's dangerous."

"Don't worry about her," my mother said. "She's a smart girl. She knows what she's doing."

"Yeah, that's what everyone says." I rolled my eyes. "Can I tell Michael about this whole thing?"

"No, don't tell him," she said. "The less people know, the better. We don't want it to get to the press or end up in the wrong hands."

"Okay." I was slightly tired from everything that had happened today. "Would you like to see my ball gown?"

"Sure." She smiled, and I went to get the bag, which was still standing near the door where I had left it. Well, it was my lucky day after all. I had bought the perfect dress, my parents didn't mind that Michael was my boyfriend as long as we didn't get married, and Paula would never find out about my betrayal. Things were looking up for me.

Chapter 9

I shared my happiness with Michael and Paula the next day. Paula was apparently curious enough to leave Adrian for a moment and join us for lunch. I told them only that my parents didn't want me to marry Michael but that they were okay with us dating for now. Paula was happy for me, but Michael looked suspicious. I just hoped he wouldn't try to find out the truth.

"So, did you and Adrian have a fight, or did you just want to hear what had happened with my parents?" I looked at Paula.

"Nope, Alan's having a conversation with him," she said gloomily. "And yeah, I was curious, too."

"A conversation? Will they kick him out of the university?" I grinned.

"Hey! Don't say that!" She shot me an angry glare.

"A girl can hope," I said.

"Is he still failing everything?" Michael asked.

"Yeah," Paula said. "He says there's no point in studying. I wish he realized there's still hope."

"You could find a real guy, you know. Someone who'll truly love you and treat you like you deserve,"

Michael said. I was actually glad that someone else aside from me had noticed it, but Paula was probably thinking he'd said it because I had told him to.

"Adrian's a real guy, and he gives me all I deserve," she said, lifting her head up and trying to look indignant.

"Don't think you can change him," Michael said. "I lost a friend because of him. I don't want to lose you, too."

"Lost?" I looked at Michael in surprise.

"Well, it's not what you think. She moved away, and I haven't had any contact with her since then," he said. Relief flashed across Paula's face. I must have looked disappointed.

"What happened?" I asked when I realized Paula wasn't really interested and wouldn't ask any questions.

"Her name is Amaya," he said, his voice full of sadness. "We were good friends since high school, and she came to study here. She fell in love with Adrian as soon as she saw him. They dated for a while, and then he left her for another girl. She suffered from depression, and her parents decided to take her far away from here."

"And she hasn't called you or anything?" Paula asked.

"No, and she didn't answer any of my calls," he said. "I just hope she's fine now."

"Who was this other girl?" Paula said, looking more interested in the girl who could be her competition here than some poor girl far away.

"Tanya."

"Tanya?" we both said at the same time. Tanya was a girl who usually gave Paula angry looks, but we'd had no idea why. Now we did.

"Yeah. Adrian has a huge list of girls he dated. And girls are still waiting in rows for him," Michael said disapprovingly.

"Well, they don't have to wait anymore." Paula smiled. "He's just mine now."

I wanted to tell her that she should reconsider that, but I kept my mouth shut, which was a surprise. I didn't want to risk losing her again, and I really hoped that the temptation wouldn't get unbearable.

"Do you really think you changed him, Paula?" Michael looked deep into her eyes, and she actually flinched and dropped her gaze. I had a feeling that even she doubted it sometimes. Good. Maybe she would finally see what was right in front of her eyes.

"Everyone can change." She got up and left us alone.

"Yeah, everyone except Adrian," I said, playing with my glass, when I was sure she couldn't hear me anymore.

"She loves him, Ria," Michael said. "There's nothing you can do about it. Only he can."

"I expected him to leave her already."

"Why?" He raised an eyebrow at me. "Did she…?"

"Yeah, she did."

"Oh." He couldn't hide his surprise.

"Don't tell anyone," I said. "And don't tell Paula I told you."

"Sure." He smiled again, and we kissed. Maybe Adrian was just waiting for a perfect victim before he broke up with Paula, but I didn't want to worry about it. I had a new mission in my life; I was going to turn that ball into the best night of my whole life.

The long expected night came faster than we all had thought it would. The whole university had been talking about it this week, and everyone wanted to be well prepared for the ball, especially the girls. There would probably be some unofficial beauty contest.

I was standing in front of the mirror, trying to make my hair perfect. I'd been doing that for the past two hours and still didn't know what to do. My hair just didn't want to stay in the position no matter how much hairspray I used. I was getting more annoyed by each second. Someone knocked on my door and completely startled me. I opened it carefully, hoping it wasn't Michael. It was Paula. And she looked gorgeous.

"Are you done?" she asked as I let her inside. Her beautiful curly hair was lifted up, but a few curls were left to fall down her face. Damn, I'd kill to have that kind of hair.

"I don't know what to do with my stupid hair." I sighed. "Anything I do is useless!"

"Why don't you just leave it down like it is?"

"No! That's too ordinary." I scowled.

"But you need something simple with this dress," she said. "Maybe I can braid it for you."

I looked at her and shrugged. I was so desperate that I would take almost anything. Almost. I actually closed my eyes while she was doing something with my hair.

"Okay, I think you're done," she said, and I opened my eyes.

"Wow." I looked at the two tiny braids she'd made for me on each side of my head. It looked good against the rest of my straight hair, like waves. Or maybe I was just seeing waves everywhere now. Oh whatever, it looked good because my hairstyle still looked simple but not plain… if that made any sense.

"Do you like it?" she asked uncertainly.

"Sure, thanks!" I went to hug her, then realized that wasn't such a good idea, so I just took hold of her hands.

We hurried down the hallway, hoping that no one would see us before we got to the ballroom. The guys were already supposed to be there, waiting for us. I couldn't wait to see Michael and the look on his face when I appeared in front of him.

The ballroom was completely bathed in a golden glow of hundreds of crystal lamps, and it looked absolutely amazing. The dance floor was to my left, and the tables were opposite from it and mostly occupied by those who were waiting for someone or didn't like to dance. I realized we were among the last people to come because I was overwhelmed by the amount of faces I could see in front of me.

All the girls looked gorgeous in their dresses, and I suddenly felt the urge to find Michael before some other girl set her eyes upon him. But it was hard to find a familiar face among all those guys in their tuxedos. Paula seemed equally lost next to me, and we slowly slipped into the crowd. People were mostly standing between the dance floor and the tables, chatting and drinking.

Adrian reached us first, which wasn't a surprise considering he had an annoying ability to sense Paula's element. Her face lit up when she saw him, but she didn't go all over him. It wasn't for my benefit but because people still weren't drunk enough not to notice any make-up or dress imperfections caused by getting too close to someone.

"You look amazing, darling." Adrian smiled at Paula, and she couldn't have looked prouder or happier. I really hated the effect he had on her. But hell, even *the monster* looked decent tonight.

"Ria." I heard Michael's voice behind my back, and I spun around a little too fast. His mouth opened, his eyes widened, and he was speechless for a moment. His reaction made me smile. I got what I wanted.

"You look…" He was struggling to find the right word. "Beautiful."

"Thanks," I said, "you, too."

And really, he did look gorgeous in his black tuxedo. His usually wavy brown hair had been carefully combed, and his green eyes were more noticeable that way. I wanted to kiss him, but just like Paula, I didn't want anything to ruin my looks for the first hour or two.

"Michael!" Paula said. "You look great."

"Thanks," he said. "You and Ria are truly gorgeous tonight."

"They always are, aren't they?" Adrian said, obviously trying to unnerve Michael. When no one said anything for a minute or so, I believe we all started to feel uncomfortable. I wanted a drink, but the waiter was passing on the wrong side, next to Michael and not me.

"Michael…" I started to say and knew I wouldn't be fast enough to explain what I wanted, especially not with all that noise around us. Adrian glanced at me and took two glasses of champagne from the tray. He offered one glass to me.

"You wanted this, I believe," he said, and I took the glass.

"Thanks," I said and took a sip, hoping that this awkward moment would pass. It seemed weird that he would take a glass for himself and me and not for his girlfriend. Paula, however, seemed pleased, because in her eyes Adrian was trying to get along with me. How nice. Michael obviously found it rude that Adrian hadn't given the other glass to Paula, because he frowned.

"Don't you think your girlfriend would want a drink, too?" Michael asked.

"She doesn't drink champagne," Adrian said, taking a sip. That answer couldn't be good enough for Michael.

"Paula, can I get you something? I'm going to get myself a drink, so…" Michael tried to make it sound casual, but Paula blushed slightly. She glanced at Adrian, who just flashed her a smile and made no movement.

"Okay," she finally said. "Could you bring me some water?"

"Water?" Adrian and I said at the same time. Great. We definitely had to get away from each other, like, yesterday.

"Get her some wine," Adrian said, and Michael's face reddened. He definitely didn't like Adrian's attitude.

"I didn't ask you anything," Michael said through his teeth and then smiled at Paula, who was looking at both of them with wide eyes. "Paula?"

"Wine is just fine," she said, a forced smile spreading across her lips. "It's a party anyway. I guess we can't drink water, can we?"

Michael just stood there for a moment, but then he left. I tried my best to ignore Adrian and turned to Paula.

"So, what do you think? Is it going to be a great party?" I asked.

"Probably," she said. "Look at all these people. When the music becomes louder and everyone gets drunk… Yeah, it'll be great."

"We don't have to wait for that," Adrian suddenly said, pulling something out of his pocket. His cold gray-blue eyes met mine for a moment, and then I looked at what he was holding in his hand. It was a small black box, and when he opened it…

I nearly dropped my drink as I saw round white pills. Drugs? I stood there, unable to move or say anything. Hundreds of thoughts were passing through my head. Was Adrian a drug addict? Had he made Paula take the pills too? Oh, shit.

"Adrian!" Paula said in a hushed voice. "Don't take that out here!"

"Why? Are you afraid someone's going to try to take them for himself?" He smiled. "Don't worry. I have plenty."

Michael returned just as I was about to drag Paula out of there, and I stopped dead in my tracks. The little black box disappeared, and Adrian was acting as if nothing had happened. His nonchalant posture almost made me believe I had imagined it. My mind was in overdrive, and when I got back to reality, Michael was asking me for a dance. I realized Adrian and Paula had gone to dance too.

I left my glass on an empty table and let Michael lead me to the dance floor. I had no idea what to do. I definitely didn't want to make a scandal here or ruin the party for Paula, but this wasn't some silly thing. Michael looked at my worried face and reached out to touch my cheek with his soft fingers.

"What's wrong?" he asked. We were still dancing, and I was really pissed off at my dress because it prevented me from getting close to Michael and burrowing my face into his chest. I wanted to tell him what bothered me, but I couldn't. I was sure he'd immediately go find Adrian, and I didn't want to know what would happen in that case.

"Nothing," I said. "I think I saw a girl in a dress similar to mine."

That was such a lame lie, and I wished I had come up with something else, but I guess I wasn't creative enough for that. Besides, that was something I could be upset about after all I'd gone through to get the damn dress.

"That's impossible," Michael said. "And even if it is similar, you look ten times better than her in it."

"Just ten?" I faked indignation, but then burst out laughing.

"Okay, billion then." The warmth of his eyes reached all the way to me and made me feel better. Suddenly there was nothing but us on that dance floor, and I was grinning at Michael as if I had just won the lottery.

"I love you," I said and meant it. Michael stopped moving and looked deep into my eyes. I supposed he was trying to see if it was the champagne talking or me.

"I love you, too," he finally said and bent his head to kiss me. I didn't move away this time because the dress was the last thing that mattered at the moment, and Michael tried to be as careful as possible. His warm soft lips touched mine gently in the sweetest kiss ever, and I was afraid I was going to melt.

The party finally started in its true form when the press and cameras were gone, and then the lights dimmed, making the atmosphere even better than it had been. Even the music got much louder. People could now relax and worry a little less about how they looked. It was hard to recognize anyone around us, but I did recognize Paula when she approached us. I had no idea how long Michael and I had been dancing and even less of an idea as to how many glasses of champagne I'd had.

"Hey, there you are!" Paula said, nearly crashing into us. She looked a bit drunk… or high. Oh crap, I'd totally forgotten about the pills. Had she taken one? I wasn't sure as I stared into her glassy eyes. For all I knew, my eyes could be looking the same.

"You promised," she yelled so I could hear her over the music. I had a hard time understanding what she was talking about.

"What?" I yelled back.

"I want you two to get along," she said. "Dance with him, please. For me."

I was staring at her for a full minute until her words sank in. Did she want me to dance with… Adrian? Just as I was about to tell her that I couldn't do it, she grabbed Michael's hand and pulled him with her to dance with him. Michael looked as confused and nervous as I was, but he let her take him away. I turned around and ended up face to face with Adrian.

"Come, my Ice Queen." He extended his hand toward me. I looked around and saw Paula watching me while she rested her head on Michael's shoulder. She smiled at me. I had no choice but to take Adrian's hand.

He pressed me close to himself, closer than necessary, and his hand ended up low on my back. At that moment, I cursed the dress with a low back cut because he was touching my bare skin, making this truly uncomfortable.

"I'm not an ice queen," I said, hoping that talking would distract me from the fact that his body was pressed against mine.

"Then why are you wearing her dress?" he asked, and I frowned.

"What?"

"The dress," he said. "It looks like ice."

"No, it doesn't," I insisted. "It's…"

I thought about it for a moment. Maybe it *was* ice… pale blue shining crystals… Oh, never mind. It depended on your point of view. But what the hell, you got ice out of water anyway. Maybe I should… No, this wasn't it; I was supposed to say something else… Then somehow, in my hazy mind I managed to remember it.

"You drugged Paula!" I glared at him angrily. He didn't react to that at all.

"Oh, don't be so dramatic," he said. "Sometimes she needs a little boost, you know. To help her relax."

I really, truly wanted to kick him in the face. "I'm going to tell her parents. You can't blackmail me anymore. This is serious."

"Really?" He raised an eyebrow, clearly amused. "Do you want me to break her heart? Trust me, I'd enjoy doing that. You can get her away from me, but what will that do to her?"

I stood there, frozen. I hadn't thought about that. Michael's story about his friend Amaya came back to me. What if Paula's parents took her away from here? Away from Adrian, but away from me too. I wouldn't be able to stand that. Surely, Paula wasn't some easily depressed girl, but who knew?

"Let's make a deal," he said, taking my hand and twirling me around. I ended up with my back pressed against his chest and his arms around me.

"What kind of a deal?" I said, hating the way he was pressing himself against me and making me move to the rhythm of the music. He moved my hair aside, and it made me feel vulnerable.

"Walk with me to the restroom," he said, his lips nearly touching my ear.

"What?" I wanted to turn around, but his grip on me was too tight.

"I will never ever give a pill to Paula if you take one now in the restroom," he said. What kind of a twisted game was he playing?

"So, what do you say?" he asked. "Will you risk Paula becoming an addict and a depressed little girl, or will you save her?"

"I don't trust you," I said.

"I'll swear on anything you want." This time he licked my earlobe. I shivered, suddenly feeling so cold from inside. I wasn't sure what to do. I should have kicked him and run, but I guess I wasn't smart enough.

"All right," I said, hoping I'd come up with a good idea before we reached the restroom. Adrian took my hand, clearly satisfied, and led me through the crowd. I was glad people were too drunk and too involved with each other to notice us. And Paula and Michael had disappeared from sight long time ago, which was a good thing, or maybe not.

We reached the restroom faster than I'd thought we would, and I hadn't really come up with a good plan, so I let Adrian lead me inside, hoping no one would see me going into the men's restroom with my best friend's boyfriend.

There was just one guy inside, clearly drunk, and Adrian waited for him to get out. The guy smiled at me stupidly before leaving, and I really hoped he wouldn't remember me. I was staring at myself in the mirror, wondering how the hell I'd gotten myself into this, while Adrian was getting out the pills.

He took one of those white things and handed it to me. I took it, examining it carefully. I had no idea what kind of a pill it was and even less of an idea what it could do to me.

"Where did you get this?" I asked. For all I knew, he could be giving me a different pill from the one Paula had taken and kill me. But what would he get from that?

"I have my sources," he said.

I rolled my eyes at him. "What is this anyway? Are you trying to kill me?" I waited for some kind of a reaction, but his face remained unreadable to me.

"Oh, come on. If I wanted to kill you, I'd do it with my own hands." He grinned. Of course, he'd take my element, and you couldn't do that if you weren't nearby right before your victim died.

"Yeah, but that would get you in trouble. Me taking a pill and dying of it at a party wouldn't make you suspicious," I pointed out, playing with the pill in my hand.

"I don't want you dead," he said. "And Paula would get depressed if you died, so… you can trust me or not, but if Paula becomes addicted, you'll know you had a chance to stop it and didn't use it."

"You're such an asshole." I looked back at the pill. It didn't seem like something dangerous, but that didn't mean it wasn't. And Adrian was most likely lying to me.

"What will it do to me?" I asked. "Just don't tell me I'm going to feel great because I'll hit you."

"You'll feel lighter, no worries, no problems… and you'll lose the feel of your element for some time," he said. I looked at him and suddenly realized why he had given the pills to Paula.

"You gave them to her so she could have sex with you," I said accusingly.

There was a hint of surprise on his face, and then he smiled. "How did you know?"

"You said it made you lose the feel of your element," I said. "And you didn't want to risk something happening during sex… You didn't want to lose control."

"Maybe," he said, but I was sure I was right. "She needed to relax."

"Which all only leads me to believe you're trying to trick me, since I don't think you aren't planning to have sex with her again."

"Don't worry. I got what I wanted from her. I'm only keeping her for... display," he said, and I turned around to face him so fast that he actually backed away.

"What? She's happy," he said. "Look, are you going to do it or not? Michael will get worried."

I considered calling the police, but Adrian had enough money to bribe them. Telling Alan probably wouldn't help since he was Adrian's guardian. Calling my father to get rid of him... Well, that was weird, and it would probably bother me for the rest of my life. Trying to make Paula see reason seemed the hardest of all of it.

Fuck. One small pill couldn't kill me, right? I let the water flow in the sink and swallowed the pill. I looked up at the mirror and saw Adrian watching me in amazement as I got some water. I had most likely done the stupidest thing ever.

"Happy?" I turned off the water and turned around. Adrian got so close to me that I gasped.

"Not yet," he whispered, his gray-blue eyes boring into mine. He reached up and placed his finger on my lip. I looked at him in surprise, and my lips parted. He must have been waiting for that because the next thing I knew, his lips were on mine. He plunged his tongue into my mouth, exploring every part of it.

I was too stunned to move. Something was telling me that I should push him away, but I wasn't quite sure why. It did feel good. Different. Hot...

Wait, what? I blinked as Adrian moved away from me, surprise written all over his face. He regained his composure in a second, smiling at me from the door.

"I didn't think you'd really do it," he said. I nearly asked what, but then I remembered I'd taken some strange pill. Ah, that was why I was feeling so weird. Just how had it worked so quickly? Or was it the kiss? The kiss? Oh, shit. I'd kissed Adrian? Or better said, he'd been looking for the pill in my mouth... with his tongue... ewww!

"Stay away from me," I managed to say, supporting myself on the sink. I just hoped it wouldn't break.

"Sure," he said. "You impressed me. Not everyone would do this for a friend. Now go find Michael before he gets worried."

Michael? Ah yeah, my boyfriend. Why was my mind suddenly so slow? I let go of the sink and figured I could still walk. Great. I was out of the restroom, bumping into people as I passed by. Where the hell was Michael?

Someone grabbed me from behind, and I would have fallen if that person's grip hadn't been strong enough.

"Ria, where have you been? I've been looking all over for you." I peered at the guy talking to me and realized it was Michael, my extremely hot boyfriend.

"Heeey!" I said, throwing myself around his neck. He eyed me suspiciously, and I pulled him with me to the dance floor. The weird feeling I'd had in my stomach was completely gone, and I felt better than ever. I wanted to dance, and soon Michael and I were ruling the dance floor. The colorful lights around us were so beautiful, so alive...

I was laughing and Michael was spinning me around, lifting me in the air, and I was flying. Flying like a bird... light and free...

Chapter 10

I woke up, feeling pain in my whole body. The headache was pressing on my head like a huge hat full of stones. I didn't feel like getting up or even opening my eyes. My arm hit something as I moved, and I heard a groan. I opened my eyes in panic and saw Michael lying in bed next to me.

"Hey, careful." He smiled at me, moving my arm away from his face. I looked around and recognized his room. Horror washed over me as I realized I couldn't remember how we'd gotten here. And more importantly, I couldn't remember what had happened at all. I saw my blue panties on the floor next to my dress, and I clutched the sheets closer to me. Oh, shit.

"What's wrong? Are you cold?" Michael's brow creased in concern. I just nodded, and he put his arms around me, pulling me closer to him, so I ended up resting my head on his chest. Clothes on the floor, weird, slightly painful sensation between my legs… Oh yeah, we'd had sex. But why couldn't I remember anything?

"Last night… It was amazing," Michael said, kissing the top of my head.

"Yeah," I found my voice and realized my throat was a bit sore. Had I screamed? Sung too much at the party? Party. Yeah, I remembered the party. And I remembered Adrian giving me that damn pill, some of the partying, but nothing else.

"What time is it?" I asked.

"Nine."

"Shit, I have to get out of here!" I knew that if someone saw me coming out of Michael's room in the dress I'd been wearing at the party last night, there would be trouble. People would be talking about it just because we had different elements; I was sure of it.

"I can lend you my shirt." He grinned. I glared at him, grabbing my clothes. Suddenly putting my clothes on in front of him seemed embarrassing. But he'd seen all of me already, hadn't he? Still, I didn't feel comfortable.

"Um, could you... look the other way?" I asked. He rolled his eyes in fake indignation but looked away anyway. I hastily put on my underwear, despite my whole body protesting against the movements. The dress, however, was impossible to put on. I sighed, wondering if I should just rip it and tie it around me. That definitely seemed easier.

"I'll give you my shirt," Michael said, getting out of the bed and walking over to the closet. He was stark naked. I stared at the perfection that was his body and wondered how the hell I couldn't remember touching any of that. He threw me a green t-shirt, which came to my thighs after I put it on.

"I don't think there'll be many people in the hallway," he said, getting dressed. "Everyone had a crazy night."

"I hope so." I looked for a bag for my dress. And I really hoped there wouldn't be anyone because my room was on the other side of the building, and I was dressed just in my boyfriend's t-shirt. Running to my room as fast as I could seemed like a good idea until I made a step toward the door and realized how stiff my muscles were. At this point walking appeared to be one of the hardest things to do.

"Well, I'm going now," I said, glancing back at Michael. "See you later."

"Okay." He gave me a smile that could melt any woman's heart. "I love you."

"I love you, too," I said and walked out of the room. On the way to my room, I cursed Adrian, his damned pills, the person who made them, and myself. Yeah, I knew it was my fault more than anyone else's, but I preferred to blame Adrian. Why had I been so stupid to take the pill? I was sure I'd never take any pill again, not even for a headache. I didn't want to forget anything, especially not something as important as my and Michael's first time.

I hadn't seen anyone on my way, and I was just about to turn the knob when I sensed someone behind me. I turned around and saw Paula. I let out a breath I hadn't even known I'd been holding.

"Oh, you... Oh!" Paula squeaked when she took in my appearance. I rolled my eyes at her delight and opened the door.

"Wanna come in?" I asked, and she followed me, grinning all the time as if she had won the lottery. I settled the bag with my dress on the floor and sat on the bed. Paula came to sit next to me.

"You spent the night with Michael," she said, and it wasn't a question. I just smiled shyly, knowing that if I could remember it, I'd probably be out of my mind from happiness.

"What are you doing in the hallway so early?" I suddenly asked, trying to change the subject. "And looking so... great?"

"Is that a compliment?" She laughed. "Well, I had some sleep, unlike you. Did you look at yourself in the mirror?"

I frowned. In all that mess, I hadn't had a chance to really do that... Oh crap, who knew how I looked? I immediately grabbed the mirror from the drawer. The person who was looking back at me had really messy hair, dark circles under her eyes, and looked a lot like a zombie. Oh, shit. And Michael had seen me like this!

"I need to use the bathroom," I said, and Paula just nodded. I was about to enter the bathroom when I remembered something.

"Wait, you said you had some sleep. Didn't you and Adrian, you know?"

"No." Her smile faded a little. "He said he was tired, so we just went to our rooms."

He'd been tired? Yeah, right. But if he had wanted to sleep with her, he'd have had to give her the pill... No, I didn't even dare to hope that he would keep his promise. Or maybe he had gotten tired of her; he never slept with the same girl twice, from what I had heard. I waved at Paula, told her we'd talk later, and went to shower.

What kind of a game was Adrian playing? First he had tried to get me away from Paula, and now he seemed to want to get her closer to me… or maybe not. Damn, he was truly a psycho. Was he planning to leave her? But why all the threats to break her heart if he was going to do it anyway? His weird logic didn't make any sense. I guessed he just enjoyed playing with people, no matter who and why.

The cold water felt good on my skin, but it didn't help me clear my mind. The headache was still present, and I felt more tired than ever, almost as if I hadn't slept at all. I managed to wash my hair, which was sticky and tangled, and clean up my face from what little was left of my make-up.

I dragged myself to the bed, barely keeping my eyes open. I was lying on the soft pillows and wondering why Paula didn't seem to suffer from the same symptoms. Or she just hadn't told me. Maybe she didn't remember but would never admit it. Funny, I wasn't willing to admit it to anyone either. With those thoughts, I drifted off to sleep.

I hadn't remembered anything else from that night even though a whole week had passed. It seemed impossible that I would ever remember, so I just stopped trying. I had spent hours and hours crying because of it. Michael was nice and sweet as usual around me, and I just couldn't help but feel bad about not remembering the night he kept reminding me of. And even worse, he'd said it had been the best night he'd ever had in his life, and I probably hadn't been me at all at that time.

"Is something wrong?" Michael asked, rousing me from my thoughts. I realized I'd been playing with the food on my plate, completely oblivious to the world around me.

"No, everything's fine," I said, getting up from the table. "I just need something to drink."

"I can get it for you."

"No, I'll go." I smiled at him and walked to the bar. I nearly bumped into Adrian when I got there.

"Whoa, Ria. Watch where you're going." Adrian's lips spread into a wide grin. "Unless that was deliberate."

"Oh, please." I frowned. "Now get out of my way before I punch you in the face."

"Why are you so moody?" he asked, getting out of my way but staying near me. "Problems in paradise?"

I turned to him to say something really not nice, but I changed my mind at the last moment. "Is memory loss one of the aftereffects of that pill of yours?"

He looked at me in surprise and then laughed. "Well, you'll need to find someone else to get you pills for that. Why do you ask? Do you want Michael to forget about something? Is it bad?"

"Shut up."

"Did you sleep with someone else and Michael found out?" he asked cheerfully.

"I'm not you," I said, trying to get past him, but he wouldn't let me.

"Ouch." He put his hand over his heart. "You hurt my feelings."

"You don't have any," I said, finally getting the drinks I wanted and walking away from him. I was glad to see that he didn't follow but instead started some small talk with the waitress. Good, except I was worried now.

Memory loss didn't seem to be on the list of the pill's effects, if Adrian was telling the truth, but why the hell had it happened to me then? But then again, weird drugs never brought anything good with them, and if they did, then you just thought it was good while in fact it wasn't. Maybe I should ask Adrian to tell me the name of the company that produced the pills so I could warn them about a new possible side effect. Yeah, right.

I slammed the drinks a little bit too forcefully on the table and some of the liquid spilled, startling Michael, who was actually reading a book.

"Hey, watch it!" he said, lifting his head up and frowning. A few drops had managed to get on the perfectly white pages of his book. Oops.

"Sorry." I smiled apologetically.

"I just bought the thing! Now it has drops all over it!" Michael narrowed his eyes at me, but only for a second. I sat next to him and pressed my lips to his. Warmth spread all over me in a huge wave, and strangely enough, it almost felt like water... I gasped, moving away from him.

"We shouldn't be doing this here," he said, looking nervous. I noticed that some people were looking at us, so I took Michael's hand and pulled him with me. When I was sure we were alone in the hallway, I stopped and turned to him.

"Were you using your element while kissing me?" I asked.

"No, why?"

"Um, no reason. I was just wondering," I lied.

"Wondering what?" He looked at me intently.

"Wondering if I made you lose control," I said, trying to make it seem playful. I must have imagined that feeling of water around me then.

"Impossible. My control is impeccable. But you almost had me that night we...made love..." He whispered it into my ear, sending shivers all over my body.

I bit my lip to stop myself from saying something stupid like: *Really, I wouldn't know*, or, *Can we do it again*? Michael smiled at me, and then he left for the library. I let him go alone because we couldn't really do anything fun there, and I didn't want to bother him, so I just headed to my room.

Chapter 11

I was sitting in my History class, staring through the window, and wondering how time could fly so fast. Four months ago, I had spent a night with Michael, and we still hadn't had a chance to repeat it. Stupid exams and stupid classes!

"Ms. Milanez," the professor said, and my attention switched to him. "The counselor wants to see you in his office. "

I blinked, trying to figure out who that was. Counselor? Ah, would that be Alan? Oh, great. Just what I needed. I got up, putting my books in my bag, and left the classroom, followed by everyone's looks. I didn't have to go far because Alan was waiting for me in the hallway.

"Ah, there you are, Ria," he said. "I wasn't sure if your professor would remember to tell you."

"He remembered," I said, and we started walking toward Alan's office. "Am I in trouble?"

"I don't know. Are you?" He smiled, and I fought hard not to roll my eyes at him. He was annoying me almost as much as Adrian. Okay, maybe not that much, but I still didn't enjoy his company. I wondered if he knew about Paula being Adrian's girlfriend, especially because she seemed to go talk to him a lot. He probably did.

"Obviously not," I said. "But why do you want to talk to me then? I mean, you got me out of class for this. It has to be important."

"Actually, I got you out of class because it's the only time when I'm not busy." He flashed me a smile as we entered his office. It looked just the same as it had when I'd been here months ago. Still horribly claustrophobic.

I settled myself in one of the red chairs and waited. Maybe he could get anyone in a chatty mood in a second, but not me.

"Does the name Oliver Milanez mean something to you?" he asked, the look on his face kind but also inquiring. I actually cringed when he said the name.

"Yeah, Oliver is…" I said hesitantly, "…my brother."

"Oh really?" He didn't seem surprised, which meant he had known it all along. "You never mentioned you had a brother."

"Why should I? I don't need to explain my family tree to anyone."

"True," he said. "It's just that you left the brothers and sisters field empty in your admission papers."

"I forgot to write it." Actually, I hadn't written it on purpose.

"All right, then I'll just add it," he said. "So, how close exactly are you to your brother?"

"I'm sorry, but that's none of your business." I gave him a polite smile even though I didn't feel like being polite with him at all. Was he this nosy with other people too? I'd have to ask Paula.

"You're not very talkative, are you?" His smile was a bit bitter now. "Fine. But when was the last time you heard from him?"

"I don't remember," I said, and that was the truth. As far as I was concerned, I didn't have a brother.

"Do you know that your parents are planning to report him missing?" he suddenly asked, and I stared at him with wide eyes.

"What?"

"Your parents haven't heard from your brother for two weeks now," he said, his face serious.

"They didn't tell me anything."

"They asked me to do it," he said. Now I was frowning. Why the fuck would my parents tell this guy something so personal instead of contacting me directly?

"Oliver can take care of himself," I said. "Maybe he simply got stuck somewhere without a phone signal during his trips. He'll be back. But what I don't understand is what do you have to do with all of this?"

"I told you. Your parents asked me to tell you this."

"Why? This is personal stuff," I said. "They could have told me themselves."

"Your father and I have been good friends for years."

My eyebrows shot up in surprise. My father knew a lot of people, even called some of them friends, but that didn't mean he confided in them.

"Oh, great," I said, unsure what else to say to that.

"We met at one of the EP meetings."

"E... what?" I'd never heard that acronym before.

"Element Preservation," he said. "Your father is a part of the Council."

I knew that, but I had no idea what being in the Council meant, except making some decisions or whatever about our elements. I'd never really been interested in finding out.

"Are you a part of the Council, too?" I asked.

"I was," he said. "Not anymore."

"Why not? Isn't that a better job than being a counselor here?"

"It is." He laughed, then his face became expressionless. "I had to give up on that job when I became Adrian's guardian."

"Oh," I said, "and why did you become his guardian?"

"I was chosen."

"Chosen?" I didn't know much about how someone became a guardian. Well, it wasn't like anyone ever talked about it. Anything that had to do with magic disease was usually kept secret.

"Yeah, most of the Council members voted for me. I had to decide whether I would accept or not," he said. "And I accepted."

"So you could have refused?"

"Yes," he said. "You can always refuse. But if I had done it, they would have killed Adrian right there with his parents."

I was shocked. Dang, why hadn't he refused? I'd be so much happier if Adrian had died that night. I almost asked him why, but I guessed that would be rude. At that moment, the door swung open, and Alan's face darkened. I glanced behind me to see Adrian, a pinched expression on his face.

"How many times have I told you to knock before entering?" Alan rose from his chair, frowning.

"Oh, don't bother," Adrian said. "Why is she here?"

And by *she*, he meant me. Of course, he could sense I was here, but why was that a problem? Ah, right, he probably thought I'd tell Alan something against him. Funny. I wasn't even planning to tell him anything, because of what use would it be? I was sure Alan would cover it all up.

"What's your problem?" I rose from my chair and hurried over to Adrian, pushing him against the wall farthest from Alan. Adrian was so surprised that he actually let me do it.

"This isn't about you," I whispered.

"It's not about you either." He smirked, and started to yell. "You're not going to get between me and Paula!"

I was completely aghast. What the hell was he talking about? As he continued to rant about me trying to break him apart from Paula, I realized something. He'd just used me to make sure Alan knew about him and Paula. But why?

"I'm out of here," I said, getting out of Alan's office before I got blamed for something I hadn't done. Okay, maybe for something I wanted to do, but what did it matter when I hadn't really done it? I sighed. Sometimes I was confusing myself... and sometimes Adrian confused me even more. What did the big bad wolf plan to do now?

At this point, I didn't really care. But I promised myself that if it were something against me, I'd just tell everything I knew about him or do something else to make him pay. I was getting sick of him. And maybe, just maybe, he was getting sick of Paula. Suddenly his outburst in the office made much more sense. He was going to break up with her and was probably trying to make it look like someone else had forced him to. It would certainly hurt Paula less, but he didn't care about her feelings.

Or did he want her to be his secret girlfriend so she'd quit being around him in public? Oh, crap. What if he didn't want to break up with her? What if he wanted more girlfriends? Surely, it hadn't been easy for him to stay just with her all these months... if he had actually stayed only with her. I wasn't sure.

Even though I'd been on the way to my room, I changed my plans and went to Paula's. At least Adrian wouldn't be around. I knocked on the door, hoping that she was there and not in the library. The door opened, and she appeared in front of me, looking pretty as usual.

"Ria!" she said, her shoulders slumping. "I wasn't expecting you!"

"Hi!" I said. "Can I come in?"

"Sure," she said and let me in. I was almost sure she'd been waiting for Adrian to show up. Her room was in real chaos; papers on the floor, tons of books lying around, some weird graphs I didn't even understand... I'd been in her room like a week ago and none of it had been there then.

"I didn't know there'd been a tornado here," I said, moving some old yellow-paged book off the bed so I could sit down.

"Sorry, I was just investigating something… and had a big fight with Adrian." She cradled another book as if it were a baby.

"You had a fight with Adrian? Why didn't you call me?" I asked, since lately we'd been talking to each other about boyfriend troubles. I hadn't told her anything about that night with Michael though. Some secrets just couldn't be shared with anyone, no matter how close that person was.

"I didn't have time," she said, looking sincere. "I believe I'm close to discovering something. Well, I'd have more chances if I could actually get Adrian to cooperate with me. But he's just being a jerk."

Wow, Paula actually admitting Adrian was being a jerk was a big thing. Maybe Adrian was tired of her using him for her research, but he had never truly helped her anyway. I had no idea why he didn't want to participate in something that could save his life later. I guessed he just didn't believe in her.

But now I was a little bit more certain he wanted to make her his secret girlfriend. If he wanted to simply break up with her, he'd have accused her of using him for the research or something. As much as I didn't want to admit it, the bastard wasn't stupid. Only I couldn't figure out why he would want to keep her. Paula herself had told me they hadn't had sex for a long time. Apparently, he had told her he was afraid he'd lose control and hurt her. Yeah, right.

"Did you rob the library?" I asked. "Or a museum?"

Some of the books really looked like the ones I used to see in museums; ones that looked like their pages were going to turn into dust if you touched them.

"No." She laughed. "I borrowed most of them. And I bought some on the Internet. I can't believe some people are willing to sell such valuable books."

"Um, not everyone finds those books valuable," I pointed out. "Well, better for you in any case."

"Yeah. Did you know that there's a place near here where they keep all the documents related to magic disease ever found in any part of the world?"

"No, I didn't." I frowned. "Why don't you go there then?"

"It's not a public place," she said. "It doesn't say anywhere where exactly it is. Besides, it's under the government's protection. No one can get into that kind of a place anyway."

"Oh please," I said. "There are always ways to break in or bribe someone to let you in."

"Not in this case." She sighed. "The government keeps something really important there, and I don't think they'd let someone in… not even for a price. And the security must be heavy."

"How did you find out all that stuff?" I looked at her, and she grinned.

"I read between the lines. No one mentions it directly, but I believe that's the only reason why this book didn't end up locked up in that place."

"Why would they want to hide things about magic disease from us? It can't be that bad, can it?" I asked. "Or maybe there are more influential families who do the same as Adrian's parents did."

"Maybe." She shrugged. "But why don't they allow more research to find a cure?"

"Um, because people from the government are stupid and would rather take money for themselves than try to find a cure for some disease? I bet none of them has a magic disease carrier in their family, or it would be another story. I'm sure they allowed Adrian to be here just like that only because none of their children go to our university." I chuckled.

"I don't know," she said. "It's just that… with all the school work, limited resources, and secrets I'm not getting anywhere!"

"I told you it wouldn't be easy. You have plenty of time to figure something out. Get your degree first, build your own laboratory… whatever you want."

"Perhaps, but I'm not sure about the plenty of time part." Her face was grim.

"Why?"

"Adrian might not…" she choked on her words, tears starting to pool in her eyes.

"Paula." I got up, walking over to her and pulling her into a tight hug. "It's okay. Don't worry about it. Everything will be fine."

"How can I not worry?" She hiccuped. "What if…?"

"No, stop it," I said. "He's fine. You'll figure it out. Don't waste time on worrying."

"Right." She wiped off the tears. "I can do this."

I could feel the wind crashing against me, whispering my name… I jumped away from Paula as if she had burned me.

"Ria! What's wrong?" Paula stared at me in surprise.

I looked at her, gasping for breath. "I don't know…I just… I need some air." I gave Paula a reassuring smile and ran out of the room before I choked or fainted.

What was happening to me? It almost seemed as if Paula being upset had made me upset too, but upset to the point of pain. Nah, she'd probably gotten too emotional and lashed out with her element, and I'd been too close to her. It was much easier to breathe in the hallway, so I just decided to go find Michael.

I couldn't find Michael. He wasn't in his room, and he wasn't in the library. I had no clue where else to look. After trying to call his phone and getting voicemail, I decided to return to my room. I figured he'd call me eventually.

I opened the door and immediately smelled roses. Roses? I looked around the room, confused, and surely enough, there they were, right on my desk. A beautiful bouquet of red roses. I reached out to touch one of the soft petals and saw a note lying under the crystal vase. I picked it up, a smile creeping up my face.

"I didn't believe in soulmates until you appeared. You are everything I have ever wanted. Meet me in the park at 7 p.m. and I'll show you how much I love you. Michael." I read it out loud, my heart thudding like crazy in my chest. Michael really knew how to make me melt from sweetness.

"I love you, Michael," I said, hugging the note to myself.

Chapter 12

I was waving a Magic Studies book in front of my face to get cooler. It turned out the book actually had some use. Oh, well. I was sweating way too much in my strapless silk green dress, which I'd chosen because the color reminded me of Michael's eyes. Why couldn't I be less nervous? It wasn't as if I were going out with him for the first time.

After making sure that everything was in its place, I sneaked out of the room. I didn't want anyone to see me and ask questions. The park was just behind the university, and it was full of trees and flowers, almost like a labyrinth. It was also a very romantic place, and many people went there to relax, read a book, or propose marriage… Oh.

I hoped that wasn't what Michael had in mind. We were too young for something as complicated as marriage, especially after what my mother had told me. I still wasn't sure I believed her. The sky was getting darker, twilight bathing the whole park in a beautiful reddish glow. I took a deep breath, enjoying for a moment the breeze that was caressing my face, and then went to search for Michael.

I found him standing under an oak tree, looking devastatingly handsome in his black suit. He held out a red rose to me, and I took it, smiling.

"So, how exactly are you planning to show me your love?" I teased.

"Come." He offered me his hand and led me deeper into the park. I heard noise coming from behind a large tree that sounded almost like… a horse. I frowned. What the hell would a horse be doing in the park? Michael led me around the tree, and sure enough, right in front of my eyes, there was a white horse. I must have looked completely stunned because Michael squeezed my hand gently.

"Do you like him?" he asked.

I blinked. "Honey, I'm not sure. I think I'm having visions because I'm actually looking at a white horse."

"It's real." He chuckled. "I brought him for you. I want to be your prince and make you my princess."

"Oh, Michael." I gasped as the full realization of what was happening hit me. That was so… so… I didn't have words to express how I felt. That was the most beautiful thing anyone had ever done for me.

"Come," he said, taking me closer to the horse. I was still slightly shocked, and a part of me wondered if it was all just a dream. But it was only Michael making dreams come true. I patted the horse's white mane and felt a smile spreading across my face.

"How did you… get him here?" I looked into Michael's deep green eyes.

"I'd do anything for you," he said. "I thought you'd like this."

"Oh, I do," I said, my eyes teary. "Thank you."

"You're welcome." He smiled and made a move to get onto the horse's back. I frowned. I couldn't ride a horse in a dress. He looked down at me and extended his hand.

"Come on, don't be afraid," he said. "Let me pull you up."

"I'm wearing a dress," I said as if it weren't obvious.

"So? You'll just have to sit in front of me and hold on to me really tightly."

I wasn't sure if I could do that. I was too afraid of sliding down and getting hurt. But the idea of holding Michael close to me was very tempting. Would I let him carry me on the horse like some princess he had saved from an enchanted castle? I decided I would.

I nearly fell off a few times and needed to tighten my grip on Michael. Stupid silk dress! I was almost sure Michael's suit would be full of wrinkles when we got to our destination. The good part of all of it was that I could enjoy in the warmth of Michael's body, his scent, his love for me…

There was a guy waiting for us in front of the restaurant who helped me get down. It was good to be on the ground again. But damn, this had to be the most exciting and the most romantic thing I'd ever done. Michael really knew how to make a woman happy.

After spending a few hours in an exclusive restaurant and enjoying delicious food and good wine, we were returning to the university. This time with a taxi. Riding back surely wouldn't have been comfortable because of the dark and us being slightly drunk, so Michael had had the horse returned right after we had arrived.

As we were getting closer to our rooms, I was wondering where we would go. Surely, this night couldn't end just with a goodbye kiss in front of the door. I wanted more. I wanted to experience everything I couldn't remember from the night that Michael and I had spent together.

"My room or yours?" I asked as we entered the hallway. Our rooms were at the opposite side of the building, and I really hated that sometimes.

"Yours," he said.

"Aren't you afraid of getting caught in a girl's room in the morning, Mr. Teregov?" I teased.

"No, not at all." He laughed, running his fingers down my back. Desire spread over me like fire, burning away any other thought that didn't include him. I didn't remember at what point we'd started kissing, but we were all over each other when we reached my room. I nearly dropped the key while trying to unlock the door.

I pushed Michael down onto the bed, getting on top of him. He kissed me, running his hands through my hair and holding it up so it wouldn't end up in his face and mouth. I smiled at him, realizing how beautiful his face was, surrounded by all that soft brown hair. He let his hands slide down my bare arms, and it sent shivers all over my body.

Our lips met again in a passionate kiss, and I started to fumble with the buttons of his shirt. He finally helped me get him out of it, and I was left staring at his muscular chest. The moment my hand touched his smooth, warm skin, I thought I could feel water around me. It was funny, considering that I felt as if I were on fire, and he appeared to be exactly what I needed to quench it.

I bent my head down, pressing my lips gently against his. But it wasn't enough. Of course it wasn't. I parted his lips with my tongue, trying to drink up that cold, refreshing water I wanted and needed so much. Just I couldn't reach it. It was there, and I was really thirsty, but it seemed to be getting away from me with Michael's every breath.

My hands went around his neck. I wanted him to stop breathing. I wanted to get to the water, or I'd die. I could feel his breath on my face, burning me even more, making my lips dry. Maybe if I could just cut off his breath for a moment… and some energy inside of me agreed with it. I tightened the grip I had on his neck, and his eyes widened.

He tried to push me away, and I didn't understand why. I only wanted some water. What was wrong with that?

I blinked and found myself almost choking Michael to death. I suddenly let go of him, and he gasped for breath. I wasn't sure who was more shocked at that moment, him or me. I jumped off the bed, unsure what had just happened. My head felt light, and I could feel my element rising inside of me, wanting out.

"Ria," Michael said, trying to get off the bed. I couldn't let him come near me. I couldn't. I ran for the door, getting out of there before something bad happened. Michael was yelling my name, and I knew he'd go after me. I didn't want that.

I had to hide somewhere from him. Somewhere where he couldn't find me, but where? I thought of going to Paula's room, but that was probably the first place he'd look for me, and I didn't trust myself enough to go near her. One part of my brain recognized the symptoms; the other part was in denial.

No, it couldn't be... I couldn't be having the symptoms of magic disease. It wasn't possible. I came from a family with a pure element, and I hadn't slept with someone who had the disease, that much I was sure of. And my element was still in me, wasn't it? I could still feel it, so maybe it wasn't that...

There was only one person who could help me, and I believed Michael would never look for me there. The only problem was that he probably wouldn't want to help me. Pushing those thoughts aside, I ran for Adrian's room. I knew it had to be late, but maybe he was still up... if he was in his room at all. And I really hoped he didn't have a girl staying over.

I banged on his door so hard that I thought it would fall down. After what seemed like a long moment, Adrian opened it with a sneer on his face.

"What the...?" His face changed from annoyed to shocked in a second. He was staring at me as if he were seeing me for the first time. I opened my mouth to say something, but instead I burst out crying. The look on his face was enough to confirm that there was something seriously wrong with me. He grabbed my arm and pulled me inside, closing and locking the door.

"What happened?" he asked, not hiding the surprise in his voice.

"Am I...? Can you...?" The words didn't come out like I wanted. I was still in shock, but I wasn't feeling thirsty or warm anymore. That was a small improvement.

"If you're asking if I can feel your element," he said, taking my hand and leading me toward the bed, "then the answer is no. You feel… like another person with magic disease."

"No, no… it can't be," I said. "I can still… feel my element."

"Huh." He grabbed a ceramic bowl from his nightstand and some paper. I was sitting on the bed and watching him, trying to at least stop crying. I could deal with this. I could. But my brain wouldn't believe it.

"Try to put it on fire." He gave the bowl to me.

I took it in my shaking hands and stared at it for a moment. I concentrated enough to feel my element swelling inside of me, and the paper burst into flames in a second. Adrian's face was calm as he watched me do it, even though he was standing very close. I was happy that I could still use my element, but him not being bothered by it made me suspicious.

"I still have my element," I said, unsure what to do with the bowl. Maybe I could set something on fire, but I surely couldn't put it out. Adrian said nothing, watching the flames dance in the bowl. Just as I was about to ask him why he wasn't bothered by it, he reached for the bowl and suddenly the fire was out, and a thin layer of ice was starting to form inside of it.

"What…? How did you…?" I wasn't even sure how to put it together. Adrian took the bowl out of my hands and put it back on the nightstand.

"Now you know my secret," he said, "and I know yours, so let's keep that safe. You can't tell anyone about what you just saw, understand?"

There was an edge of a threat in his voice, and I nodded. Things suddenly clicked into place; that was why I felt so cold around him sometimes, why the bottles had had ice on them after an encounter with him at the party... But I still didn't understand how he'd done it.

"Yeah," I said. "But, please, tell me how you did that."

"I can do things with ice." He sat on the bed next to me. "It's like... my element."

"Ice is not an element." I shook my head. Well, it surely wasn't in the books.

"Then what is it?" he asked. "It definitely acts like an element."

"You have a point," I said only because I couldn't come up with anything smart to add, and because I didn't know much about this whole ice thing. Suddenly something else came to my mind. "Wait, so you don't have magic disease?"

"I do. And judging by this, so do you. Who infected you?" He made that question sound as if I were a cheap hooker.

I frowned. "I didn't sleep with someone with magic disease. But what do you mean I have magic disease? It's impossible. People with magic disease lose their element."

"That's what they claim." He flashed me a smile. "But there isn't much information about it. Maybe they don't know or they're lying to us."

"Um, did you tell Alan? Are they doing research?" I asked, getting interested in the topic. I had never dreamed I could be talking to Adrian about something serious. It seemed wrong. And yeah, I still didn't believe I was completely screwed.

"No, no one knows. And you're not going to tell anyone." His cold gray-blue eyes bored into mine. "And if you do, I swear to God of Magic, I'm going to kill you."

I believed he'd do it, but I didn't know why.

"But wouldn't it help? They wouldn't treat you like a…" I couldn't say the word. I could be turning into a murderer myself.

"They wouldn't do anything, or they would simply accuse you of killing someone to get the element. They kill first and ask questions later, and even if somehow they believe you, guess what, they don't fucking care," he said. "Believe me, staying alive for longer than they planned is the best thing you can do. If your element stays, you can control yourself better around others… except in situations with lots of emotion or element usage."

"Maybe I don't have the disease… maybe it's something that will pass," I said, trying to convince myself to what I was saying.

"Do you feel other people's elements?" he asked.

"Well, I don't feel yours… but sometimes I felt air around me, and I just felt water when I was with Michael," I said, and something must have shown on my face because Adrian suddenly looked worried.

"You didn't kill him, did you?"

"No. But I almost did."

"Huh, wish I could have seen it." He seemed amused for a second. "How did that happen?"

"We were… um, you know, kissing, and… I got thirsty and I only saw water in front of me… I almost choked him to death!" I was again on the verge of tears. Somehow saying it out loud seemed twice as bad.

"Ria, Ria, Ria." He reached for my hand. "I'm actually a hundred percent sure you have magic disease, so you could as well stop lying and tell me where you got it."

"I'm not lying," I said angrily. "I'm not sleeping around like you! I just don't know! What if the disease mutated somehow? What if it can be transmitted differently now?"

"Not likely," he said. "It looks like you're the only person who has it here, so if you're right about the mutation, where are the others?"

He was right, but that didn't make it more real to me. I still hoped I'd wake up from this nightmare.

"You'll learn how to live with it," he said. "It's not as bad as you think."

"Are you insane? I can't live like that!"

"Yes, you can! Especially because no one will know! Your life will stay the same." His hand somehow ended up on my thigh. I frowned.

"Don't you dare think I'm going to sleep with you." I pushed his hand away.

"Pity. But you might change your mind eventually," he said. "There isn't a girl who can resist my charm."

I laughed. He really was an arrogant bastard. "What? Are you making me your next target?"

"Yes, I think I am. Sex with you could be a lot of fun since your element doesn't bother me anymore." He smiled.

"You're an idiot." I sighed. "And what about Paula?"

"What about her?" He seemed completely oblivious.

"Are you going to leave her?"

"Nah, probably not. I just don't want to have sex with her again. She's so boring."

"Why are you staying with her then?"

"So I can keep an eye on her research and stop her before it becomes dangerous for me," he said. "And yeah, she's pretty, smart, and from a rich family. It looks good on my record."

I rolled my eyes at him but decided to leave that for now. Yeah, I was being egoistic, but I didn't want to worry about Paula's life now when I had so much trouble in my own. I didn't know how to deal with this. I couldn't tell everything to Michael because I was sure he'd hate me. Paula would probably start doing experiments on me, and I wasn't ready to do that.

Telling someone else here I had magic disease and my element would most likely result in my execution. Adrian was right. They didn't really care; they just wanted to get rid of the danger. I had wanted that too, and now I was the danger. My parents didn't have any symptoms of magic disease, and they were strongly in favor of pure elements, so telling them might make them renounce me. There was always my brother, but I didn't trust him, and he was missing anyway.

I was suddenly so alone in the world. How had this happened? There wasn't any logical explanation. It also didn't make any sense how Adrian had developed something element-like when everyone kept saying people with magic disease didn't have an element unless they killed someone and stole it; but once they did that, it would be gone in some time, and they would have to kill again… and again…

I realized I was crying, and Adrian was cradling me in his arms. It should have horrified me, but it didn't. I didn't feel anything at all. I was tired and sick of everything.

Chapter 13

I woke up from a bad dream. I was sure it had been only a nightmare, but I didn't remember any of it clearly. When I opened my eyes, I realized I was in an unfamiliar room. I blinked. There was sunshine coming from the window, which was behind my back. It took me a moment to recognize Adrian's room. I'd never seen it bathed in sunshine before.

Oh fuck, so it had been all real. I panicked, and it wasn't because I might have magic disease, but because I was lying in Adrian's bed. That was a very scary thing, but luckily, I still had my dress on. I slowly turned around, holding my breath. He wasn't on the other side of the bed, which strangely enough, didn't look used at all. I lifted my eyes toward the window and there he was.

Adrian was sitting on the windowsill, his knees drawn up to his chest. He was leaning his head on the glass and looking outside. His face looked beautiful and sad. Golden rays of sunshine were falling down on him, giving his black messy hair a bluish shine. Damn, he almost looked likeable. I shook my head. Nah, I was still too sleepy and shocked to think rationally.

He turned his head to look at me. I started to smile at him but caught myself in time. We weren't lovers, and smiling at a guy after you woke up in his room to thank him for letting you stay over somehow didn't feel right.

"You're awake," he said, not moving from the windowsill. I wanted to see his face, but I couldn't because of all that sunlight behind his back.

"Um, I'm sorry. I didn't mean to fall asleep. Thank you for letting me stay." I couldn't believe I had actually said it, but I'd felt like I had to.

"Don't worry about it. But you should probably leave before Alan comes or Michael tells someone you went missing."

"Right," I said, getting up. At this angle, I had a better view of the dark circles under his eyes.

"Have you slept?" I asked.

"No," he said. "I figured you'd kill me if you found me lying next to you, and I didn't feel like sleeping on the floor, so... I just stayed up. Oh, and the sunrise looked nice."

"I wouldn't have killed you." I frowned. Really, I wouldn't have. Maybe I'd scream, but I didn't think I had an appropriate weapon to kill someone... except maybe my high heels.

"I know. But you'd make a fuss." He smiled. "And someone reporting noise from my room wouldn't be a good thing."

"Um, yeah," I said. "I'm going... I just..."

"Act as if nothing had happened. Invent something believable for Michael. Say that you got carried away. I don't know."

"Carried away? Right," I said, a hint of anger in my voice. "It would mean I'm a psycho who gets excited by choking people to death!"

"Ah, so you really tried to choke him? Interesting." There was a cocky smile on his face now. Good. He was returning to his usual self, and I knew how to deal with that.

"Shut up!" I said and went for the door.

"Come back any time you want," he said. I looked back at him to tell him that wouldn't happen, but I wasn't sure of it.

"Thanks," I said instead and left.

I slowly opened the door of my room and let out a sigh of relief when I saw no one was there. I'd half-expected to find Michael waiting for me. My phone was lying on my nightstand, and I picked it up. I had twelve messages and fifteen unanswered calls, mostly from Michael. Well, there was no reason to draw this out further, so I dialed his number. Maybe it was 7 a.m., but I believed he was awake.

I was right. He answered on the second ring.

"Ria!" His voice was urgent and full of worry. Damn, what had I done to him?

"Michael, listen," I said, "we need to talk."

"Yes, we do. I'll come immediately."

"All right," I said.

He knocked on my door a minute later, which meant he hadn't been in his room. Had he been looking for me somewhere?

As soon as I opened the door, his hands went around me, and he hugged me as if his life depended on it. I let him do it, hoping the whole time that his element wouldn't wake and turn me into a monster. But I could feel his element deep inside of him. A picture formed in my head as I concentrated on his water, and I saw a clear stream that was glittering in the sun. Somehow, I knew that if I drank from it, the water would be cold, refreshing, and pure. Only I couldn't let that happen.

"What happened? I've been looking everywhere for you," he said, and I noticed for the first time a few dark bruises around his neck. Oh, shit.

"Michael, I'm sorry. I just…"

"It's okay. I'm glad you're okay," he said. I couldn't believe it. I had nearly killed him, and he was worried about me! I didn't know what to say to him.

"Really. You don't have to feel bad." Michael smiled. "I know you lost your balance and your hands ended up on my neck. You probably weren't even aware it was my neck. It was too dark to see."

I opened my mouth, closed it, and then just nodded. He'd offered me a perfect explanation. I would have never come up with something as original as that.

"I didn't want to hurt you," I said, and that was the truth. I definitely hadn't had that in mind when we'd been kissing.

"I know. I told you already. It's okay," he said. "Don't think about it anymore."

He kissed me gently, and I returned the kiss after I was sure I wouldn't try to kill him. What had my life turned into? His arm slid around me and our kiss deepened. I finally pushed him away as gently as I could.

"I need to talk to Paula," I said.

"Okay. But you have to tell me where you've been all night. I know you weren't here."

"I was outside," I said, hoping he'd leave it alone. I would have said I'd been at some friend's room, but he could easily check that and discover the lie.

"All night? Something could have happened to you!"

"I've been in the park," I said. "It's locked for everyone outside the university at night."

"I know, but still…" He took my hand and pressed it to his lips.

"I'm fine." I smiled. "See? Everything's just fine. But I really want to catch Paula before class."

"Do you have a class together?"

"Yeah, we do, and you know what that means. I can't talk in that class." I felt immediately sick after I said it. Magic Studies wasn't the class I wanted to go to. Not now when we actually got to work with our elements. Oh, crap. I hadn't thought about it at all! No, that couldn't be happening! I survived the shitty part, and now I couldn't go to the awesome part! Fuck!

"Are you sure you want to go to that class?" Michael asked cautiously. "You've been outside the whole time. You need sleep. I don't want you to faint or something."

"You're right. I probably shouldn't go to class," I said. "But I still want to talk to Paula about something."

"Okay, as you wish." He kissed the top of my head. "I'm going now. There are some books waiting for me in the library. See you later. And get some sleep."

"Yeah, sure." I waved him goodbye. When the door closed, I threw myself on the bed, unsure what to do. I'd had more than enough sleep, so staying in my room didn't seem like a good option, even though I had some unfinished homework and lots of stuff to study. But with all of this on my mind, I didn't think I could really concentrate on studying.

After a little trip to the bathroom, I was feeling fresh and clean again, so I decided to find Paula. Michael was nowhere to be seen, and I tried to figure out if I could find him like Adrian could, but I failed. I really needed to ask Adrian about that.

Paula was the only person waiting in front of the classroom, but that wasn't unusual. People usually got to class a minute or two before the beginning, just like me. But Paula wanted to make sure she got there in time, so she always went earlier. She smiled at me as I approached her, then she suddenly frowned.

"Ria, where are your books?" She raised an eyebrow.

"I'm not going to class today. I don't think I can stay concentrated long enough."

"But you can't miss this class! We'll be doing some fun things with our elements!" she said. "You love doing that!"

"I'm tired." I leaned on the wall next to her. "It's been a long night. But listen, I wanted to ask you something."

"Sure," she said cheerfully. "What is it?"

"Well, Michael and I were at a fancy restaurant yesterday, and I overheard someone talking about magic disease."

"Oh, you two were out? That's awesome." Her blue-green eyes shined with excitement. "Where did he take you? Was it romantic?"

That wasn't exactly what I wanted to talk to her about, but as I remembered that part of last night, it seemed like something worth talking about.

"He actually brought a white horse here, and we were riding together to the restaurant," I said with a shy smile on my face. I wasn't sure whether I should brag about it or be embarrassed because I had let Michael put me on a horse while I was wearing a dress.

"That's so romantic!" Paula said, looking genuinely happy for me, but I knew she wished it had happened to her. It was her dream that her boyfriend did something romantic for her, but I didn't think Adrian was the right guy for that.

"Yeah, it is," I said. "I'll give you the details when we have more time, but I was wondering about something I overheard in the restaurant. One guy said it might be possible for people with magic disease to keep their elements. What do you think about that?"

"Impossible. If they kept their element, then they wouldn't have to kill to have it. They wouldn't have magic disease then."

I frowned. If she was right, then what Adrian and I had wasn't magic disease. But why did we have symptoms of magic disease? And why had I almost choked Michael to death then? Another point against her theory was that Adrian's parents had both had the disease for sure, and there was no way he hadn't inherited it, unless Adrian's mother had cheated on her husband. But even then, the chances of not inheriting the disease were very, very low.

"But let's just say they could have the disease and keep the element," I said. "What would happen in that case?"

"Um, I'm not a science fiction expert." She laughed a little. "I don't know. Maybe they could collect elements when they killed? That could be very dangerous if you ask me. But don't worry. That guy was probably reading some kind of a novel."

"Yeah, you're right," I said. "Well, I have to go now. Not showing up for class is much better than running into the professor and then not showing up."

"I'm going to bring you my notes after I'm done."

"Thanks." I smiled and headed down the hallway, as far away from the classroom as I could. I was glad that going to classes wasn't obligatory, because I didn't feel like coming up with some stupid excuse. But, of course, missing a class meant a lot, especially Magic Studies practice class. You could get the notes, but no one could show you exactly how the thing was done. Well, they could show you how they thought it went, but that was never going to be perfect.

I was getting closer to the lunchroom, and suddenly I could feel various elements around me, and yeah, each one seemed different in a way. It was almost overwhelming. Maybe I should just stay away from big crowds for some time. And I really needed coffee. The café where I usually went with Michael felt like the best choice, so I hurried outside.

I spent the day mostly sitting in the café and reading some of my university books. Sitting was easy, but reading took some effort. I couldn't concentrate on History or Geography when my thoughts were drifting away. I also decided not to show up for any other classes, but I took the risk and went to lunch with Michael. Luckily, no one died.

In the evening, Paula came to my room to bring me the notes, and we talked about my romantic date with Michael. Paula was just about to show me what was supposed to be done with the element when her phone rang. Her face lit up as she answered, and I knew immediately it was Adrian.

"Can he come here?" Paula asked, holding her hand over the phone. "I was supposed to meet him half an hour ago, but the time flew by. And I really want to show you this."

I wasn't really sure I wanted to see her use her element in front of me, and I didn't know what to invent to avoid this. I had to learn how to control myself. And somehow having Adrian around when that happened seemed like a good idea. I just had to stall Paula until he came, because I was sure she wouldn't want to use her element in front of him. If only she knew.

"Let's do this," she said after exchanging a few words with Adrian. From what I gathered, he was on his way here. I just hoped he'd come in time.

"Wait, can you explain first what this means?" I pointed at a random sentence in the notes.

"Yeah, but I want to show you this before Adrian comes. I don't want to use my element in front of him," she said impatiently.

"I know. But what's the point in showing it to me first if I don't get it?"

"Um, there's a point in showing it. You'll know what result you're supposed to get. It's the same for all elements, so I can show it to you without a problem." She sighed. "You'll never get it otherwise. Ah, what are you going to do when we start having separate classes for each element?"

"I'll be lost." I chuckled, but she just pressed her lips together in what looked like an angry line.

"Just let me do this, okay? Maybe I'm not perfect at showing it, but it might make things easier for you."

I didn't have time to answer because there was a knock on the door. I immediately jumped to open it and felt relieved to see Adrian. Relieved to see Adrian? Oh yeah, this world was going to end soon. I could feel it.

"Hello, my ladies," Adrian said, a sly smile on his face. I frowned at him, but his expression didn't change. It was almost as if I had dreamed everything from last night.

"Heeey." Paula threw herself into his arms, and they kissed. I rolled my eyes.

"Have you missed me?" she asked, stepping away from him and putting her notes back together.

"Yes," he said, looking directly at me, "I missed you."

I looked away, suddenly feeling heat coming into my cheeks. I remembered what he had said last night about making me his next target, and I couldn't help but feel upset and angry. But why in hell was I blushing then? Keeping secrets from Paula really was a difficult thing.

"Damn, now I can't show her the exercise we did in Magic Studies." She pouted.

"Sure you can," he said casually. "I'll survive. Besides, I'm sure Ria would kill me before I even got to you."

"I agree." I grinned. It was Paula's time to roll her eyes at us.

"You two are impossible, you know?" she said. "All right. But, Adrian, tell me to stop if it bothers you."

"I'll leave the room if it bothers me," he said.

"Why don't you leave now? I can meet you…" Paula started to say, but Adrian interrupted her.

"More standing in the hallway? No, thanks," he said. "You made me do that too much today already."

"Sorry." She smiled apologetically.

"Stop talking and do it already!" I said, and Paula frowned, but she went through the notes again. While she was checking out some things, Adrian came to stand behind me. I wanted him to assure me that everything was going to be all right, but I got nothing from him.

"Okay, here it goes," Paula said. I'd seen her use her element numerous times, but this time it wasn't just the tingling sensation I was feeling. I could feel the air all around her, and it wasn't a breeze exactly, more like a tornado. Maybe Paula wouldn't hurt a fly, but this tornado that was her element was meant to destroy things.

According to the notes, she was supposed to slowly call her element to life, bring it to full force, and then shut it off. I guessed the task was supposed to teach us to shut our element abruptly in a second if necessary. Maybe it seemed easy, but it wasn't. Shutting all that energy down after it was full force wasn't the same as my usual medium power turned into heat inside of me before dying out completely.

I could now feel her element completely, and it was suddenly hard to breathe. I wanted to stop her. I wanted to take her out before I suffocated. I blinked. No, that was wrong. I was still breathing, but my chest felt so heavy, and that element would feel sweet in my possession...

The pressure in my chest intensified as I was struggling for breath. There was no air in my lungs. I had to... I felt Adrian's hand behind my back. I put my own hand behind me, and he took it. The air was back and I could breathe just fine. I could still feel the power of the air, but I didn't feel like I wanted it.

Paula's eyes were closed now, her hair flying around her and the papers rustling as she was trying to stay concentrated and do this as best as she could. I didn't want to risk a glance at Adrian to find out how he was feeling with me holding his hand. It seemed that we got back in control of ourselves when we touched. Creepy, but it might be useful.

In a blink of an eye, Paula's element was no more than a gentle pulsation inside of her, which I could feel only because of my condition. I was still in denial, actually. Maybe this thing would pass. Adrian let go of my hand, and we both pretended that nothing had happened.

"Did you see it?" Paula asked proudly. "I used my element to make that bit of paper twirl and stopped it completely in a second! I can't wait until we learn how to get rid of other things flying around as well." She said the last sentence while she was trying to make her hair look good again.

Oops, I hadn't even noticed the twirling paper. Damn. I knew that in my version of this task there would be something on fire, and I was hoping I could get rid of the temperature rising inside of me when I used my element... if I got to keep my element at all, that is. All my wishes and dreams needed a makeover.

"Yeah, it was great!" I said, smiling.

"Why don't you give it a try?" Paula asked, and then her face darkened as her eyes fell on Adrian. "Oh, sorry. Fire bothers you the most. I forgot."

"Ria can try that later," he said. "And you have to come with me. Now."

"Okay," she said and looked at me. "Do you need anything else?"

"No," I said. "Thanks."

"Well, see you soon," Paula said from the door. And Adrian, who was standing behind her, mouthed "in my room" to me. I just nodded, and then they were gone. Great, Adrian wanted to see me. I wondered how Paula would feel about it, but I needed to see him. And it wasn't as if I were going to sleep with him or something. Michael was my one and only, and I swore to myself nothing was going to change that. I'd find a way to keep him. I had to.

Chapter 14

I wasn't exactly sure when Adrian expected to see me, but I'd figured that I could just go to his room, and if Paula was there, I could say I was looking for her. I'd invent something. But from what I had heard from her, they mostly stayed in her room. Adrian apparently told her something about the danger of someone finding her in his room. Maybe he was afraid she'd come and catch him with another girl. But for some reason, I didn't believe he took girls to his room; he stayed in theirs.

I knocked on his door somewhere around 11 p.m. Paula usually went to sleep at that time because she needed to be well-rested in the morning and ready for classes and research. He opened it in a moment, a big grin on his face.

"It's so weird not to know when you're coming," he said as I stepped inside.

"Whatever." I sat down on the bed, looking at him expectantly. "You told me to come, so I'm here. What now?"

"Oh, please. You've been dying to see me," he said, getting two beer bottles out of somewhere and handing me one.

"You're an idiot. If you're trying to get me into your bed, it's not going to happen."

"You've already been in my bed." He laughed and came to sit next to me.

"That's not what I meant." I frowned and took a good swig of the beer.

"Are you going to tell me how you got the disease?" he asked, a hint of amusement in his gray-blue eyes.

"No, because I don't know," I said. "My parents are not telling me something, but I can't just ask them directly because I'm not sure. I'm kind of still hoping it's all going to go away."

"You really didn't…?" he asked in surprise.

"No!" I said before he could finish the sentence. "And I'm not ready to find out that I'm not my parents' daughter or something equally complicated."

"But you'll have to find out someday."

"Yeah, but not today or anytime soon. I'm still dealing with this…whatever it is that I have." I sighed. "Hey, I wanted to ask you how you could find people by recognizing their element. I tried to figure out where Michael was but didn't know how to do it."

"I don't think you'll be able to do that anytime soon," he said. "It takes time to learn it."

"Crap! It would definitely help to avoid trouble." I certainly wouldn't have to invent silly excuses because I'd know if Paula or anyone else was here.

"Yeah, it comes in handy."

"What do you think happens if… we get in possession of another element?" I looked at him, wondering if he would know the answer.

"You mean if we kill someone?" He chuckled. I started to say no, but damn, there wasn't another way.

"Yeah," I said reluctantly.

"I don't know." His eyes flashed dangerously. "Wanna try and see?"

"No!" I yelled, and then put my hand over my mouth. I just hoped no one was outside to hear me. I really had to be more careful.

"Fine, you don't have to get upset," he said. "It was just a thought."

Yeah, a thought, right. But I didn't say anything.

"Wait, are you thinking someone like us could be collecting elements?" He suddenly looked interested in the topic and not just because he thought I could be his partner in crime.

"Are there even people like us?" I asked.

"I don't know, but we can't be the only ones, can we? They must be hiding."

"Yeah, no one would admit to being a murderer just to let everyone know it's possible to have more elements," I said. "What about your parents? Did they have an element like you?"

"I don't think so." His voice was strained.

"So your mother had an affair…" I couldn't even finish the sentence because he turned to me completely furious, his face only inches from mine.

"Don't you ever say something like that!" he said through his teeth. "Or we might find out if I get to keep your element or not."

He moved away from me and took a swig of his beer. For a moment, I just sat there, trying hard not to shake and show him my fear. But he had scared me. He had really, truly scared me. Mentioning his parents in a bad context obviously wasn't a smart thing to do; even I should have known that.

"Sorry," I said, trying to change the subject. "So you can't feel my element when I'm using it, and touching helps while others are using their elements nearby?"

"Yeah," he said. "Touching and being together with another person who has magic disease helps you to stay in control and to be able to stay longer around people with elements. Of course, having an element helps you even more, so you can actually live without killing someone… at least for some years."

"Why? And if that's true, how did you go all these years without another person with the disease?" I raised an eyebrow at him. Maybe I shouldn't take everything he said as the truth. He could as well be trying to manipulate me into something.

"Because you're always surrounded by people who have elements, and their elements are using up your energy. Imagine them like bees buzzing around your head and tempting you. Sooner or later, you're going to snap," he said. "And once the disease gets stronger, you'll be able to feel people's elements almost a mile away from you. It's almost impossible to stay completely away unless you go to an abandoned island in the middle of nowhere."

"Why don't people with magic disease stick together then?"

"Because no one is willing to put an ad in the papers asking for a partner with magic disease. Try telling someone you have magic disease and watch how people start to treat you. Some would find you interesting, but they would still be watching carefully for any sign of danger. But, then again, you must already know that because you decided not to tell your boyfriend."

"You're right." I didn't have to ask people what they thought about magic disease carriers, because I knew all too well what I had thought... or maybe I was still thinking it.

"Hey, you didn't answer my second question," I said suspiciously. "How did you manage not to kill someone this whole time?"

I was gripping the beer bottle so tightly in my hands that I thought it would burst. What if he had been lying to me? No, I refused to feel intimidated by Adrian again. Not now. And yeah, I must have thought that countless times by now.

"The disease first showed," he said, "when I was fourteen. My element, or whatever it is, came when I was sixteen."

"Okay, it isn't that many years, but," I said, and he lifted his finger in front of his mouth. I stopped talking and stared at him.

"Give me a chance to tell you," he said. I just nodded to let him know I wanted him to continue, and he did exactly that.

"At fourteen, I could only do what you can now, and that's just feel the elements when they are especially strong or when they are close," he said. "But I didn't try to kill anyone, so you're just more advanced."

I knew he was teasing me with the last part because the corners of his lips were going up a bit.

"I was seventeen when the disease got stronger, and since then I've been learning how to keep it down," he said. "It wasn't easy at first, and that was why Alan took me someplace for some time until he was sure I could control it. There I learned a lot of things about elements, the disease, and everything else."

"Wait, so Alan could help me learn all that stuff like he helped you?" I asked hopefully.

"No, you wouldn't want to go there, trust me," he said, his face deadly serious. "It's the worst thing that can happen to you, actually. I think you and I can keep you in control just fine. I can tell you things I know, and if you avoid dangerous situations, everything will be fine."

"If you say so." I let the doubt show in my voice. I wanted him to know that I didn't trust him.

"Think whatever you want," he said. "I'm telling you the truth."

"All right."

"Any more questions?" He looked at me expectantly. Actually, I was full of questions, but I just didn't want to or couldn't discuss them with him at the moment.

"Why did you make a fuss in Alan's office when I was there?" I asked.

He flinched back but quickly regained his composure. "I wanted Alan to know I have good intentions with Paula. Maybe make him believe I love her."

"Why?" I asked. "You don't love her."

"True, but I want him to believe it. It's a guy thing."

No, it wasn't. And it didn't make any sense. Oh well, all magic disease carriers were a bit crazy… um, wait a second. That would mean I was crazy too. Stupid logic.

"Why are you frowning?" He came really close to me, studying my face.

"Just don't tell me I'm less pretty when I'm frowning because I heard it from, like, twenty drunk guys at parties," I said.

"Nonsense. You're always pretty."

"Oh, please." I snorted. "You just want to get into my pants."

"Yeah, I do." He smiled. "And what's wrong with that?"

I got up from the bed, walking a bit closer to the window. Adrian followed me like a shadow at my back. I placed the empty beer bottle on the desk to my right and took a deep, shaky breath. I knew he was going to touch me. And of course, he did. He placed his hand on my shoulder, letting his fingers slowly slide down my arm.

His touch sent shivers of delight down my spine, and that was making me angry. He wasn't supposed to cause that kind of a reaction in me because that was reserved only for the person I loved, not for some random good-looking, manipulative bastard. I turned around suddenly, stunning him for a moment, and punched him in the face.

"Don't you ever touch me like that again," I said as he stared at me in surprise, his hand touching his lip and coming away with blood. The expression on his face turned into an angry sneer.

"You bitch," he said.

"I'm not a fucking toy! You can't play with me like you do with Paula and the other girls," I said. "So if that makes me a bitch, fine. I'll be a bitch then."

I pushed past him and went for the door. Maybe I needed him to get through this, but I wasn't going to let him play with me. Not him and not anyone.

Chapter 15

I was feeling just fine in the morning, so I decided to call Michael. He agreed to meet me at the park, even though he sounded surprised. I didn't have anything romantic planned, but an early walk in the park seemed like a perfect thing to do with the man I loved.

I couldn't help but smile when I saw him coming toward me. His wavy brown hair was shining in the sun, and he looked devastatingly handsome in faded blue jeans and a yellow t-shirt. Whatever I had to do to keep this man... I'd do it. I was sure of it.

"Hey, my love." Michael smiled and gave me one of the hottest and sweetest kisses ever. There was a glint of amusement in his eyes.

"Why are you looking so... happy?" I asked, trying to ignore the image of running water that I had somewhere in the back of my mind.

"Can't I just be happy to see you?" He laughed.

"Yeah, but that's not it."

"You're right," he said. "I just saw Adrian Liandre. He has a nice bruise on his jaw. Finally, someone got the better of him. Too bad I couldn't see it."

I froze. Uh oh. That wasn't good. If only Michael knew it had been me who'd done that… Maybe he'd be proud of me. Yeah, right.

"Really?" I didn't know what else to say.

"Yeah, and now he's in trouble." He smirked. "Looks like we won't be seeing him at the party tonight."

"What party?" I frowned.

"Where do you live, my love?" Michael laughed. "The ads for it are all over the university!"

Yeah, they probably were. But I hadn't had time to notice them while I kept getting images of different elements in my head!

"Are we going?" I asked, smiling up at him and putting my arms around his neck.

"Sure we are," he said. "I'll come for you at nine."

"Great!" I said. "Where are we going exactly?"

"To that awesome club in town. They're finally opening it, and the party is for students only."

That club really was a big thing. We had all been so excited when we had heard about it being built. I wasn't sure of the name exactly, but I thought it was Scarlet Kiss. It was supposed to be a five-floor club with many dance floors, rooms, a restaurant, and all kinds of music. It surely sounded like a lot of fun.

"They're finally opening it? That's amazing!" I said, realizing that I'd need to plan my outfit carefully for such an event. "I need to talk to Paula. We need to pick outfits!"

"Are you sure Paula is going?" Michael asked.

I looked at him in surprise. "Why wouldn't she? She's been waiting for this as much as everyone."

"Well, I'm not sure she'll go without Adrian."

"Without Adrian?" I blinked at Michael in confusion.

"Yeah, I told you he was in trouble. They won't let him go."

"What? Why?"

"I told you about the bruise. He got into a fight again, and Alan decided that unless his opponent came alive to his office and signed a report, Adrian couldn't go anywhere."

"What?" I nearly yelled. This could not be happening.

"He has magic disease, Ria," Michael said. "And he really needs to stop getting into fights, especially those without witnesses. Alan's finally had enough of him, and I'm glad. We don't want him to kill anyone."

"But that's insane! So someone hits him in the face where no one can see it or doesn't want to admit it, and he's accused of murder?"

"He's dangerous. And don't worry about him. No one would dare to go against him alone, and he wouldn't let anyone do anything to him. You're underestimating him. Maybe he did kill someone."

Ah, fuck.

"Maybe he just fell," I said. "Surely they can't blame him for that."

"Well, that's probably what he claims. But then he'll still miss the party, and who knows how many other parties until the police checks all other options. But why aren't you happy? I was sure you'd enjoy the news. You hate him, honey, and you told me you wanted him dead or locked up. This is the best you can get."

"Um, it's because of Paula," I lied. "I really want her to go and be happy."

"Aww, you're such a great friend," Michael said and kissed me. I looked away, thinking what I could do that didn't include me going to Alan's office. I couldn't come up with anything. Great.

"I'm going to find Paula." I put a fake smile on my face.

"Okay," Michael said. "See you later."

I nodded and headed for the university.

Adrian was right. I couldn't tell anyone that I had symptoms of the disease. They would treat me like a criminal. And part of me could actually understand it, because I was dangerous. But I didn't want to live my life like that.

I went straight to Alan's office before I changed my mind. Maybe I should leave Adrian to deal with this on his own. Maybe being away from others would help him become a better person... Yeah, and if that happened, I'd have to go look for flying pigs. He'd probably just be pissed off at everyone and everything.

And I needed him, especially now that I was supposed to go to a party with lots of people around me. Besides, he was in this whole mess because of me. Okay, he had provoked me. It was his fault, but still... I sighed. All of this was making me tired.

As soon as I entered the office, I saw Adrian, who was leaning on the wall as far away from Alan as he could get. And that wasn't far considering how small the damn office was. I often wondered how Alan didn't get claustrophobia from being in here all the time. Adrian's eyes flashed with fury as he saw me, but he just stood there with his arms crossed. The dark bruise on his jaw in combination with his attitude made him look pretty scary.

"You have nothing to do here," he said, glaring at me.

"Adrian!" Alan said disapprovingly, and then gave me a smile. "Ria, what can I do for you?"

"I need to talk to you," I said, "in private."

"Adrian, wait outside," Alan said.

"Aren't you afraid I'm going to kill someone?" Adrian asked sarcastically.

"Will you go out, or do I have to call the guards?" Alan asked, the expression on his face perfectly calm. Adrian rolled his eyes and slowly started going for the door, his arm brushing against mine as he passed by. I let out a breath of relief and looked at Alan, who offered me a seat.

"So, what can I do for you?" Alan asked politely after I had gotten comfortable in the chair.

I took a deep breath, let it out, and smiled. "I was the one who punched Adrian in the face."

Alan's smile faltered for a moment, and then he looked at me carefully, almost as if he were trying to see through me and find out if I was lying.

"Are you sure of what you're saying?" he finally asked.

"Yeah," I said. "Totally."

"Do you know that you have to sign an official statement? You could be convicted as his accomplice."

"Wait, you really think he killed someone?" I scoffed.

"I had to warn you," he said. "Will you sign it?"

"Sure."

"Why did you punch him?" he asked as he gave me some kind of a document and a pen. I studied the text for a moment and realized it really was a true statement. Unbelievable.

"He tried to seduce me despite the fact that he's dating my best friend," I said calmly as I signed the statement.

"Oh. Then I'm not surprised you did it, but next time you better ignore him. Don't put your life in danger. I might be reconsidering my decision to let him have a girlfriend, too. What do you think? Is Paula in danger?"

"No, she's not. She loves him," I said. "And he wouldn't hurt her."

"I hope you're right." He sighed. "But if you notice anything strange in his behavior, tell me immediately. I explained to Paula already how she has to act around him and gave her my number in case she needs anything."

"Great," I said, even though I was considering punching him in the face too. "Can I go now?"

"Yeah, sure." He smiled. "Oh, and don't punch anyone else in the face. It could get you suspended."

I just nodded, getting up. Yeah, I'd get suspended for punching a *normal* person, but not for punching a magic disease carrier. Awesome. Once, I would have approved of that, now that I had magic disease it didn't seem funny anymore.

Just as I came out of the office and closed the door, Adrian grabbed my shoulders and pushed me hard against the wall.

I glared at him. "Get your hands off me. I don't feel like signing another statement."

That made him hesitate, and then he slowly moved away from me.

"What have you done?" he asked, rage still shining in his eyes, which now seemed almost silver to me.

"What I had to," I said, trying to walk away, but he caught my arm. This time his hold on my arm was gentle.

"You better take Paula to that party tonight," I said. "I might need you there."

"You're such a selfish bitch," he said, letting go of me.

"Yeah, I guess I am." I smirked. "And that's actually fortunate for you today. So, are you going to the party?"

"Yeah."

"Good. And I really hope you didn't kill anyone in the meantime."

"Maybe I should have."

"Yeah, you should have," I said and left before things could get ugly.

I found Paula in her room, and, of course, she was sitting on the floor surrounded by books. She immediately cheered up when I told her the good news, but I left out the part that involved me in the whole thing. I suggested that we should skip class and go shopping, and she almost threw a book at me, accusing me of being irresponsible.

She also told me she already had a dress for the party, so I decided to leave her to her books and find someone willing to go shopping with me. I didn't really have any good friends like Paula. There were those girls who talked to me during lunch or went to classes with me, but I didn't feel like taking them with me. Then I got a crazy idea; I grabbed my phone and dialed Michael's number.

It took me a while to persuade him to come with me and skip his favorite History class, but he couldn't say no to me in the end. We ended up in one big mall, which had tons of different shops, and I had no idea what I wanted. Michael nearly lost his mind with me, but he followed me everywhere. He almost begged me to choose something after two hours of walking from one shop to another.

I settled for a denim miniskirt, orange top, and black high heels. Michael approved of my choice, and that was the only thing that mattered. I also realized I was starting to feel thirsty. Not really thirsty, but thirsty for Michael's element, so I had to let go of his hand. I probably shouldn't have spent so much time around so many people with elements. I could feel the element of almost any person near us, and yeah, that was starting to bother me.

When I returned to my room, I realized my hands were shaking. Touching Adrian earlier today obviously hadn't been enough, or maybe I'd be in even worse condition now if he hadn't touched me at all. Why did it have to be him? I took a shower, ate a bit of chocolate, and went through some books, but nothing helped to get rid of that anxiety inside of me. I wanted someone's element. It didn't even matter whose.

I decided to look for Adrian because that was the only thing I could do so I wouldn't freak out and kill someone. Okay, maybe I wouldn't kill anyone, or at least I liked to think that. Adrian was in his room when I arrived, and he let me in without a word.

"I need your help," I said almost breathlessly.

"I know." He came closer to me but didn't touch me. He just stared at me with his cold gray-blue eyes, his face serious. I licked my dry lips and looked at him.

"I'm sorry for hitting you," I said, even though I wasn't.

"You're not," he said. Oh well.

"It would be easier if we could just cooperate." There was something on his face that told me he knew just how much I needed him right now.

"Yeah, it would." He took a step closer to me, so we ended up standing only inches apart. "Can I touch you now, or are you going to hit me when you don't need me anymore?"

Ouch. It did sound mean when you put it that way.

"Please," I whispered, closing my eyes. I felt him pull me into a hug, and I pressed my head against his hard chest. The world immediately started to feel like a better place. I couldn't feel any of the elements anymore. Damn, that felt good. We stood there like that for a long while. I half-expected him to try something with me, but he didn't.

"Feeling better?" he asked.

"Um, yeah," I said, moving away from him. "Let's make a deal."

"A deal?" He raised an eyebrow at me. "What kind of a deal?"

"We touch only when we need to," I said. "And I don't want anything sexual on your part."

"All right," he said confidently. "But I'll get you to have sex with me, you'll see."

"Oh, please." I rolled my eyes. "I wouldn't have sex with you even if you were the last man on the planet."

"We'll see what you'll say when time passes and you realize you can't have sex with your dear boyfriend."

"Maybe I'll just drug him like you do with your girls."

"But you won't," he said. "And do you know why? Because you would worry too much."

I just glared at him because he was right. I wouldn't give Michael some pill that could ruin his life, especially not after what had happened to me. It was easy for Adrian to give the pills to girls because he didn't care about them at all after he got what he wanted.

"Well," I said, going for the door, "I guess I'll see you at the party."

"Wait," he said, "I want to give you my number first. If you can't find me at the party, text me."

"Okay." I took my phone and saved the number he told me. "Thanks."

"See you there." He smiled.

I went for the door and stopped to look back at him. "Do you think things could get ugly with so many people at the party?" If a few people in the mall bothered me, then who knew what would a building full of drunk and crazy students do to me?

"We'll see," he said. "Last time I'd been to a party of that size Alan gave me some weird pills, and he wants to give them to me tonight, too, but I think you and I can survive without that."

That almost made me laugh. I couldn't believe he was complaining about someone giving him unknown pills when he was doing exactly the same.

"Wait, there are pills for us, too?" I frowned, a bit annoyed that he hadn't told me about it before. I wasn't really thrilled about any kind of pills, but that would definitely be better than having to run to him every time the disease showed its ugly face.

"Yes, there are," he said. "But you don't want to try that, trust me."

"Why not?"

"Because you don't lose just the feeling of other people's elements, you lose any other feeling. You're just perfectly calm. If you took that pill and someone told you the room was on fire, you'd just stare. It's like being in someone else's body, and everything that happens to it doesn't affect you at all."

"Ah, creepy." I didn't know why I'd expected there could be something good in a pill. "So how are you going to get out of taking the pill?"

"Hey, I'm an expert in hiding pills in my mouth." He chuckled. "I had years of practice."

And I didn't want to know the details, so I just shook my head and left.

Chapter 16

I was already dressed and ready to meet Michael in the hallway when someone knocked on my door. I opened it, slightly annoyed, but then I saw Paula smiling at me. She was wearing a tight pink cocktail dress and pink high heels, which all together seemed like she was desperately trying to get Adrian's attention, because I could see the edge of her bra peeking out. I smiled back at her simply because what I thought about her looks didn't matter. If she was happy with it, so was I.

"Hey, are you ready?" she asked.

"Yeah. Where's Adrian?"

"Waiting in the hallway." She grabbed my hand. "Come on. Michael's there, too. I don't want them to get in a fight before we get there."

"Oh, then we better hurry," I said, and we left my room. The whole idea of the four of us going together to the club seemed both crazy and dangerous. I wondered who'd come up with that idea. Probably Paula.

"I managed to cover Adrian's bruise with make-up," she said, and I nearly tripped on the stupid dark blue carpet.

"Cool," I said cautiously. "Did he tell you how he got the bruise?"

"No, he didn't." She sounded a bit worried. "I'm just glad that they allowed him to go to the party."

I really hoped no one would find out the truth, especially not Paula. I just didn't feel like explaining how exactly that had happened.

My heart skipped a beat when I saw Michael just standing there and looking incredibly good. He was dressed in dark blue jeans and a black shirt, which fitted him perfectly. The way he smiled at me made me feel warm all over. I hurried over to him, and we kissed, not caring about my lip gloss.

I was still in Michael's arms when I glanced at Adrian and Paula. Paula had done an awesome job and covered his bruise almost completely. I was sure no one would see it at all under the dim lights in the club. Adrian was wearing blue jeans, a white shirt, and a black leather jacket, and there was no doubt Paula would have to be careful of her man, or someone might steal him.

There was a limousine waiting for us outside, and we must have been a bit late, judging by the small number of remaining cars. Some of the students were going with their own cars, which were mostly very expensive and fast. Actually almost everyone had a car, but not everyone wanted to keep their precious baby parked near the university. Besides, we rarely needed transport since everything was so close.

We reached the club in five minutes. I couldn't see much except lots of blinding lights, a red carpet in front of the entrance, and heavy security. The building seemed huge, almost like a hotel or something. Adrian opened the door and got out first, offering me his hand. I took it, but not because I needed help getting out. His touch let me take a short break from the world of elements. Michael helped Paula out, and he seemed really annoyed, so I took his hand as soon as I could to prevent him from saying something to Adrian. Not that Adrian would care.

We were almost attacked by the press when we reached the entrance. The security did a good job of keeping them away, but the cameras still caught us. Of course, who wouldn't want a photograph of a living magic disease carrier with his girlfriend? I wondered how much more expensive photographs of me would get if the world found out the truth about me.

The camera flashes were completely forgotten when we entered the dimness of the club. The room was huge and full of people who were already dancing to the music, which was as loud as it could get. I felt as if I had dived into a sea of elements and realized that the same types of elements were mostly gathered in small groups. We must have been a strange group since we all had different elements… Oh, and two of us had magic disease, and one had a completely unknown element. We were definitely special.

As we pushed through the crowd, I managed to see a huge bar to my left and stairs in front of me, which led to another floor. There were also other stairs not far from the first ones, but those led down. I couldn't see the doors that led to the other rooms, but they had to be somewhere.

Michael pulled me away from Paula and Adrian, and soon we were lost in the sea of people. We passed numerous rooms with different music; some rooms even had comfortable-looking chairs, but we didn't have time to sit around. After we had seen most of the place, we decided to pick one room and stay there. I managed to stop Michael from taking me too far away from the exits.

We danced for some time, and I was becoming more and more aware of the elements around me, especially Michael's. Maybe I could survive a bit longer, but different kind of thirsts started to exchange in me, and I figured it was time to take a break. I sent Michael to get us some drinks, and when he was gone, I sent a message to Adrian. He replied within a minute, telling me to come out through a side door. I followed his instructions.

The air outside was fresh, and it cleared my mind a bit, but that still wasn't enough to help me get away from the elements. I realized I was shivering from the cold, and I ran my hand through my damp hair. Great, I'd stepped outside into the cold night from a hot club in sweaty clothes. I'd be lucky if I didn't catch a cold or pneumonia.

The slight pain in my legs forced me to sit down on the low stone wall that surrounded the building. Sitting down was probably another step toward pneumonia, but my high heels were killing me. It almost felt scary to sit there alone in the dark with no one around. I let out a sigh of relief when Adrian came around the corner. He must have been in a completely different room.

He smiled at me, taking off his jacket and putting it over my shoulders. I shivered as the warm leather touched my cold skin, and I could smell his, now too well-known, scent of pine, musk, and other trees. He sat down next to me and put his arm around me. I rested my head on his shoulder and enjoyed in the warmth of his body and in complete obliviousness to the elements in the building behind my back.

"I discovered something. I feel cold when someone has fire as their element," I said. And I desperately wanted to get closer to that fire to get warmer. "Did you feel that way around me before?"

"Yeah," he murmured against my hair. "Until I made you feel cold, too."

"Oh. And when I want earth really badly, I feel like I'm floating around, and only getting down to earth can save me from falling into the abyss."

He didn't say anything.

"Why does this thing make me see images in my head?" I asked, not willing to sit there in silence with him.

"Maybe because you're now an insane murderer just like I am."

"Whatever," I said. "What did you tell Paula before you came here?"

"Nothing," he said. "She lost me."

I moved my head off his shoulder so I could look at him and show him my disapproval.

"She loves you," I said angrily. "You can't do this to her!"

"Sure I can," he said. "She lets me."

I sighed. Fighting with him because of Paula was useless. I didn't want him to leave her and break her heart, but I also couldn't watch him treat her badly. I'd expected her to open her eyes earlier, but she still kept seeing him for what he wasn't.

"How did you get rid of Michael?" he asked.

"I didn't get rid of him," I said. "I sent him for some drinks."

"Oh well, easy for you girls." He laughed. "Just send a guy for a drink so you can meet with another one."

"Hey! I'm not doing this for fun!"

"Whatever," he said. "You should go inside now."

"Right, Michael must be looking for me."

"You're going to freeze if you stay here." He smiled. Ah, that too. I got up and handed him the jacket. Damn, I really *was* freezing, especially without the jacket and his arm around me. The elements were back, but they weren't strong. Good.

"See you later," I said and went for the door. I shivered when the hot, damp air of the club hit me along with the horrible smell of alcohol, sweat, and smoke. Michael found me a few minutes later, pushing through the dancing crowd just like I'd been.

"There you are! I've been looking all over for you," he said, kissing me on the cheek and then moving away in surprise.

"I danced with some guy." I grinned before he could say something. Adrian's cologne must have stayed in my hair somehow.

"Really? And where is that bastard who dared to touch my girlfriend so I can punch him in the face?" Michael asked, amusement showing in his green eyes. He gave me the beer bottle he was holding, and I took a big swig before responding.

"He was drunk." I laughed. "Told me I looked pretty."

"No one can resist you, my darling," he said. "Ready for some more dancing?"

"Of course."

I met with Adrian outside two more times. Damn, the night was long. When it was finally time to go, I felt completely drained. My feet were killing me, and I wasn't sure if I could even walk normally. My hair was tangled and sticky, and it smelled like smoke and alcohol, just like my clothes. But it had been a good night. We'd had a lot of fun. I took a long shower and fell asleep as soon as I touched the pillows.

The ringing of my phone woke me up, and I realized I'd been asleep for nine hours. It was Michael, and he brought me breakfast to my room. That was so sweet of him, and I wondered for a second if I should tell him the truth. But I decided I wanted to keep things like they were.

"Well, last night was amazing," Michael said as we were drinking orange juice and eating the last bits of our breakfast.

"Yeah," I said. "I had a great time."

"But now we have to prepare for the exams," he said, and I sighed. Exams were such a fun spoiler.

"Right. So when will I get to see you?" I asked.

"Not before nine."

I looked at the time on my phone and frowned. "Wait, you're planning to study for six hours?"

"Sure, and that probably won't be enough."

"You've been studying for those exams for weeks," I said and realized that I was even more behind with my work than I had thought.

"Yeah, but I want to nail it." He touched my cheek lightly. "And I really want to know all that stuff. How will I ever be good at what I do if I can't remember anything I learned?"

I didn't answer because it would most likely lead to an argument. I was okay with him being ambitious for both of us. Studying had never been my thing, and I did it only because I had to pass the exams. History and Geography had always interested me, but that didn't mean I enjoyed every field.

"See you later then," I said, and we kissed. "Happy studying!"

Michael gave me another kiss that warmed me all over and then waved me goodbye. I actually opened some books and read a few pages, but then water, fire, air, and, occasionally, earth filled my mind and I had a hard time concentrating. I seriously considered going out and screaming at everyone to get out of the damn building, but that wouldn't just put me on the list as someone with magic disease, but also as a crazy person.

When I realized I'd done nothing for almost an hour, I texted Adrian, and he replied that I could come to his room if I wanted. I picked up some of the books and took them there with me. Adrian raised an eyebrow at me when he saw the books in my arms.

"What exactly are you planning to do with that?" He pointed at the books. "Make a big fire?"

"No," I said. "I have an exam in two days, and if I remember correctly, so do you."

"And?"

"Oh, right, you're failing everything. Almost forgot. But I have to study, and I can't do that with stupid elements buzzing around in my head."

"Well, that sounds like fun," he said. "Not."

"I know." I sighed. "But I need your help."

"All right, but you owe me, Ice Queen," he said, walking toward the bed. "And I know exactly how you're going to make up for it."

I didn't like the way he made that sound, but I hoped it wasn't anything illegal. Maybe I should have asked, but I'd lost too much time already and didn't want to lose any more. Adrian was already lying on the bed, and I went to join him. I felt way too comfortable lying there next to him with my head on his chest and his arm around me.

We spent some time like that, and I managed to read and memorize a few pages, even though I was aware of the fact that I'd never get to learn it all in time. But I had two more days, so maybe I'd learn enough to pass.

"Did you know that they had planned to introduce the law about not killing magic disease carriers 200 years before it actually happened?" I asked as I closed the book and got up so we could change our positions.

"They were more bloodthirsty back then," he said. "Now they want to discover more magic disease carriers so they can watch over them."

"Why do you say it as if that law were a bad thing? They would have killed you already if it hasn't been passed."

"True, but they didn't pass the law because they wanted magic disease carriers to have a better life. They passed it in hope that people like you would come out and admit they had the disease in order to get more rights for magic disease carriers. But it only gives the government an excuse to track you down."

I didn't really get his logic. Why would it be a bad thing if both parts got what they wanted? Or was there another thing they were hiding from us? I wasn't sure, and I didn't really want to get involved in politics.

I sat down on the floor, leaning my back against the wall. Adrian watched me for a moment, and a small smile spread across his face. Then he came to lie down on the floor and placed his head on my lap. I raised an eyebrow at him.

"Wait, don't you hate lying on the floor?"

"Not with such a gorgeous pillow." He smiled, and I rolled my eyes.

"I'm not having sex with you, so you may as well stop trying."

"I never stop until I get what I want," he said, his gray-blue eyes flashing dangerously. I had never doubted that, but I wouldn't give him what he wanted. He may be freaking hot, but that didn't mean much to me. I hoped.

My phone rang at that moment, and I sighed when I saw my father's number. My parents called me every day, but we never really talked about anything important. They would have told me already if they suspected I might have magic disease. Or maybe they wouldn't. Maybe my parents weren't who I thought they were. However it was, I didn't trust them. I couldn't. Not after what they had told me to break me apart from Michael. I still didn't believe that story completely.

"Yes, Dad?" I said.

"Honey, how are you?" he asked cheerfully.

"Any news on Oliver?"

"I'm glad you're asking," he said. "He called your mother this morning."

"So he's fine?" I let the annoyance show in my voice. My parents always made a big fuss whenever Oliver didn't feel like talking to them, and this time he'd even gotten me worried. That son of a bitch.

"Yeah," my dad said, and I could hear the nervousness in his voice. Oh yeah, Oliver was perfectly fine, as usual.

"Great," I said sarcastically. "Now we can go back to being one happy family."

"Ria, is something wrong? Are things fine at the university?"

Yeah, there always had to be something wrong when I was trying to point out the obvious. "No, everything's fine," I said.

"Is that worthless magic disease carrier bothering you again?" he asked.

"No, Adrian's not bothering me." I glanced down at Adrian who was watching me curiously. We both nearly burst out laughing. Ah, if only my father knew.

"Good," my father said. "Mom says hi."

"Um yeah," I said. "Bye, Dad."

I didn't wait for him to say anything; I simply ended the call. So now I could reach my brother and actually talk to him. Great. Adrian observed me while I played with the phone in my hand.

"Call whoever you want to call," he suddenly said.

"I'm not sure it'll be a pleasant call. And I'm not really sure what to ask."

"Just do it." He reached up and placed his hand on my cheek. "Or you'll be thinking about it until the chance is gone."

I took his hand and moved it away from my face. Maybe he was right. It was hard to guess when Oliver would disappear again, so I found his number in my contacts and pressed the button. Oliver answered on the third ring.

"What do you want, little sister?" he asked.

"I want to ask you something," I said, wondering if I was doing the right thing. Oh, well, only one way to find out.

"Shoot."

"Am I adopted?" It was the question that bothered me the most, because that would be a perfect explanation for me getting the disease. I was almost sure my parents would lie to me about it even if I asked. Oliver had no reason to do it.

"Unfortunately, sis, you're not." He laughed. "Anything else?"

He seemed sure of it. Shit. It wasn't that then.

"What do you know about our great-grandfather?" I asked.

"Aaah, you know. I can't believe they told you about the deal. Have you been dating someone inappropriate?"

"That's none of your business," I said coldly. "Just tell me if that shit is true."

"Yes, it is," he said. "Luckily for us, the old guy was living in different times. Marriage meant something then. You can still fuck your boy and nothing will happen."

"You're such an asshole," I muttered.

"You know it, and yet you called."

"Yeah, I don't know what I was thinking." Could I ask him about the disease?

"Anything else?" he asked impatiently. He probably had some hot girl waiting for him. I had no doubt about that. He was really handsome for an annoying guy.

"Are you sure our family has a pure element?" I asked, holding my breath for the answer. Just the answer didn't come. "Oliver?"

"Yeah," he said hastily. Something was wrong. Very wrong.

"Uh huh," I said, hoping he'd notice that I didn't quite believe him.

"I assure you. Just don't bother our parents with it, understand? You mustn't ask them such a silly question. Dad could get a heart attack." He laughed. "Look, sis, I'm going to come to see you as soon as I can. Love you, bye."

And with that, he hung up. I was still trying to understand what he'd said. But if he'd said he was coming and that I shouldn't tell my parents, then it had to be something serious. Maybe this disease wasn't a result of some weird mutation or my bad luck after all. And he also believed someone was listening to our conversation.

"Well, it looks like my family has a secret, and I shouldn't talk about it with them," I said. "Apparently, my disease didn't come by accident."

"Of course it didn't," Adrian said.

"And my brother's coming here." I said it and still didn't believe it. What was he going to do? Kill me? Yeah, I believed that more than I believed he'd actually help me.

"Damn, I don't know my own family," I said, tears threatening to come out. Adrian touched my arm, and I looked into his gray-blue eyes. I realized his eyes weren't as cold as they usually seemed to me. There was something else there; something I couldn't quite identify... I shook my head. This conversation with my brother was making me see things.

Chapter 17

I'd learned, or at least I hoped I'd learned, one more chapter of the book, and then I was too tired and too annoyed to continue. Adrian was more than happy when I threw the book away from me.

"Are you finally done?" he asked, picking up the book from where it had fallen. "Because if you're not, then I might just throw this out of the window."

"I'm done." I laughed. "I can't believe you actually did this for me."

"Yeah, me neither." His lips spread into a smile. "But now you have to do something for me."

"All right, as long as it doesn't involve sex," I said, and he gave me a disappointed look, which faded in a second.

"I want you to come somewhere with me," he said.

"Where?" I narrowed my eyes at him. I just couldn't help but be suspicious about it.

"Don't you trust me?" There was a playful smile on his lips.

"Of course not," I said.

"It would be more fun if you didn't know."

"You're just afraid I'll refuse."

"All right. I need you to help me do something half-illegal," he said.

"Half-illegal?" I gave him a doubtful look. "There's no such thing as half-illegal."

"Sure there is," he said. "It's when something is illegal, but you consider it to be perfectly legal."

"So it is illegal." I frowned. "I should have known."

"Whatever." He shrugged. "You're coming with me."

"You can't make me." I clenched my jaw, getting annoyed. "Just tell me what the hell it is."

"I need to get my father's journal."

"Wait, what's illegal in that?"

"It's somewhere in the Council's quarters," he said. "It was among the few things that survived the fire. They took it as evidence and refused to return it to me."

"Don't tell me you're trying to break into the Council's best kept building," I said, remembering what my father had once said about the security.

"There isn't any other thing to do. Besides, now I have you to help me. And you'll help me because my father's journal could maybe give you some answers."

"Why would *your* father's journal give *me* answers?" I raised an eyebrow. Did he really think I was so stupid to believe that? Tricking me into something wasn't a nice thing at all.

"Because my father might have known someone from your family, and there's a list of names in that journal that includes every carrier he met." His face was completely serious. Maybe he wasn't lying. Maybe.

"No way," I said. "They would have come for everyone on that list if it really existed."

"Well, it's not exactly written for everyone to see. You need to know what you're looking for to find it. No one from the Council noticed it, or they'd have arrested many people already. But they found it suspicious enough to keep it there."

"And why do you want it now?" I asked suspiciously. He could have paid someone to go with him to get the journal, and he wouldn't have had to explain anything, so why look for it now?

"Because you appeared," he said. "I want to know if there are more benefits of you being around, and how we can use that. My parents might not have kept their elements, but they were in the same situation as us, and maybe that can help us."

"All right. So the journal might be useful," I said. "But the Council is like two hours from here."

"So what? We have time."

"You know something that I don't, so you better spill it out." I crossed my arms.

"There are special guests from another country visiting the Council's building tonight." He winked at me.

"Let me guess. They're extremely important guests who'll need a lot of security. But the guards still won't leave everything else unprotected. There are cameras and alarms, you know."

"Oh, but they'll stop working." He smiled, and I shook my head. That was completely insane. We couldn't pull off such a thing. I wasn't some super spy or a master thief, and neither was he... as far as I knew.

"You're crazy," I said.

"Look, you'll only have to create a diversion. I'll take care of everything else."

"Diversion?" I gaped at him. "I can't do that!"

"Yes, you can," he said. "You're pretty enough to do that."

"Pretty, huh?"

"Be charming, seduce a guard, ask him to take you to the ballroom because you got lost, and when you get there, faint," he said as if he were giving me a shopping list.

"No, I can't! Besides, the guy will recognize me, and I can't just pretend to faint! I'm not an actress."

"You could be. No one will recognize you if we buy you a wig, use some fancy make-up, and maybe buy colored contacts," he said. "Come on, we don't have time to waste."

"No, I'm not going."

He got closer to me, and his gray-blue eyes were like ice, making me shiver. "Fine. I'll go alone. But when they catch me, you're on your own, sweetheart." He went for the door, not looking back.

I stood there for a moment, calculating his chances of doing this successfully on his own. Crap. I needed him more than he needed me. He'd be just fine, but I wouldn't.

"Wait," I said, already regretting my decision. "I'm coming with you."

It turned out Adrian had a really nice black Lamborghini parked outside the university, and soon we started the craziest journey of my life. I should have probably left Michael a message, but I didn't know what to say, because I was sure he'd come looking for me if I told him I was tired or something. He'd surely want to give me a kiss before going to sleep. And thinking about it only made me feel guiltier.

"Nice car," I said over the music, which Adrian had turned on as soon as we got inside. He didn't say anything, but the corners of his lips went up. My Audi had stayed at home since I'd figured I wouldn't need it. It was much easier to walk or get a taxi anyway, but Adrian didn't really have a home, so I assumed he didn't have anywhere else to leave the car.

"Do you have a house somewhere?" I asked. "I mean, do you have a place where you plan to live after university?"

"No. I could buy one, I guess. But why bother when no one expects me to live that long?"

"Magic disease doesn't kill," I said more to myself than to him.

"No, but people do." He glanced at me. There was a sad look in his eyes, which again seemed warmer somehow. I blinked, and it was all gone.

"Do you really think… they would kill you even if you didn't do anything?"

"Yes," he said. "Alan will want to have a family soon, and he can't have that with me around."

"Wait, can't he quit or something? Maybe they could give you someone else. And he isn't really forbidden to have a family, right?"

"He can't quit. It's for life. Of course, no one expects magic disease carriers not to give in to the disease. And tell me, a few months ago, would you have accepted that you and your children live with someone who has magic disease?"

"No," I admitted. "I wouldn't even accept it now. I mean, we're like exceptions, right? Having any kind of an element is much better than having none."

And really, if I felt like this while I still had my element, then how would I feel without it and without Adrian's help? I couldn't even imagine not having my element at all. I was still freaked that I'd wake up one morning and it would be gone.

We hadn't talked much for the rest of our trip. On our way, we only stopped at a few shops and bought the things we needed. I got a wig that reminded me of Paula's hair because it was blonde and curly. I'd finally have curly hair! It took me a while to stop laughing, which wasn't easy, considering that we'd bought green contact lenses and a red dress, which showed way too much skin for my liking. I couldn't recognize the woman that was staring at me from the mirror when I finished applying heavy make-up.

"I look like a freaking porn star," I said, twirling around so Adrian could see me better.

"You look hot." He smiled. "But I prefer the original."

"I suppose you don't have one of those fancy voice changers from the movies," I said, turning back to the mirror. Damn, this whole make-up mask I had on my face was making me itchy, but I didn't want to smear my black mascara or my bright red lipstick. And I hoped that the red gloves I was wearing would prevent me from touching my face. Yeah, I needed gloves because we couldn't afford to leave any prints.

"Nah, nothing like that. But you can change your accent a bit," he said, observing me so carefully that I felt warmth coming into my cheeks.

"It would sound fake." I frowned. "Stop staring at my butt!"

"It's a nice butt," he said, and I turned around and flipped him off. He just gave me one of his arrogant smiles.

"Where did the 'I'm going to kill you and steal your element' thing go?" I asked.

"Well, you're more interesting to me now than you were then." He shrugged. "But that doesn't mean you're completely safe."

"Thank you very much. That's really comforting to hear a moment before I go out to help you and risk everything."

"Nothing bad will happen." He took a step forward and got a hold of my hand. "And if it does, run like hell and get out of there."

"You bet I will."

"Good," he said, taking my other hand. "Are you sure you're feeling good enough not to accidentally kill someone in the next hour or two?"

"Yes," I said, realizing that I wasn't only risking being caught, but also risking doing something horrible. A wave of panic hit me, and Adrian noticed it.

"It'll be all right," he said reassuringly. "No one's supposed to have any strong feelings at the ball, and you've spent enough time with me. Besides, those are not university students who lose control of their element so easily. But if the alarm goes off or people start to panic, just get out."

I took a deep breath, trying to clear my mind of all bad thoughts. I wasn't going to do anything hard, except pretend I was someone else at some stupid party. It shouldn't be different from a few formal parties I had gone to with my parents. I could do it.

"Let's do this," I said, adrenaline surging through my body. I had no idea what Adrian was planning to do, except that he would wear all black. He was definitely risking more than I was, but he didn't want me to worry about it, so I didn't.

I was walking down the hallway of a nicely decorated part of an old building. There were lots of lights everywhere, and there were vases with flowers in almost every corner, making me wonder who the idiot who had put them there was. My black high heels were already making my feet ache because I'd had to walk all the way to the building; we'd had to leave the car farther away from there so it wouldn't be suspicious. And yeah, who'd forget that kind of a car?

It hadn't been hard to get inside of the building since there was actually some kind of an exposition in the lobby open to the public. I wondered why they hadn't closed it because of the special event that was being held upstairs, but that would have probably drawn even greater attention. There were definitely no signs of any kind of a thing happening in the other part of the building, but it was a huge building; big enough to both hide the important stuff and host huge balls or expositions.

Of course, there was a guard at my side as soon as I stepped into the nonpublic area. And he had a gun tucked into his belt. I averted my eyes from the gun and smiled at him.

"Miss, you shouldn't be here," he said politely. "This isn't a public area."

"Oh, really?" I batted my eyelashes, which felt a bit heavy under who knew how many layers of black mascara. "But I really wanted to see the ballroom. They say it's amazing."

"Yes, it is." He swallowed. "But you need a special invitation to go there."

"And how do I get one?" I asked, slightly biting down on my lip. The guy's face was getting redder and redder. He couldn't have been much older than twenty-one, and he wasn't exactly the hottest guy, but he was cute… if you closed one eye maybe. Somehow bribing him seemed like an easier thing, but that would be suspicious.

"Um, it's not like that," he said.

I touched his shoulder. "Come on, I'm not a threat," I said in the sweetest voice I could manage. "I just want to see it. You can come with me. It'll only take a minute."

"Miss, I can't…" he said. "There are… some people there right now."

"Perfect! Then you can let me have a peek, and everyone will think I'm just another guest," I said, moving my hair out of the way and giving him a better view of my cleavage. The control he had on his element faltered, and the familiar pull of fire made me anxious to start moving as soon as possible. I was really glad he wasn't gay, so I leaned forward, close enough to whisper into his ear.

"Please," I breathed. "You won't regret it."

My hand *accidentally* brushed against his groin, and he suddenly smiled at me as if he knew all my secrets. He moved away from me, reaching for the earpiece and taking it out. Great, one thing less to do.

"Come on, sweetheart," he said, suddenly looking too sure of himself. He had to be thinking that I was genuinely interested in him, and that had made him feel all brave and happy. God, the guy was an idiot. I wondered how he had gotten a job here because I'd expected the men here to be well trained and professional. But then again, I wasn't about to complain, not when I planned to do something dangerous.

I started walking upstairs, and he followed me, no doubt staring at my behind. Good, I didn't need him focused on security anyway. Maybe he'd lose his job if Adrian and I managed to pull this off. Somehow, I didn't really care.

As we neared the ballroom the chatter became louder, but that wasn't the only indicator that the party was there. There were around fifty people of all elements inside as far as I could count. And, thankfully, no one was out of control, but that didn't mean I could stay around them for long.

There were two more guards at the door, and they looked startled when they saw us approaching. The one to the left had earth and the other one had air. And it was the air guy who eyed us suspiciously.

"What's up?" He looked at me and then at the guard following me.

"Nothing," the fire guy replied. "I brought this lady here to see the ballroom."

"Are you insane?" the air guy asked. Oh, so apparently they weren't all stupid. The fire guy said something, and both the air and earth guy turned on him. I used their quarrel as an opportunity to slip past them and walk into the ballroom. The damn room was much bigger than I'd thought it would be, and people were chatting and dancing, dressed in expensive suits and dresses. No one even glanced at me as I made my way through the room.

I really hoped Adrian was on his position, because I was about to start a little bit of chaos. The guards must have realized where I'd gone; there was a bit of commotion behind my back. But I didn't have time to think about it. I grabbed a glass of red wine from the tray and bumped on purpose into an important looking guy, spilling the red liquid all over his suit. He swore, and I noticed the guards moving from their positions toward us.

I spun around and hurried to the area the waiters were coming from. There was a lot of shouting behind me, and the guards had their attention on the guy who was still completely outraged because of the red stains on his shirt. But, of course, I could feel the elements in the room getting stronger because not everyone could see it was only wine, so people were afraid and trying to find a guard.

I entered the 'waiters only' area despite the protests of an elderly waiter. I looked around and found the door I needed. Adrian had actually shown me a map of the building so I could escape easier. The emergency door that I was just about to open was under an alarm. But if everything had gone all right, it shouldn't go off.

I opened the door before anyone could notice and disappeared down the stairs. I didn't hear the sound of the alarm, but that didn't mean it hadn't gone off in some security office. The guards were probably not far behind me, but I hoped that panicked crowd had managed to slow them down. I could feel their elements still pulsing rather strongly. My shoes were a bit uncomfortable for running down the stairs, but I managed. Just like I managed not to look up in case there was a camera somewhere.

The stairs led me to one of the side exits, but the damn door was locked. I had to take another door and ended up in the lobby, where the guards were trying to evacuate people who had come to the exposition. I merged into the crowd and hurried outside before the guards from the ballroom could give my description to the others.

I felt a wave of relief wash over me as I found myself in the dark outside the building. But it wasn't over yet, so I hurried in the direction opposite from where Adrian's car was. Luckily, no one was following me, and there were only a few cars passing by on the street. I found the abandoned warehouse where we were supposed to meet and got inside through a half-collapsed door. Not so long ago, I would have been scared to enter such a place, but now I was sure there weren't other humans inside… unless they had magic disease and I couldn't sense them. That almost made me hesitate, but I couldn't see anyone.

I hastily got a plastic bag out of the backpack we'd brought there before going into action, and I took off the wig, stuffing it into the bag. I was glad no one had come here in the meantime and found our things. We'd been careful not to leave anything personal, but it would have been a bit of a problem if someone had stolen it. I removed the contacts from my eyes after the fourth or fifth attempt. Damn, those things were irritating. Removing the make-up was another difficult thing, and I had to wipe my face a few times before it was more or less clean.

The dress and all I'd worn ended up in plastic bags, and I was dressed in plain jeans and a black t-shirt with a picture of a bird on it. I was really grateful when I got rid of my high heels and put on a pair of comfortable black sneakers. The door rattled a bit and I froze, my heart beating like crazy. Then I heard footsteps but couldn't feel anything.

I let out a sigh of relief when Adrian came into view. He took off his heavy black coat and the hat, tossing them to me. I immediately started to put his things into another plastic bag because the speed was what mattered now. He removed the mask and changed into blue jeans and a blue t-shirt.

It was all nicely packed in white plastic bags, and we were almost ready to get out of there when I looked into his dark eyes. "The contacts," I said.

"Shit!" He handed me a leather journal, which was probably the thing he'd been looking for, and hurried to get the contacts out. We checked the place for any possible traces, and when we were sure there weren't any, we headed outside.

As we neared the Council's building I felt more and more nervous, but we didn't start walking faster. We didn't want to draw attention to ourselves, so we just tried to act like a couple coming from a grocery store. That was why we'd taken the plastic bags of a nearby supermarket. And I really hoped no one could sense the rapid beating of my heart. There were police lights flashing in front of the building, and I was wondering what they were thinking about everything that had happened.

It seemed like an eternity until we reached our parking spot. We put the bags in the trunk, which, to my surprise, was in the front, and just stared at each other for a moment before getting into the car. Adrian laughed as I closed the door, but it was a nervous laugh.

"Let's get the fuck out of here," he said, starting the engine. I couldn't agree more. This had to be the riskiest and stupidest thing I'd ever done.

Adrian stopped the car in the dark part of the woods, some twenty-five minutes away from the university. We got out and took the plastic bags, placing them on the ground in the middle of a small meadow we'd found, which was completely surrounded by trees, and therefore out of view. I took a deep breath and found my element deep inside of me. In a few moments, the bags burst into fire, turning everything inside into ashes. The smell of melting plastic was horrible, but the fire actually warmed up the cold night air a bit.

I was staring at the flames when Adrian came closer and put his arm around me.

"Thank you," he said, kissing my cheek. I didn't really think he was used to thanking people, so maybe I should feel honored. But I was too tired to feel anything anymore.

When our things were no more, Adrian used his ice, which turned into water when it touched the heat, to get everything wet and scatter it a little. We hoped no one would come here soon and find the remnants, but by wetting them, we were trying to make the fire look older than it was. It would be crazy if someone connected a random fire in the woods to the theft miles away, but you never knew.

As we were driving to the university, something came to my mind.

"The car!" I said, and Adrian glanced at me in surprise, mostly because we hadn't talked at all during our trip.

"What?"

"The car was clean," I said. "And that path we took to the woods was dusty. Someone's going to notice you used it."

He swore and steered the car in the direction opposite from the university.

"Do you think Alan knows you've been away the whole time?" I asked as we neared a self-service car wash. It was a good thing that these things were open 24/7. I just hoped Adrian had enough coins.

"No, I don't think so." He shook his head. "He would have called me if he suspected I wasn't somewhere at the university."

"I still don't know why they allow you to walk around unsupervised. You could totally leave and they would never find you. Or you could kill someone during the night miles away and pretend nothing happened," I said.

"Yeah, but if I left, they would look all over for me. I wouldn't be able to use any of my money, and they would kill me on sight. Actually, anyone who recognized me would be allowed to kill me and earn a large sum of money for it." He sighed. "As for the killings, it would be hard since they actually check with Alan where I was at that time for every suspicious murder in this area."

"But that way someone can frame you for a murder if Alan can't account for you." I frowned.

"Yeah, well. I hope I won't be at the wrong place at the wrong time." He smiled, but it didn't reach his eyes. I had always thought he had it all, but maybe it wasn't like that. However, it was one more reason in favor of not telling anyone about my disease.

I stayed in the car while Adrian fumbled with the spray wand. He'd probably never washed a car on his own before, and this was a whole new experience. But who was I to say anything? I had never washed my car by myself either.

It was very late when we returned to the university, and we used the back door to sneak inside. Even though we weren't forbidden to go out at any time of the night, there was a guard at the main door and people rarely wanted to be seen. The back door was locked, but Adrian had the key. I knew that a few people at the university had it, too, mostly boys from the third year. Someone must have stolen it, made a copy, returned the key before anyone noticed, and then sold the copies.

My room was closer, and we ended up there. I threw myself on the bed and sighed. Damn, what an insane night! Adrian sat down on the bed near me and stared at the journal in his hands. I almost couldn't believe we had done all that to get some old notebook. He ran his fingers gently over the leather cover, and then I realized it was more than just an old journal to him.

"I'm going to take a shower," I said, leaving him there alone because I thought he wouldn't want anyone around when he opened that journal. He didn't say anything, so I just went to the bathroom, carrying my stuff with me.

My shower took longer than I'd expected, and putting my clothes on my still damp skin was a bit difficult. But I couldn't come out in a towel when Adrian was there... if he was still there. Maybe he'd gone to his room at some point.

I slowly got out of the bathroom and immediately saw him lying on the bed, the journal open and cradled in his arms. As I neared the bed, I realized his eyes were closed.

"Adrian?" I whispered, just in case he was still awake. But he didn't answer. He really was asleep. I carefully sat on the bed next to him and gently removed the journal from his hands. His arm twitched, but he didn't wake up. I wasn't really sure what to do now. He couldn't stay in my room, but I didn't want to wake him.

I studied his face and couldn't help but think he looked so harmless when he was asleep. And he had such beautiful thick eyelashes, which were as dark as his hair. I found myself wanting to touch the smooth skin of his face, to touch his lips... I blinked. What the hell was wrong with me? Just because the guy had good looks didn't mean I could forget everything else.

I let my hand drop onto the pillow next to his face and was completely startled when something vibrated on my nightstand. It was my phone, and I went to grab it before the noise woke up Adrian. Luckily, the sound was off because I couldn't have afforded it ringing during my mission. Later I'd simply forgotten to turn it back on.

Michael's number flashed on the screen, and the message symbol appeared above it. I pressed the right button and opened the message. Michael said he was sorry because he'd forgotten to call me this evening but that he'd been studying and hadn't even realized what time it was. Which meant he hadn't gone to dinner either, and I wouldn't have so much explaining to do. But it scared me a bit that he'd spent hours studying and hadn't even noticed the time. I would have gone mad.

I didn't reply because I didn't want him to come here to see me. It was better if he thought I was already asleep. It was late anyway, and I should have been in bed, but I couldn't sleep, even though I felt more tired than ever. I turned off my phone and placed it back on the nightstand. My eyes fell on the journal and I picked it up, opening a random page.

The handwriting was careful and beautiful, and it seemed as if the person who had written it had spent a lot of time on it. I hesitated for a moment, unsure how Adrian would feel about me reading his father's personal journal. But he was asleep, and I was curious.

I read a few pages, and they all mostly talked about what Adrian's father had been doing that day… only the date was missing, and there was absolutely no indication when the events had happened. I didn't know why, but I always assumed a journal should at least have a date or year written, because how would you remember it if you didn't know when exactly it had happened?

There was only one small number in the right corner of each page, but it seemed weird. Many pages in a row had number zero, and then a good deal of them had one and so on until six. I wasn't sure what that meant. If it meant anything at all. Maybe the guy had been writing in chapters. Who knew?

After flipping through a few more pages, I still didn't find anything interesting. It seemed to be just an ordinary, boring journal. The guy talked about his day at work, how he watched something on TV or read a book… but nothing about magic disease. Was it possible that Adrian had tricked me and that the journal had only emotional value for him? Yeah, it was. But he'd have stolen it a long time ago, unless… unless he hadn't known before where the journal was or how to breach the security.

I closed the journal and went to put it down on my desk. Adrian better had an answer in the morning. Speaking of the morning, it was really time for me to go to sleep too. But Adrian was still sleeping on my bed, and I couldn't decide between waking him and simply lying down next to him. Waking him seemed rude since he'd let me sleep in his room once. Sleeping in the same bed with him somehow seemed much scarier than everything we'd done when we were awake.

I wasn't really sure what I was exactly afraid of. Maybe I was just uncomfortable to sleep next to a guy who wasn't my boyfriend but in fact my best friend's boyfriend. Would he use the opportunity to touch me inappropriately if he woke up? Would he somehow lose it and try to kill me? Okay, my mind was definitely too tired because I was jumping to insane conclusions. But I was still a little bit suspicious because he had actually stayed awake that night I slept in his room, and I wasn't sure he'd done it just because I might have felt uncomfortable. Why would he care how I felt?

In the end, I gave up, because I could barely keep my eyes open. And my double bed was more than big enough. I pulled the covers over both of us and was asleep in a second.

Chapter 18

Something like a whimper woke me up, and I opened my eyes in surprise. Then I realized Adrian was still in the bed with me. But what I didn't expect was that the sound had come from him. He was murmuring something incoherent in his sleep and clutching the sheets as if they were the only thing keeping him alive. I reached out and touched his arm.

"Adrian?" I shook him a little. His eyes fluttered open, and he nearly jumped off the bed when he saw me.

"You had a nightmare, I think," I said, pulling my hand back. He got up from the bed, his breathing ragged, and turned his back to me. It took him a moment to calm down, and when he turned around to look at me, I thought he would kill me. I'd never seen him that furious before. There was something deadly in his gray-blue eyes, which now seemed colder than ice.

"Don't you ever do that again," he said. I slowly slid off the bed and took a step toward him.

"Do what?" I said calmly. "Wake you up? Sorry, but I didn't want my sheets to get destroyed."

"I have to go." He took the journal, pushing me out of his way, and went for the door, only to realize it was locked, and I had the key.

"No," I said," you're not going anywhere while you're upset."

"I'm not upset!" he yelled, and I crossed my arms, giving him a quizzical look. If he wasn't upset, then I had no idea what he was. But I couldn't let him go and take out his anger on someone with an element, like Paula, for example. I was almost sure she'd be waiting for him near his room. I just wasn't sure why exactly he was angry.

"I have no idea what's going on," I said. "But please stop for a moment."

"I could have hurt you, Ria."

"Oh, please." I waved my hand. "You're not *that* dangerous. Did you dream of killing someone?"

"That's none of your business," he said, but I could see he suddenly seemed relieved.

"You thought you'd said something in your sleep, didn't you? Well, you did say something, but I couldn't understand a thing, so I guess whatever you're hiding is safe."

"Just unlock the door," he said.

I went to get the key, and then realized I had one more question. "Did you lie to me about the journal?" I searched for any sign on his face to see if I was right.

"No." His face was expressionless.

"And I'm supposed to believe that?" I raised an eyebrow. "I checked the journal last night and there's nothing about magic disease in it."

"I told you it wasn't that obvious." He smirked.

"Well, you better tell me what it is then." I frowned. If he had tricked me, he was going to be in trouble.

"Do you really think my father was so stupid to have proof that he had magic disease in his house?" He glared at me.

"I guess not," I said. "But it's hard to believe there's anything important in that journal."

"Just because you don't see it doesn't mean it isn't there."

"Yeah, whatever," I said impatiently. "Just tell me already!"

"Well, I'll need to do some underlining."

I stared at him, completely clueless, which only made his smile become broader. I was glad we were past his furious and killing mode, but now I was the one who might get furious if he didn't stop playing games with me. "Underlining, huh?"

"Yeah, if you underline the right letters, you'll get the hidden meaning."

"Yeah, right," I said skeptically. "That way you can underline whatever you want and get a hidden meaning in any book you take."

"Not if you underline every sixth letter."

"Why sixth?" I frowned.

"That's a secret." He flashed me a smile. "You'll see."

"Fine, I'll see."

He was crazy if he thought I was going to forget about it. But now I just wanted to get him out of my room, so I reached for the key and went to unlock the door. When he was gone, I picked up my phone to call Michael. I needed someone less complicated to talk to; someone I trusted completely, and that could only be him.

I wasn't even a tiny bit surprised when I saw the Council's building again… on the TV, of course. The news was talking about someone breaking into one of the offices with classified information, which had happened exactly during a commotion at a party for very important people. One of their theories was that someone from the attendees had caused the commotion on purpose to steal some important information, but ended up stealing the journal by mistake.

Another theory was that everything had been organized by the leaders of the Magic Disease Carriers Association, an organization that fought for the rights of magic disease carriers. The press thought that the journal had been stolen simply because it had belonged to a person who'd had magic disease, or because of some weird political reason that I couldn't quite understand. But no one ever mentioned whom exactly the journal had belonged to or why it was so important. Maybe it wasn't important, but it still seemed suspicious.

And while they fought about who and why had done it, they only mentioned a mysterious blonde woman as a possible suspect. Great, I just hoped no one would recognize me. But if I was lucky, none of those people should ever see me again in their life anyway. Besides, they didn't even have a picture of the woman since the cameras had gone off. There was absolutely no proof against me even if someone came to suspect me one day. At least that was what I thought.

"Why would someone steal some stupid journal?" Paula asked, taking a bite of her sandwich. She, Michael, and I were sitting together at lunch. I had no idea where Adrian was, and Paula hadn't said anything about him. Michael kept apologizing for missing dinner, and I couldn't have felt more guilty about it.

"Politics." Michael shrugged. "MDCA just wanted to prove they could get inside the Council's building and steal something."

"But why?" Paula asked. "That's stupid."

"The Council probably refused to give them some classified info they wanted to use for their cause," Michael said. "Who knows?"

"Well, that's still stupid," Paula said and looked at me. "How's studying going?"

"Um, fine," I lied. "But it's all just too much."

"Tell me about it." Paula sighed. "I don't even have time to be with my boyfriend!"

And it was better like that, but I couldn't say that to her.

"Yeah, studying is taking over our lives," Michael said, turning to Paula. "I didn't even make it to dinner last night! Completely forgot about the time. And it robbed me of some precious minutes with my gorgeous girlfriend."

He kissed me, and the world seemed like a better place, but only for a moment because elements started raining down on me. I abruptly moved away, and Michael's brow creased in confusion. Damn, it looked like I would have to forget about kissing in public. There were just too many emotions in that small act. I wasn't sure whose control was slipping, but it didn't really matter.

"I don't want people to stare at us," I said in an attempt to make things better.

"Why not? Let them stare." A smile tugged at Michael's lips. "We're in love. No one can hold that against us."

I smiled at him, but he didn't try to kiss me again. Paula gave me a suspicious look, and I just shrugged. My phone vibrated in the pocket of my jeans, startling me. I got up, and both Michael and Paula turned to look at me.

"I need to... get back to studying," I said, giving Michael a kiss on the cheek and getting out of there before someone started asking questions. I flipped my phone open and saw an unknown number.

"Yes?" I said.

"Ria." I recognized my brother's voice even though it sounded as if he were speaking through something.

"Oliver?" I asked. "What's up?"

"It'll take me more time to come visit you than I thought," he said. "Are you okay?"

"Um, yeah, why wouldn't I be? You don't have to visit me if you..."

"I'll come," he said. "Have to go now. Bye, sis."

And with that, he hung up. What the hell? This conversation was even more awkward than the first one. Not to mention that this was probably a record amount of time we had spent talking in a year. He obviously wanted to tell me something but didn't want to do it over the phone. Huh, maybe he'd gone mad and thought some spies were following him. It wouldn't be the first time in our family history. And for all I knew, he could have been in some kind of an institution and not really in school like my parents had told me.

Actually, at this point in my life, anything was possible, even the craziest ideas. I went to my room and locked the door, determined to learn at least a few more pages for the exam, despite the constant buzzing of elements at the back of my mind.

Chapter 19

I failed the exam, which wasn't surprising to me, but it was to everyone else. Michael and Paula were the first ones to ask what had happened and wondered if I needed help. My parents got all worried and kept asking if they should send me something or come to visit me. I was half-annoyed after all that, and there was only one person that could help me get myself back together... well, only to prevent me from choking someone to death. Besides, I was curious what he had done with that journal so far.

I knocked on the door of his room, and when no one opened, I turned the knob. It was unlocked, and I peered inside. He was nowhere to be seen, but the bathroom door was closed. Oh, well. I could wait. I went inside and sat down on the bed, looking around for the journal. Of course, it wasn't anywhere I could see it, so I just waited for Adrian to appear.

My mouth fell open when he came out of the bathroom, because he was wearing only a towel. I tried to say something, but the words just wouldn't come out. Maybe now I could understand better all those girls who were running after him, because damn, he looked hot. His jet black hair was wet and nearly covering his eyes. Drops of water were gliding down the smooth skin of his muscular chest… I bit my lip, trying to look away, but I didn't.

"Would you like me to drop the towel?" he asked teasingly, his gray-blue eyes sparkling with amusement.

"No," I said, reminding myself that I didn't want to be one of those silly girls who got fooled by his good looks. Michael was just as gorgeous as he was, maybe even more… only I couldn't really touch Michael because I risked killing him, so maybe… I blinked. No, I hadn't just considered having casual sex with Adrian just because I couldn't do it with Michael. No, no, and no!

"I know you want me," he said, "so you may as well stop pretending you don't."

"You're so full of yourself." I finally managed to concentrate solely on his icy blue eyes.

"Maybe." He smiled. "But that's not the point."

"No, that's not the point," I said. "What did you do with the journal?"

"I discovered some… things," he hesitated, and I frowned. Maybe I was just pessimistic, or there was really something bad. It was hard to tell.

"What things?"

"Can I get dressed first or are you still hoping the towel will fall off?" he asked.

"Get dressed." I rolled my eyes, getting up from the bed and walking to the window. "I'll wait."

He gathered his things and went back into the bathroom. A few minutes later, he was back, his hair still a bit damp, and he locked the door before getting the journal out of his black backpack. We sat down on the bed, and he opened one page. I looked at the underlined letters and realized they really did make sense.

"Being with Elisabeth helps me stay in control, but it also makes me weaker," I read out loud and looked at Adrian. "What's that supposed to mean? And who's Elisabeth?"

"My mother," he said. "This is explained later on. It means that when we're together, we help each other stay in control... as you have already seen. But, according to my father, the more time we spend together, the harder it'll be to stay in control when we're away from each other."

"Oh," was the only thing I managed to say.

"I think that's why people with magic disease tend not to get attached to anyone," he said. "Touching is very helpful, but you also become dependent on that person."

"Great. Then we should just stay around people with no element," I said gloomily. I definitely didn't want to become dependent on Adrian. That would be some creepy nightmare material.

"Not exactly. People aren't really born without an element. It's just too weak for the person to use it. And it's the same with those who give up on it. The element is weak, but it stays there."

"And how exactly did your father know all that?"

"It says here that he read it in reports from different scientists. They did all kinds of research on the topic."

"Impossible," I said. "We would have known about it. Well, maybe not us, but Paula certainly would, and there were no books, no research, and not a thing about that."

"I know. The government has to be hiding it from us. My father mentions that all the documents are stored in Pandora's Box, and I have no idea what that means."

"Ah, great," I said sarcastically. "As if hiding the true meaning of the words in the journal wasn't enough, now we have cryptic names, too."

"I don't know. Maybe it means something to someone, just not to us." He shrugged. That was actually a good point, but we couldn't ask anyone without revealing too much.

"Okay, we have one mystery place to…" I suddenly remembered something Paula had said to me. "…discover."

"What are you thinking?" Adrian gave me a curious look.

"Paula mentioned some secret place with tons of security. She read about it in some dusty, old books, but she couldn't figure out where exactly it was… just that it was near here. All info about magic disease from all over the world is supposed to be kept in that place."

"And you didn't mention this to me before because…?" He raised an eyebrow at me.

"Well, why would I? We have no idea where that place is. I thought it might be the Council's building, but we have seen the security there, so I don't think that's it. The Council's building probably keeps less important things, and they make everyone believe the opposite."

"Yeah." He nodded. "We would've never gotten the journal if they thought it was important."

"True, but they still didn't want to simply hand it over to you."

"Right." He sighed. "I guess I'll have to do some more underlining. That's such a boring task."

"I could help you. If you're willing to tell me how you know it's every sixth letter we have to underline."

"All right." He laughed. "My father started writing the journal when my mom got pregnant. I was the reason he wanted to find out everything about magic disease... to make it easier for me. But he knew he couldn't write it just like that, so he found a way to hide it. And my name is the key to it."

I looked at him, trying to figure it out.

"Ah, your name has six letters," I said, and he nodded. "So your dad started to write it when they knew they were going to have a baby boy?"

"Not exactly. He started it earlier." He smiled. "They just agreed on six letters in the name no matter if it was a boy or a girl."

"Aah, but what about those numbers in the corner of the page?" I asked. "They also come to six."

"Yes, but for a completely different reason," he said with a hint of sadness in his voice. "Number zero represents the time from when he started it to the time when I had my first birthday. So each number represents my age at the time he was writing it. It comes only to six because... he died right before my seventh birthday."

"Wow, he'd been writing it for years," I said, surprised. "I'd expect a lot bigger journal for all those years, but I guess it's difficult to find what to write so that every sixth letter has a meaning." Actually, I was sure that if I tried, I would fail. I couldn't even come up with a normal journal and especially not one with a secret meaning inside.

"Yeah, it's difficult."

"What were they like?" I suddenly asked, and his eyebrows shot up. "Your parents?"

"Why?"

"I was just wondering."

"They were the best parents in the whole world." A sad smile spread across his lips. "My mother… she was… she was beautiful. She had long dark brown hair and light blue eyes. She was nice, gentle, smart… And she worked as an architect."

I had probably seen a picture of her in the newspapers, but that had happened a long time ago. Her eyes must have been the same as Adrian's. I could remember Adrian's father a little bit better. He'd had the same hair color as Adrian and he'd been a very successful company owner. As far as I knew, the company sold furniture, and it was now in Adrian's hands.

"You must have loved them a lot," I said.

"Still do," he said, focusing on some point on the wall. Well, he probably saw them differently, because it was a little bit hard for me to imagine two people who were all over the news for various murders as nice people. I always imagined them as cold, heartless monsters. But according to the popular belief, I was a heartless monster now too.

"How did they meet?" I asked. He gave me a look that wasn't even a bit friendly. It was probably hard for him to talk about it, but I was curious. Besides, he didn't have to tell me if he didn't want to.

"During a project," he said. "Mom was supposed to design the building, and Dad was supposed to get the furniture. It was a very important project, so they were both present at the meeting. Of course, they immediately discovered the secret that could have ruined both their lives... and soon they fell in love."

"Someone could discover me like that," I said.

"Yeah, but we all like to keep a low profile." He touched my hand. "And I don't think anyone else except me is a known magic disease carrier."

"Right. So even if someone saw me, we could make a deal not to tell anyone about each other." I hoped that I wouldn't accidentally run into another person with the disease. I mean, how many of us could be out there? Probably more than everyone thought, but why would they be near here?

"Yeah," he said. "Or find a way to make sure that person never talks."

"What?" I glared at him. "You'd kill someone?"

"Don't look so shocked. You wanted all magic disease carriers dead, didn't you? Besides, how can you trust a murderer?"

"Um, that's a bit complicated." I swallowed. "It's true I wanted everyone with magic disease dead, but now..."

"Now you don't want that because the same rule applies to you." He gave me a bitter smile. "It's all right when it happens to someone else, but when it happens to you... suddenly it's different. Why, Ria? Why?"

"I didn't understand it before. Now I see everyone needs a chance to prove their innocence. But I'm still not sure what I would think if I ended up killing someone. It seems so unreal."

"You didn't understand because you didn't want to. Paula understands, and she doesn't have the disease."

"Hey, don't blame me!" I said, my blood racing. "You were the one who said you'd kill another magic disease carrier to shut him up!"

"Survival is a completely different thing," he argued.

"Survival? Well, that's what I was talking about when I wanted all magic disease carriers dead!" I yelled. "They were a danger to me!"

"Really?" he asked. "Did you really feel so threatened by me?"

"No, but…"

"There are dangerous magic disease carriers who go around killing people, but not everyone is like that. And you'd have just sentenced them all to death even though not everyone was a threat to you or anyone else! But now that you belong to that dangerous group…"

"Yeah, yeah, whatever!" I got up from the bed and went for the door. I knew it wasn't smart to go outside angry, but I didn't want to stay near him. And I wasn't used to being told I cared only when it concerned me. Deep down inside I knew he was right. Not that I would ever admit it to anyone, especially not to him. He didn't try to stop me or anything as I stormed out of the room.

Chapter 20

One Friday I was sitting in Paula's room when she suddenly took my hands into hers.

"So what are Michael and you planning for next week?" she asked cheerfully, and I blinked at her in surprise.

"I'm not following you." I wondered if I had automatically said 'yes' to something she had asked without realizing.

"Well, the holidays are next week!" she said. "We can do whatever we want and go wherever we want! Some people are going home, but that's silly. Others are going to some exclusive destinations far from here, but I think that's boring. I'm sure Michael and you have something better in mind."

I certainly hadn't expected the holidays to come so fast, but now that I knew that was already next week, a small smile started to creep up my face. After weeks of exams and being busy, I could finally spend some quality time with Michael. We hadn't really talked about what we would do during the holidays, but I had something in mind. And I was sure he'd accept, because how could he ever refuse me?

The only problem was that I needed Adrian's help to do it, because having a romantic day with Michael would cost me a lot of my self-control. For the last two months, Adrian and I had spent less time together. He was busy working on the journal, and I came to him only when I needed to, but only for a few hours. Neither of us wanted to become dependent on the other.

"Sure we have," I said. "What about you? Are you going somewhere?"

"Um, I don't know yet. Adrian told me not to count on him."

"Why not?" I wanted to know more for me than for her. His plans could ruin mine, and I didn't want that to happen.

"He said he had other plans. So I think I'll just stay here and do some research."

"But you're doing that all the time!" I had no idea how she managed to both study and do research, but I guessed she was just that crazy about it.

"Not as much as I want to." Her lips pulled into a smile. "And there's nothing much I can do anyway, except go home. I don't want to go home."

"Yeah." I couldn't force Adrian to be with her, but I also couldn't take her with Michael and me.

"Don't worry about me," she said. "So, you said you had something in mind?"

"I haven't told Michael yet, but I'd like to go to that lake that's a few miles away from here. It sounds romantic."

"Wait, you're willing to spend a day with nature? With bugs and wild animals… and what else did you say when I suggested something like that a few years ago?" She laughed.

I wasn't really thrilled by it, but at least there wouldn't be a lot of people. Besides, lakes and meadows were supposed to be calm places, so everyone's elements should stay deep inside, together with my disease. "Anything for Michael."

"You really love him, don't you?" she asked, and I just nodded. "Have you thought about the future?"

"No, I don't want to," I said. "We can't know what will happen. It would be a waste of time to try to plan something."

"Yeah, I guess you're right," she said. We hadn't wanted to think about the future at the beginning of our relationship, and now even less.

"Well." I got up from the bed. "I have to go talk to Michael. I don't want anything to ruin my plan for us."

"Good luck." Paula smiled, and we hugged. I immediately hurried to Adrian's room and found him surrounded by books. That shocked me so much that I stopped dead in my tracks. He looked up at me and flashed me a smile.

"It isn't what it looks like," he said, pulling the journal out from under a pile of notebooks. "I just can't risk anyone seeing it."

"That makes more sense." I tried to remember what the hell I had come for. Ah, yeah, the holiday plans.

"What do you need?" he asked, tucking the journal back under a book.

"I really need you to be here next week."

"Why?"

"Because I want to spend some time with my boyfriend. And, unfortunately, I can't do that without your help."

"Ah, you want to have sex with him."

"No! I just want to be with him." A frown creased my brow. "There are better things to do with your loved one than just have sex!"

"Whatever you say," he said. Well, I definitely didn't expect *him* to understand.

"Look, this is really important to me. I love Michael, and the moments I spend with him are so rare now… Please, don't take that away from me."

Adrian watched me for a moment, and I tried to look as miserable as possible. Surely he could have a bit of compassion somewhere deep inside of him. Besides, I couldn't think of what he could possibly be doing that didn't include being here.

Just as he opened his mouth to say something, the door swung open. I turned around, startled. I wasn't used to anyone coming in here, especially not without knocking. Alan stood there at the door, his lips parted in surprise.

"Can't you fucking knock?" Adrian asked, annoyance filling his voice.

"I didn't know you had company," Alan said and smiled at me. "Hello, Ria. Didn't expect to see you here."

"I just came… for my notebook," I said, grabbing the first notebook from Adrian's pile that I could get hold of. "I was going anyway."

"Oh, there's no need for you to go now, Ria," Alan said. "Maybe you could help Adrian to pass an exam for once." There was an edge to his voice that I didn't like, and I was sure Adrian didn't either.

"What do you want?" Adrian asked.

"Just came to check if you're going to Riversbrough next week," Alan said, and I froze. That damn place was hours away from here! If Adrian went there, there was no way I could survive alone here with Michael.

Adrian looked at me, probably saw the panic written all over my face, and closed his eyes for a moment. "No," he said. "I'm not going."

The tension left my shoulders, but Alan's eyes went wide.

"You're not?" he asked. "Why? You go every year! You said you wouldn't miss it for anything in the world."

"I changed my mind," Adrian said grimly. Now I felt a bit lost in the conversation. Why would Adrian go to some small place every year? It didn't make any sense.

"Adrian," Alan said, "is something wrong? I can't imagine why you wouldn't want to visit your parents' grave."

I stared at Alan and then at Adrian, my mind too foggy to react.

"You heard me!" Adrian yelled. "I. Don't. Want. To. Go!"

"Fine," Alan said, frowning. "If that's what you want." With that, he walked out of the room.

"Why did you…?" I looked at Adrian, unsure of what exactly to say. His parents were obviously important to him, so why would he throw it all away… for me?

"You're alive. They're dead," he said, avoiding my eyes.

"Yeah, but I didn't know about your plans!"

"Do you want to be with Michael or not?" He finally looked at me, his eyes shining like a silver blade.

"I want to, but…"

"Then you better get the fuck out of here before I change my mind."

"Thanks." I took hold of his hand. "I will never forget this."

"You better not," he said, and I hurried to find Michael, who without any doubt would agree with my plan.

And that was exactly what happened.

Chapter 21

The lake was one of the most beautiful places I had ever seen. The water had a nice green-blue color that for some weird reason reminded me of Paula's eyes. The sun shined brightly down on Michael and me as we were lying on the grass. My head rested on Michael's chest, and he was running his fingers through my hair. There was no one else around us except the trees and flowers.

"What is it about you that drives me crazy?" Michael murmured.

"My hair?" I offered.

"That, too." He laughed and kissed the top of my head.

"So, why do you love me?" I lifted my head to look at him. The breeze played with his wavy brown hair, the sun making him squint his green eyes. My eyes focused on the fullness of his lips. I wanted to kiss him so badly.

"I love you because you're beautiful, and smart, and funny, and…" He couldn't say anything else because I pressed my lips against his. At that moment, nothing else mattered except us. I felt like I could fly. But as his hands slid under my white top, there was suddenly too much water around me. I gasped for breath, breaking away from him.

"Let's do something crazy," I said, not willing to let my disease ruin our day.

"Like what?" he asked.

"Go swimming." I got up.

His eyebrows shot upward. "It's forbidden. Besides, we don't have…"

I gave him a meaningful look. For a second, I thought I could see him blushing.

"Come on," I said. "There's no one around here."

"Yeah, but…"

"Don't tell me you're afraid!" I crossed my arms. "Well, I can always go without you…"

"Hey! I'm coming!"

"Good!" I said and started running toward the lake, not waiting for him. I knew he'd be right behind my back. Just as I was nearing the lake, I pulled off my top and threw it on the ground. I had to stop to take off my sneakers and jeans, and that was enough time for Michael to catch up with me. He was taking off his clothes too, and I smiled, walking into the lake just in my black panties and bra.

The cool water felt good on my skin as I dived into it, and that scared me for a moment. It was way too close to how I felt when Michael's element awoke. Water had always been water. Only this water didn't call to me and I didn't want to drink it all up.

I felt Michael's arms around my waist and I turned around, putting my hands around his neck. The water came nearly to my shoulders, so he lifted me up, and I pressed myself closer to his hard chest. We were frozen for a moment, just standing there and staring into each other's eyes. Every moment we had spent together passed in flashes through my mind... every moment except that one night when we'd made love, which I would never remember.

"Is something wrong?" Michael's eyes were full of concern for me, and I knew mine were pooling with tears. I loved Michael, but there were just so many secrets between us now. Why couldn't I just tell him everything? Why was I so afraid of losing him when I had probably already lost him? Looking again at Michael's face, I suddenly knew why. I wanted to keep him as long as possible. I wanted to love him. I wanted to be happy.

"I love you," I choked out, trying hard not to cry.

"I love you, too," Michael whispered, kissing my lips. Happy. That was what I had to do. Just be happy. I let go of Michael and laughed.

"Catch me if you can!" I said and started swimming as fast as I could toward the opposite side of the lake. If Michael was confused by my weird mood swings, he didn't show it. He just grinned at me and gave me a nice head start before coming after me.

We ended up lying on the shore, getting mud all over the blanket Michael had brought just in case we needed it. Well, we didn't really mind as long as that mud didn't get all over our skin and underwear. Michael held my hand while he was telling me stories about his childhood. He told me how he'd loved to climb trees and go fishing with his father. It was nice to hear more about him and his life.

"I'm going to tell you a secret," Michael said, and I raised an eyebrow at him.

"You have a secret?"

"Yeah." He laughed. "Isn't that strange? I can't seem to keep anything from you."

"No, you can't, my love," I said. "Spill it out."

"I bought a house not far from here."

I propped myself on my elbows and stared at him. "Why?"

"I saw it some time ago," he said. "It's out of town, in the countryside... it's gorgeous. And big enough for tons of children."

"Tons of children?" I said, my voice strained.

Michael looked at me and laughed. "Two at least."

I just blinked at him. "Oh, all right." It was a little bit hard to believe he was already thinking about having kids. I didn't know why, but it just felt wrong. And not only because I was sure I couldn't have kids with him... Hell, I couldn't even live with him.

"I'll do anything it takes to be with you, Ria," he said, determined. I could only smile at him and wish that this moment would last.

We spent the rest of the week visiting different places in the same area. It was surprising how many truly beautiful sights were hidden behind the trees and wild bushes. We even found a tree house and spent a while there. The whole week had been just awesome, and I was sad when it came to an end.

Chapter 22

More exams and even more exams; that was our new reality. The end of the academic year was nearing and everyone wanted to… well, survive. I was already sick of studying and everything, especially because it meant I had to spend more time around Adrian.

Paula and I were walking down the hallway when she suddenly stopped me and pulled me aside.

"I'm throwing a party," she said. "But you mustn't tell anyone."

"Oh, come on," I said. "Everyone always knows about secret parties. But why are you having one now? Don't you have to… study?"

"Yeah, but it's for Adrian's birthday." She smiled. "I got the permission to use the lunchroom and I'm going to need everyone's help."

Unbelievable. No one had ever gotten permission to do such a thing. I assumed she'd asked Alan, and since I didn't think Adrian had ever had a real birthday party since his parents' death, he'd allowed it.

"Sure, you can count on me."

"Thank you!" she squealed, throwing her arms around me. That party had to be the most important thing to her at the moment.

"So, how many people will come?" I asked.

"Everyone! At least I hope so. Even though I'm not sure I want all those girls at the party." There was something bitter in her voice, and I had to bite my lip to stop myself from smiling. It was hard not to be jealous when almost every girl at the university wanted your boy. Of course, there were girls who wanted Michael too, but Michael wasn't Adrian, so I didn't have to worry so much.

"It'll be fine," I assured her. "But I don't think you'll manage to keep that kind of a party a secret. Adrian will find out."

"No, he won't! Everyone promised not to tell."

"Yeah, sure they did," I said, but she didn't seem to notice the sarcastic tone in my voice.

"Okay, so you're coming. Tell Michael, will you?" She took out a small notebook and checked something.

"Sure."

She smiled again and then she noticed someone passing by and ran after him. Wow, who could have thought Paula would be organizing a party instead of spending all her time on doing research? Adrian was obviously that important to her. If only she would see that he didn't love her and had no interest in making her happy.

I checked the time on my phone and figured it was a good time to visit the boy in question. Michael had a Literature class and he wouldn't be free for the next two hours, and Paula was too busy hunting down people for the party. I found Adrian in his room, still working on the journal.

"Hey," I said, sitting down next to him, close enough for our shoulders to touch. That small contact took away the whole world of elements around us.

"Did Paula invite you to my birthday party?" He rolled his eyes and focused again on underlining the letters in the journal.

"Um, yeah, but you weren't supposed to know about it."

"Oh, please. When has anyone managed to hide anything around here?" he asked. "Especially if it's a huge party."

"Yeah, I guess that's hard to hide. Which one of your lovers told you?"

"I don't have lovers." He looked up at me, a glint of amusement in his gray-blue eyes.

"I don't believe you."

"You don't have to." He flashed me a smile. Maybe I hadn't seen any girls around him, but that didn't mean he hadn't gone after them when I'd been away.

"Anything interesting in the journal?" I tried to read the underlined letters, but Adrian closed the journal.

"Yes and no," he said. "There's indication that at least four Council members had the disease. But the others didn't know about it."

"Council members? There should be more information about them somewhere." I frowned. "Is there anything on the Internet?"

"Nothing suspicious. But one guy had an affair with some unknown girl and his divorce was all over the news. Maybe he contracted the disease from his lover."

"That's plausible," I said. "What about the others? I mean, are there more people mentioned who had the disease?"

"Yeah, but no one famous or anyone I've heard of."

"Pity." I glanced over at the pile of books on his desk. The books looked untouched, of course.

"Maybe I'll discover something more later," he said.

"Maybe. Are you planning to fail everything again?"

"Yeah, that's the plan."

I frowned. "You can't do that. They'll kick you out." And once I'd hoped for it to happen, but now I needed him, and I wasn't sure if I could stay here without him around.

"So?" He grinned. "Would you miss me?"

"Yeah, I would. I'd have to kill someone. And I don't want that to happen."

"I'll worry about it in the fall." He ran his fingers down my arm.

"But you have to pass the exams! Or do you keep thinking it's cool to be in the first year forever?"

"What's the point, Ria?" he asked. "It's not as if I need a degree to die happy."

I sighed. It was completely impossible to convince him that maybe things weren't so bleak, but then again, maybe he was right. But I wasn't willing to give up on anything just yet.

"Never mind," I said. "We've had that conversation already."

"Yeah, and I haven't changed my mind since then," he said, the tone of his voice implying that he didn't change his mind about things as much as I did. Gah, he was annoying sometimes.

"Why don't you just break up with Paula?" I asked. "It hurts me to see her trying so hard to make you fall in love with her. You could at least be fair to her and tell her the truth."

"What truth? That her best friend wants me just for herself?" He raised an eyebrow at me.

"Hey!" I punched him lightly in the shoulder. "It's not like that. I'm just saying you could have any other girl who isn't my best friend."

"I could have any girl, but I don't want to."

"All right," I said, lying down, and Adrian did the same. I snuggled closer to him and stared at the ceiling.

"Do you think I should tell Michael the truth?" I said after a long moment of silence.

"I can't tell you that. You're the only one who knows."

"But I don't know," I pointed out. "I'm afraid I'm going to lose him."

"He loves you and you know it. But you don't love him."

"I do love him." I looked up at Adrian.

"Not like he loves you," he said.

I frowned. "What do *you* know about it?"

"If you truly loved him, you would have told him everything ages ago. There's no true love without trust. And you don't trust him."

"That coming from a guy who sleeps with a girl and then moves on. Yeah, you're a real expert on love."

"Fine," he said. "Be in denial."

"Oh, shut up!"

"Well, you asked."

"Forget it. So, will you ever tell me how you learned to control the disease without the help of another magic disease carrier?"

"Maybe someday," he said.

"Huh, and why not now? Just don't tell me it's a long story."

"It's…" He smiled. "…not a nice story."

"Who cares? I still want to hear it." And maybe find out something useful.

"No," he said. Maybe I was right about him hiding something from me, but there was nothing I could do to get it out of him. Typical. We stayed like that in silence for a few moments, and then I went to my room to prepare for my next class.

Michael raised an eyebrow at me when he saw me. It was the day of Adrian's birthday party, and Michael had come for me so we could go together. Even though it was a bit hard to believe, Paula had managed to do everything to make the party perfect. I'd already seen the lunchroom since I'd been helping her, and damn, the place looked completely different.

"What?" I asked, smiling at Michael.

"You're going like that?" He sounded surprised. I looked back at the mirror to check if everything was all right. I was wearing blue jeans and a light blue top. My hair was down as usual, and there was nothing except my dark blue high heels that showed I was going to a party. Besides, Paula asked specifically for casual dress. Michael seemed to be surprised by it, because I usually wore something new for parties.

"Yeah, don't you like it?" I asked.

"Sure I like it."

"Good. Then we're ready to go."

He took my hand, and we walked out of the room. Michael was looking hot as usual in his dark jeans and a white shirt, but what was burning through me was the unusual force of his element. He was nervous because of something, even though his face didn't show it.

"Is something wrong?" I looked into his green eyes.

"No." He blinked at me. "Why do you ask?"

"I don't know," I lied. "I have a feeling you're not happy for some reason."

"You're right." He sighed. "I'm not really thrilled to go to Adrian's party."

"But Paula organized it. Think of it as her party."

"I'll never understand why she bothers so much for that bastard."

"She loves him," I said. "She'd do anything for him."

"Yeah, but he would never do the same for her," Michael pointed out.

"True."

We reached the lunchroom, so if Michael wanted to make more comments about the party, he couldn't. At least not without Paula overhearing something, because she was being a every good hostess by waiting for the guests at the entrance. I'd tried to convince her she should be inside and keeping an eye on Adrian, but she preferred to make sure no one appeared uninvited or smuggled drugs or something inside. I wondered if she had checked her own boyfriend for those.

"Hey!" Paula smiled at Michael and me. "Go on inside! It's awesome."

I just smiled back at her as we entered. The music was so loud that I was sure she was right about the party being awesome. And there were so many people dancing and standing around the tables with drinks and food that it seemed as if the whole university were here. I spotted Adrian near one of the tables, chatting with some girls. His eyes met mine briefly, and I pulled Michael with me toward the spot where he was standing.

I could feel Michael's hand tense in mine, but he let me drag him there. Adrian said something to the girls and they were gone. He smiled as we reached him.

"Happy birthday," I said, letting go of Michael's hand and taking a step forward to kiss Adrian's cheek.

"Thanks," he said quietly so Michael couldn't hear us. "Your boyfriend would like to see me dead at the moment."

I just smiled and returned to Michael, whose element was all over the place.

"Let's go," I said, and Michael followed me to the nearest table. He was so angry, and I was afraid to even touch him. I shouldn't have kissed Adrian, but shaking hands seemed awkward, and I needed a bit of peace from the elements to make sure I could get through this night.

"Why did you do that?" Michael asked, grabbing a beer bottle. I took another one and tried to figure out how to calm him.

"It's his birthday," I said. "It seemed like a polite thing to do. Besides, how many girls kissed you on your birthday?"

That shut him up for a second and he just angrily took a swig of his beer. Just as I hoped we were over it, he looked at me. "He could have hurt you, Ria. I'm not jealous, because I know you love me, but I don't want you near anyone who has magic disease."

"I know you wouldn't let him hurt me." I smiled and risked touching his face. He finally relaxed under my touch, and we kissed.

"Would you like to dance?" he asked, taking my hand.

"Always," I said, and we left our beer on the table so we could join the others on the dance floor. I'd never imagined I would dance in the lunchroom, but once the tables had been moved, it almost seemed like a real dance floor.

Two hours later, I was too tired to continue dancing, so we went to sit at the table that was in the corner of the room. Paula had finally come inside and was chatting with some girls, who were probably telling her how wonderful the party was or something similar.

A few girls I knew also came to tell me how my outfit looked pretty or how lucky I was to have such a hot boyfriend. Michael went for another beer as one of my friends started to talk about some cute outfits she'd seen at the shop earlier. I mostly ignored her, nodding a few times, and looked at the crowd. Adrian was standing alone near the table and drinking while everyone else was having fun.

A girl in a very short miniskirt and a top that showed more than it should have approached him, but he just waved her off. A few moments later, I saw him going for the back door and leaving. That surprised me because I had no idea why he would leave a party, especially his own party. Was something wrong? If I was feeling all right around all these elements, then he should have too. I checked my phone just in case, but I had no messages.

I waited some time for him to come back, but he didn't. And I hadn't seen any girl sneaking out after him. Paula was too occupied with the other girls to notice, and Michael was now chatting with some of his friends. And I was really glad there weren't any girls in that group of his friends. Yeah, jealous little old me.

I considered sending Adrian a message, but I wasn't sure he'd get it, and I probably wouldn't hear if he replied. No, I couldn't be worried about Adrian. I couldn't, right? I sighed and got up, walking over to the table with drinks. I glanced around, and when I was sure no one was watching, I grabbed a bottle of vodka and hurried to the back door. Adrian was probably having fun with some girl in his room, and I figured I'd need lots of vodka to erase any images that couldn't be unseen later.

I knocked on the door of his room and nothing happened. Maybe he wasn't there at all. I reached for the knob and opened the door. He was there, alone, sitting on the windowsill, and smoking. I walked inside, locking the door behind me.

"What are you doing here?" he asked, not even bothering to look at me.

"I didn't know you smoke."

"I don't," he said. "This is a special occasion."

"Special occasion, right," I said, walking over to him.

"You didn't tell me what you're doing here." He finally looked at me, and there was something in his eyes that I couldn't identify… sadness maybe or resentment. Just I didn't know what could have caused any of it.

"I don't know," I said and sat down on the bed, raising the bottle of vodka. "I saw you leaving and thought something was wrong."

"Admit it. You got bored of the party, too." He smiled, but it didn't reach his eyes.

"Maybe I did. But I can't figure out why you aren't there flirting with some girl. Oh, except if you're waiting for someone to come, and I should better leave before…"

"I'm not waiting for anyone." He put out the cigarette and threw it into the trash can. Then he came to sit next to me and ran a finger down my bare arm, making me shiver.

"Paula went through a lot of trouble to organize that party," I said. "You should at least be there with her."

"It's not my fault she decided to throw the stupid party," he said. "Besides, it's my birthday. I can do whatever the hell I want."

"And how exactly is being alone in your room better than being at a party?" I asked as he continued to trace his fingers down my arm until he reached the bottle and took it away from me.

"You wouldn't understand." He opened the bottle and took a gulp.

"Whoa, slow down with that!" I snatched the bottle out of his hand and took a sip. The bittersweet taste of it made me close my eyes for a second.

"Is Michael's element too strong for you, so you came to *recharge your batteries*?" he asked.

"Don't be a jerk. I was actually worried about you. But you seem to be just fine." I got up to leave, but he caught my arm and I stumbled, nearly dropping the bottle. He caught it, but I fell down on the bed. I couldn't help but laugh.

"Okay, let's play a game." I kicked off my shoes and pulled my legs up so I could sit on the bed.

"What kind of a game?" He sat down opposite from me.

"Truth or Dare." I smiled. I was feeling a little bit drunk, but that didn't mean I couldn't get some interesting information out of Adrian. He just eyed me suspiciously.

"Come on! Don't be a coward," I said.

"All right. But remember you asked for it. Oh, and I want to add something to that game."

"Add what?"

"We take a sip of vodka after each question," he said. I was chewing on my lip and thinking about it.

He smiled. "Coward."

"I'll do it!" I frowned.

"Good," he said. "So, truth or dare?"

"Um," I said, trying to think which one would be easier, "truth."

"How many boyfriends have you had?" he asked, studying my face curiously.

"Five, before Michael," I said, and he took a sip of vodka. I just smiled. "Truth or dare?"

"Truth," he said, which honestly surprised me, but I'd been waiting for it, so I didn't complain.

"Where did you live before you came here?" I asked, knowing that he'd probably been trying to learn how to control his element somewhere. There just had to be a place for such a thing, or maybe there were other ways to do that.

"At a special place," he said. "For magic disease carriers. Or better said, a special research place."

Ah, so there was a place, but I couldn't ask two questions, so I just took a sip of vodka.

"Truth or dare, Ria?" The corners of his lips went up, and I knew he had something evil in mind.

"Dare," I said, even though I was sure I was going to regret it.

"Take off your bra," he said, and I gaped at him.

"I won't do that!" I said indignantly.

"You started the game. It's not my fault. So do it or don't. Oh, and you can keep your top on."

I gave him an angry glare while I thought about what I should do. But he was right; it was my own fault. I sighed and reached under my top to unhook the damn bra. After a moment of fumbling with it, I managed to take it off without showing too much skin.

"Happy?" I asked, none too friendly, and saw a happy gleam in his eyes. Yeah, my top was a bit too thin. Fuck.

"Yeah, really happy." He flashed me a smile and took another sip of vodka. I glanced at the bottle and couldn't help but wonder how many sips he had taken while I'd been trying to get the bra off.

"Great," I said sarcastically. "Truth or dare?"

"Truth," he said. "But just because I know you want it."

Was that supposed to make me feel better? Yeah… right.

"That place where you lived," I said. "What it's like?"

He smiled bitterly and shook his head. "You don't want to know."

"Yes, I do," I said.

"You really want the whole story?"

"Yeah."

"Fine," he said, reaching for some pillows and placing them against the headboard so he could lie down more comfortably. "Come here."

I moved from my position and lay down next to him, placing my head on his chest and letting him put his arm around me. I half-expected him to reach up for my boobs, but he held his arm firmly around my waist.

"Have you ever been in a hospital?" he asked.

"Um, once. I went to visit someone."

"Well, it smells like a hospital in there. It's a huge place with horrible, ugly white walls. Most of the rooms are laboratories used for discovering things and doing research on the elements and the disease. But they don't discover much, or at least don't share it with the world," he said. "The other part of the building is used as a place where some of the scientists live and… for other purposes. One of those special places is a room made for carrying out experiments on living magic disease carriers."

"You were in that room," I said, my voice a little bit louder than a whisper.

"Yeah, I was in there. Too many times. I was probably the first living magic disease carrier they got."

"What kind of experiments did they do?"

"All kinds of experiments," he said. "They used elements for almost every one of them."

"What's that room like?" I asked, trying to imagine it.

"It's not much bigger than this room. It has white walls and a white floor, except for a big black piece of glass on one wall. They can watch you through that glass from the other side, but you can't see them. And there's nothing else in that room." He took a sip of vodka. I could feel his muscles tensing under me. I waited for him to continue, not wanting to push it. It sounded as if that place were a cross between a psychiatric hospital and prison.

"They would put me in there and play with their elements around me," he said. "They tried really hard to make me lose control, and they enjoyed it when they had to cuff me to stop me from attacking them. But I scared the hell out of one woman once."

"What did you do to her?" I asked, wondering what I would do if someone tried to do experiments on me.

"She tried using fire in front of me. I let her get close to me, even though it was hard as hell to stay calm. Then I swept her feet out from under her, and she ended up sprawled on the floor. It was hilarious, except she didn't think that."

"Bitch," I murmured, taking the bottle from him to take a sip.

"Yeah. She said to everyone that I was dangerous and that I should be killed. But the others wanted to do more experiments, so they just left me there. After I don't know how much time, I figured I had something like an element in me and I used it. It helped me, even though I almost froze to death."

"Froze to death? But how?" I looked up at him.

"There was nothing I could turn into ice there, and I didn't want them to know about it. I've no idea what they would've done to me if they had found out. So I just turned the air cold and stopped only when I had to so they wouldn't notice. Or if I got so cold or tired I couldn't do it anymore."

"How did you get out of there?" I asked. Maybe he was inventing it all, but why would he? My mind was a little bit hazy, and I was sure I was forgetting something, but that didn't matter. It couldn't matter if I couldn't remember what it was, right?

"Alan didn't want to work and live there. He got sick of that place and he got a job offer here, and since he couldn't leave me, he had no other choice but to bring me with him," he said. "Of course, that was already at the time when I started to control myself much better, so Alan got the permission from the Council. I got my life back on the day we came here, because they didn't just stop experimenting on me, but they also gave me back everything that belonged to me. Things my parents had left me."

"So you own that company your father had?" I asked.

"Yeah, I do. But others are taking care of it since I know nothing about business, and they would never trust me with it anyway," he said. "But it's okay since they give me the money."

"Cool." I didn't even realize I was still holding the vodka bottle until Adrian took it out of my hands and placed it on the nightstand. I started lifting myself up, and then my eyes fell on his lips.

"Your lips are dry," I said in a voice that didn't quite sound like mine. Great, I was most likely drunk. But I didn't care.

"So?" He raised an eyebrow at me.

"I can fix it," I said, going for my jeans pocket. "I have lip balm somewhere."

"Oh no, you're not giving me your lip balm." His eyes widened.

I found the little tube in my left pocket and smiled triumphantly.

"Yes, I am," I said, trying to open the stupid thing, but my fingers kept sliding off. Damn, when had those little things gotten so complicated to open? I finally opened it and squeezed some on my finger... and some of it fell on my jeans, but whatever. I moved closer to put it on his lips.

"No! Stay the fuck away from me with that!" he yelled, but I didn't stop. He grabbed both of my hands and held me at a safe distance, and I just kept trying. After his attempt to push me away, we ended up rolling across the bed. In what seemed as a second, we fell onto the floor.

Actually, I fell on top of him and that softened my fall a lot.

"Ouch," he said, wincing in pain.

"Sorry," I said, but instead of sounding like it, a giggle escaped my lips. I couldn't help it, but there was something hilarious about all of this. He looked at me and then started to laugh too. When I came back to my senses, I realized I still had a bit of my lip balm on my finger.

"No, don't do that." He moved his head away. I looked at him, then back at my finger. Oh well, if he didn't want it… I brought my finger to my lips.

"What are you doing?" He turned his head back to look at me, and I saw it as an opportunity to do what I wanted. I brought my lips down on his before he could protest again. Just this time he didn't try to push me away. He kissed me back. Kissed me? Some part of my brain knew there was something wrong with that, but my body didn't. His lips were so soft and so warm on mine, and nothing existed except us.

"Not on the floor," he said, breaking the kiss. I shakily got up and let myself fall on the bed. He was right; the bed was much more comfortable. He pulled himself up and climbed on top of me. I stared into his gray-blue eyes and smiled. His eyes had never been so beautiful as they were now.

"Kiss me," I whispered, and he did. My arms slid around his neck and his hand ended up under my top, caressing my breast. This had to be wrong on so many levels, but it felt so damn good. I just didn't want him to stop.

He kissed his way down my cheek, my collarbone… My hands gripped at his shirt, and he helped me pull it off. His lips were on mine again, sending shivers all over my body.

"Take it…" I whispered, "…off."

He looked at me, and I tugged at my top to show him what I wanted. It took him a second to understand, and soon enough my top was somewhere on the floor. His every touch, every kiss, every caress, brought me waves of pleasure. I'd never felt so good in my whole life.

He stopped suddenly and looked at me with those gorgeous gray-blue eyes. I frowned at him first, not understanding what he was waiting for. Then I looked down my body and realized that the only thing that was between him and me were his boxers. I didn't remember exactly at what point my panties had come off, but it didn't really matter.

I tried to pull him closer and kiss him, but he didn't let me. He was just looking at me intently. I suddenly knew what he wanted. This was my chance to say no. This was my chance to stop, but I didn't want to. I gave him a short nod, and he reached for the drawer of his nightstand. Maybe we couldn't infect each other with magic disease, but there were other unwanted consequences.

He was kissing me again in a second, and I dug my nails into his back and didn't care if I would leave marks. The world suddenly seemed like such a nice and happy place, and I wanted that to last.

Chapter 23

Someone was banging on the door, and it was loud enough for me to hear it through my sleep. I felt shifting in the bed and slowly opened my eyes. Images from the previous evening hit my head like a wave, making me dizzy for a second. I had slept with Adrian.

"Adrian! Open the damn door!" I recognized Alan's voice and looked at Adrian in panic. He got up from the bed, finding his boxers and jeans, and put them on. I looked around and saw my clothes scattered everywhere. I had enough time only to put on my panties because Adrian was already going for the door.

"No!" I whispered to him, but he ignored me. I had no other choice but to wrap the sheets around myself and wait to see what would happen. Adrian opened the door and moved away as Alan stormed inside. The look on Alan's face when he saw the state of the room and me there in the bed was that of shock, surprise, and then pure fury.

"What have you done?" Alan asked, turning to Adrian.

"What does it look like, genius?" Adrian asked, looking amused. Alan took a step toward him and slapped him hard across the face.

But Adrian just smiled at him. "You didn't believe I could have sex with any girl I wanted," he said. "Well, now you have the proof."

"But you, Ria?" Alan looked at me, and I just bit my lip, looking away from his judging eyes. There was no excuse for what I'd done. And I couldn't blame anyone but myself.

"I want to see you in my office," Alan said. "Both of you."

With that, he left the room. Adrian closed the door behind him and walked over to pick up his shirt, a satisfied smile on his face.

"You son of a bitch," I said angrily, collecting my things. "You knew he was going to come! You fucking knew! You used me!"

"You enjoyed every bit of it." He smirked. "And I don't care what you think."

So, that was it. I was just another girl on his famous list, and he had a witness. I wasn't sure what I'd been expecting, but last night I hadn't been thinking about any of it. How would I look my boyfriend in the face? How would I look my best friend in the face knowing that I'd slept with her boyfriend?

I got dressed as fast as I could and ran out of the room. When I was safe in my own room, tears started to fall freely down my face. I picked up my phone and saw a ton of worried messages and unanswered calls from Michael. He was concerned about me as usual, and I had stabbed him in the back. I managed to send him a message saying that I was fine and that I would see him at lunch. I wasn't sure what I would say or do, but I had to do something… anything.

Now I knew why Adrian was the way he was, but that didn't give him the right to go around and play with any girl's feelings. For a second, I wished Alan would decide to send him back to that horrible place, but what would be left of me if that happened? Why did I depend on such a hateful man? How would I ever go to him to get back in control of myself knowing that he'd tricked me? And was there anything real in that boy, who sometimes cared about me when I needed it, or had it all been a trick to get me to like him? I just wasn't sure. I wasn't sure of anything anymore.

After a few hours of brooding in my room, I decided I couldn't go back in time and change anything, so I might as well accept it. It was lunchtime, and I had to see Michael no matter what and tell him everything. If he was going to hate me, then let him. He had every right to do it. Paula, too. I was probably going to stay alone in the world, but I didn't want to think about it.

As I walked down the hallway toward the lunchroom, I noticed people were watching me differently. Some boys were laughing quietly after I passed by, and girls were giving me dirty looks.

"You bitch!" one blonde girl yelled at me. "You just couldn't be happy with one, could you? You had to have them both!"

I stared at her in shock. No, no way. He couldn't have spread the news, could he? Because if he had, I was going to kill him.

"Fight! Fight! Fight!" I heard someone yell, and I ran for the lunchroom, pushing people out of my way. I didn't have time to notice that the lunchroom was back to its usual state, because people were standing in a circle in the middle of it. Some were shouting, some were cheering… it was a total mess. I managed to get to the front and at that moment saw Adrian punching Michael in the face. They both looked as if they were in the middle of a war.

"Stop!" I yelled, but they didn't hear me or didn't care. I saw Paula standing on the other end, her hands covering her face. She was crying. Michael's element was getting stronger and stronger, and I recalled something I'd learned about magic disease, and that was that it got stronger in fights. They could really kill each other. I knew I couldn't just stand there, and I ran toward them at the same moment as Alan appeared. But I was closer to Adrian and he was closer to Michael.

I wasn't sure if Adrian had said something about me having the disease to anyone, but I didn't have time to think about it. Others joined in to help separate them, and Alan managed to pull Michael out of Adrian's reach. I ran to Adrian and grabbed his arm, but he shoved me away.

"Stop! Adrian, stop!" I stepped in front of him and placed my hands on each side of his face. His gray-blue eyes were unfocused, and even though he was looking at me, I knew he didn't see me.

"Look at me," I said. "Adrian, look at me. Please."

He blinked and surprise was written all over his face. My touch calmed him enough to bring him back from killing mode to reality. If it weren't for his split lip, I wouldn't be able to tell he'd been in a fight at all. Alan came to us and roughly grabbed Adrian by the arm to get him away from there.

"I don't know what you did," Alan said to me, "but I still want to see you in my office."

They walked away, and I turned around to see Michael and Paula standing there. A bruise was forming on Michael's cheekbone, but I knew that wasn't the reason why his green eyes were full of hurt and sadness. Paula's make-up was smeared all over her face, and she was staring at me through the tears. I took a step toward them, but Michael turned around, took Paula's hand, and they walked away from me.

From what I could hear while walking back to my room, Adrian had approached Michael and told him he'd slept with his girlfriend. Michael hadn't believed it at first, but then Adrian asked him if he knew where I'd been the whole night. Then Michael punched him and the fight started. I couldn't believe Adrian would do such a thing when he'd already done so much to hurt me. But I guessed he'd just wanted to rub it in Michael's face. They were enemies after all.

Alan caught me just as I was plotting how to avoid his office. There was nothing I could do but follow him to his annoying, claustrophobic den. When I entered, I immediately saw Adrian leaning on the wall, his arms crossed. I gave him the coldest and angriest glare I could muster, but he just watched me passively.

I settled down in one of the familiar red chairs and waited.

"Sit down, Adrian," Alan said, getting comfortable in his own chair. Adrian didn't move.

"Sit down!" Alan repeated, and Adrian reluctantly dragged himself to the chair. For some reason he avoided looking at me as he sat down as far as he could from me. Weird. Shouldn't I be the one avoiding him?

"I can't believe what the two of you have done!" Alan said. "Especially you, Ria."

"We're not kids," Adrian said through his teeth.

"I don't care," Alan said. "You were stupid enough to engage in dangerous behavior!"

I snorted. I wasn't in the mood for patronizing and especially not from the guy who had absolutely no say in my life. Besides, I had much more important things to do, like figuring out how to explain everything to the two very important people in my life, who probably didn't want to see me ever again.

"Ria, I don't think you understand how serious this situation is." Alan was frowning at me.

"Just let her go, Alan," Adrian suddenly said. "It's my fault."

"Your fault? Yeah, I figured that, but it's her fault, too," Alan said. "Unless you forced her to have intercourse with you."

"I…" Adrian seemed to be unsure of what to say. He was looking down at his hands in his lap. I glared at him. What the hell was he trying to do? Get himself killed?

"Adrian, go outside for a moment," Alan said. "I need to speak privately to Ria."

Adrian got up and went for the door, not even glancing at me. I really wished at that moment that I could read his mind, because I wasn't sure what was going on.

"Oh, please!" I said. "We had sex, so what? That's not the university's problem."

"No, it's not," Alan said. "But it's mine."

"Why?" I said, clenching my jaw in annoyance. "Because you're Adrian's guardian? Well, he slept with his girlfriend, too, and I don't remember you complaining."

"Yeah, and the difference in that is that Paula is his girlfriend and you're not. Actually, Paula told me you couldn't stand each other. She said you wanted all magic disease carriers dead. I highly doubt you changed your opinion."

"What are you implying?" I asked, wondering why the hell Paula had told so much to this man.

"That Adrian forced you to sleep with him, and you're worried about your reputation, and maybe afraid for your life too much to admit it," he said. Great, just fucking great.

"You'd love that, wouldn't you?" I glared at him. "You'd love to get rid of him forever and have a normal life."

"No, Ria, it's not like that," he said, surprised. "I'm just worried about the students' safety."

"Well you don't have to be. They're perfectly safe."

"Ria, I can make sure he never hurts you again. Don't think I forgot that incident when you hit him. And I know I told you to avoid him. I don't know how he threatened you, but I'm sure there's more to this."

"He didn't rape me," I said, trying to stay calm. If I showed any sign of the disease now, they would blame Adrian for it. I couldn't let that happen.

"All right, but did he threaten you? Blackmail you? Drug you?" he asked, and my frown deepened as he continued talking.

"How many times do I have to say no?" I asked.

"You're not convincing me." His eyes softened as he tried to look harmless and good-hearted. "Why would you sleep with your best friend's boyfriend? Especially, when you have a boyfriend. I know you're not that kind of a girl."

Well, that was a good question. Why had I done it? I'd been drunk and Adrian was good-looking, but that wasn't it. There had to be something else that had caused it. Maybe the fact that I could safely do it only with him? I didn't know and I didn't want to discuss it with this man.

"I'll take a lie detector," I said, meeting his eyes. That confused him for a moment, because he'd surely expected my admission that Adrian had somehow forced me to sleep with him.

"So you really slept with him because you wanted to?" Incredulity was written all over his face.

"Yeah."

"I guess I was wrong then. I'm sorry, Ria." He sighed. "If you need someone to talk to, you know where to find me."

"Yeah." I tried hard not to roll my eyes at him. Did that guy have to know everything about students' lives?

"You may go," he said, and I got up immediately. Adrian was waiting outside, chewing on his lip and looking nervous. I walked over to him.

"What's wrong with you?" I asked. "First, you brag about sleeping with me, then you pick a fight with Michael, and now you make it all sound as if you raped me!"

"Did you tell him anything?" he asked urgently.

"About what?"

"You know," he said, lowering his voice, "your condition."

"No. I'm not that crazy."

Relief flashed through his eyes.

"Wait," I said. "Did you think that Alan would get it out of me somehow? Did you think that saying you raped me would seem believable enough for him to drop the subject?"

"Of course not," he said, but the look on his face betrayed him.

"You're an idiot! How dare you risk your life for…" The words were stuck in my throat. I stared at him, unsure what to think.

"Okay, maybe I'm an idiot," he said. "But I was afraid you'd tell him everything since you seemed so upset before… and… I had no idea what to do."

"Why? Why do you care?"

"I don't want you to go through the same things as me," he said, looking sincere. "I don't want anyone to go through that."

"So you'd risk your own life just to prevent that?" I raised an eyebrow.

"Nah, I was hoping you'd be smart and know what to say." He smiled.

I rolled my eyes. Why had I even thought for a second that he was a nice person? He was still that arrogant, manipulative bastard who thought he could get anything he wanted. And he always got it. Damn.

"I'm going to tell the truth to Michael and Paula, whether you like it or not," I said. "I need to try to explain it somehow to them."

"Fine. But know that you're putting us both in danger."

I gave him a cold stare and left.

Chapter 24

Michael and Paula had managed to avoid me for two full weeks. They didn't return any of my calls and looked away from me when we passed each other in the hallway. Paula still waited for Adrian to come talk to her, but he didn't even bother looking for her. As far as he was concerned, their relationship was over. I was sure he had someone in mind already, but I didn't feel like talking to him about it.

One day, I decided to finally resolve the situation between Michael, Paula, and me. I'd spent the whole day sending them messages and calling them, so they agreed to meet me at the laboratory. I thought the laboratory was the best place since Paula had the key and no one could overhear us there. I didn't know if Paula had gotten the key because of her academic success or her situation with Adrian, but that didn't really matter.

They were already waiting for me inside when I showed up. I closed the door and locked it behind me.

"Hey," I said and walked over to them, sitting down on one of the chairs. They didn't say anything but just stared at me, the expression on their faces grim and unforgiving. I could do this. I had to.

"I'm really sorry about what happened," I said, taking a deep breath. "I didn't mean to hurt you. I…"

"Did you really sleep with him?" Michael swallowed, trying to keep his face expressionless. "Willingly?"

"Yes, I did," I said, and Paula burst into tears.

"Why?" she choked out. "Why with my boyfriend?"

"I don't know," I said. "It kind of… happened."

"Happened? But how?" Michael asked with a hint of anger in his voice. "You hated him! You didn't even see each other, and so suddenly you just…"

"There's something you both need to know," I said. "Something I didn't tell you because I was afraid… I was afraid to lose you, but now I guess it doesn't matter."

"Tell us what?" Michael asked suspiciously.

"Michael." I looked at him. "Do you remember that night when we almost slept together? When I lost my balance and nearly choked you to death?"

"Yeah, but I don't see what that has to do with anything," he said. They were both watching me intently, trying to figure out what I was talking about. There was a huge lump in my throat, but I had to get the words out before I started to cry or something.

"I didn't lose my balance," I said. "I did try to kill you… at first… because… because I have magic disease."

Tears welled up in my eyes as I said it. By saying this out loud in front of the two very important people in my life, it felt like everything became more real. I finally admitted to myself that I had the disease and that it wasn't just going to go away. Michael and Paula stared at me in shock, not believing what they'd just heard.

"No." Paula shook her head. "It can't be. It can't!"

"Yeah, I didn't believe it either," I said, letting the tears freely run down my face.

"How? How did you get it?" Paula blinked through tears. We were turning into a huge crying party.

"I don't know. I guess I inherited it," I said. "But I'm still trying to find out..."

"Why didn't you tell us?" Michael was suddenly in front of me, pulling me into a tight hug.

"I couldn't… I thought you'd… hate me," I cried. "And I wanted it to go away… I don't know. I was stupid, I know…"

"Ria." Paula was on the other side of me, putting her hands around me too. "We love you. We could never hate you. Right, Michael?"

"Right," he said, and we just stayed for some time like that, hugging and crying. After we'd calmed down, I told them everything that had happened to me during these past months, but deliberately avoided mentioning any of Adrian's secrets. I just told them how Adrian had been helping me to stay in control of myself and how awful it was to feel elements.

"I'll find a cure, Ria." Paula held my hands in hers. "I promise. I won't sleep, I won't care about studying… but I'll find a cure, got it?"

"I know you will, but it's okay. Don't worry about me," I said. "I'll be fine."

"Sure you will. But I think I discovered the place where the government keeps those secret files. If we break in there, we can get the files and I can find a cure and…" Paula was very excited about her plan to save me. She and Michael talked as if they had just brought me back from the dead, and maybe they had. I told them why I didn't want anyone to know about the disease, and they both swore to keep my secret. I had really been an idiot. How could I not have confided in those who cared about me so much?

"I'll help you." Michael smiled at Paula. "I'll do anything to help my girlfriend with this."

"Girlfriend?" I looked at him in surprise.

"Yeah, you're my girlfriend, aren't you?" he said, and I couldn't believe what I was hearing.

"You mean… You can forgive me for..?" I asked.

"I love you, Ria," he said. "And I know you love me, too. What happened between you and Adrian… it doesn't matter. He used your vulnerability, and that's all."

How good it sounded when he put it like that. And maybe it was true. I wasn't sure. All I knew was that I didn't want to lose Michael, not again.

"Michael… I don't know what to say," I said.

"Will you be my girlfriend?" He offered me a smile. "Again?"

"I would love to," I said. "But I'm not sure that's a good idea. I still kind of can't be around people without Adrian's help."

"I know, and I won't be angry about it. I promise," he said. "Besides, you know how it is with Adrian. He never sleeps with the same girl twice… Oh, I'm sorry, Paula."

"It's okay." She sighed. "I'm done with him. He'll never love me."

"You deserve better," I said to her, and she just smiled. It was so nice to have my best friend back. I knew it would take her some time to recover from this, but she would be fine. She had just needed something as big as Adrian sleeping with her best friend to prove that he wasn't for her and that she should quit trying to turn him into a better person. And she really was too good for him, just like Michael was too good for me…

"So, what do you say?" Michael was standing inches away from me, his green eyes shining like two emeralds.

"I'll be your girlfriend… again." I smiled, and he kissed me. I felt water all around me and I moved away.

"I'm sorry… your element," I said, turning around and taking deep breaths. I knew it wouldn't help, but this whole little gathering was too full of emotions, and it had drained me.

"Sorry," Michael said. "I'll be more careful."

"But I just don't understand why you still have your element." Paula frowned, back in her scientist mode. "I could do some tests…"

"No," I said. I hadn't told them about Adrian, so Paula basically considered me a miracle.

"But it could help!" she said. "We still don't know how you got the disease, and I can't believe you haven't looked for answers!"

"I did, but I think I should be careful with this," I said. "My brother told me not to tell my parents, so he has to know something. And I'm quite sure my parents don't have the disease… I don't know. It's all so confusing."

"We need to get those secret files," Paula said determinedly. "And according to my books, they're near here. I bet they're in that building the Council has. It's just a perfect location."

"I don't think so," I said. "It's too obvious."

"No, I think Paula's right," Michael said. I knew they were both wrong, but I couldn't tell them I'd been there with Adrian to steal that damn journal. Maybe I should have told them everything, but then there would be questions about Adrian, and I didn't want to betray him. Funny, because I was sure he'd betray me.

Paula was getting too excited about the new research and my case that I couldn't stand a minute more with them. Their elements were all over the place, and I couldn't risk snapping. We hugged hastily, and then I went to find Adrian. I almost felt guilty about doing that now that Michael and Paula had forgiven me, but there was nothing else I could do.

I shivered as I entered Adrian's room because the air inside was colder than a winter's night. Adrian was sitting on the windowsill, as usual, and staring through the window. Now I knew why he liked that spot so much. Spending too much time in a windowless room could make you love windows.

"I'm not a penguin, you know," I said, and he looked at me as if I were crazy. "The room is freezing!" I added, rubbing my hands together.

"Oh, sorry," he said, blinking in surprise. He hadn't even noticed he was doing that. Weird. I started walking toward him and reached inside of me for my element. This room needed a little bit of heating.

"Just hold me, would you?" I said, and we ended up lying on the bed. His arms were around me as usual, and it felt so good that I couldn't help but feel as if I were betraying Michael again… and myself. But Michael had agreed to this, right? Right? There was no one to answer that question.

"Did you tell them?" Adrian asked.

"Yeah. They forgave me," I said. "I'm still Michael's girlfriend. And I didn't tell them anything that involved you… if that's what worries you."

"Good," he said. Why was I even trying to be nice to a guy who had toyed with me so he could add me to his list? For some unknown reason I hoped that everything hadn't been just an act to get me to sleep with him. Something was seriously wrong with me.

"Paula and Michael believe there are files that could help Paula discover a cure for magic disease," I said. "Maybe scientists have discovered it already and are hiding it from us… I don't know."

"I don't care," he said. "There's no cure."

"How can you be so sure?"

"Stop living in dreams," he said. "Let them research whatever they want, but keep your mouth shut about me."

"But they think that place is the Council's building! We can't let them go there! It would be an unnecessary risk! And I don't want to go near that place again. If I could just tell them the whole truth…"

"No," he said. "If they want to go there, let them. You don't have to go with them."

"But…"

"Shut the fuck up, will you?" he yelled, and I looked up at him.

"Ah, so now that you had sex with me, you don't have to be nice anymore," I said angrily.

"Well, I didn't kick you out of the room, did I?"

"No, but I think you would have if you didn't need me," I said. "Why don't you just tell me what's wrong? There's a reason why you turned the room into a freakin' penguin playground!"

He just stared at me with his cold gray-blue eyes.

"I know where the secret place is," he suddenly said, and I blinked. He was changing the subject. Great. But he got me there.

"How?" I asked suspiciously. Maybe it was just another thing he invented to trick me again.

"My father wrote about it." Judging by the look on his face... no, I was clueless again.

"Show me." If there was really something written in that journal, then I wanted to see it. No more believing anything without proof.

"The journal's in the drawer," he said. I frowned because the drawer was on the other side of him. But, no, the bastard wouldn't even lift a finger to help me. I had to reach over him to get to the drawer. Great. I got the journal and just as I was settling back on the bed next to him, he snatched it out of my hands. He went through a few pages and gave it back to me open on one.

"Um, thanks," I said sarcastically.

"No problem." He smiled, and I rolled my eyes. Well, better to focus my attention on the journal before my fist decided to flirt with Adrian's jaw again.

"Scientists have discovered more than anyone could imagine, but the government wants to keep it away from people. Magic disease is still a great way of manipulating people. If you want to get rid of someone, simply accuse him of having magic disease. If you want to marry into a rich family, spread the word about how magic disease is dangerous, and soon enough, if you're of a pure element, your dreams will come true. And, after all, it's easier to manipulate people if they hate each other," I read out loud, because I hoped that way I would understand it better. I continued reading.

"There's an international deal, and Councils from all over the world signed it. The deal is that everything that mentions magic disease should be stored in a safe place. That way the scientists believe their materials go to other scientists across the world in order for their theories to be checked or compared, and no one doubts it when negative results come back. If not the negative results, then they are told someone else had already discovered it somewhere in the world. The files are stored only to keep an eye on the discoveries and to have proof against everyone who dares to think something strange is going on."

"I have reasons to believe that place is underground. Somewhere near the Council's offices, but not quite there. I would have found it already, but being a member of the Council doesn't mean you have access to all the information. Actually, most of the information is hidden from the Council members, only a few families get a special pass, and there's nothing anyone can do about that. Anyway, as for the location of that secret place, I believe it is exactly under the Hotel Blue Moon. The man who built it there was a member of the Council. And the University of Magic is near enough."

I stared at the page because I was getting dizzy from all the underlined words. When I looked back at the real text, it seemed as if a lunatic had written it. The word 'enough' was actually made from the sentence: 'Eleven nights of her pure fragrance have me crazed.' Adrian's father probably hadn't had time to come up with the sentences, or he'd gone mad because of all of it. And Adrian was probably tired of underlining because he'd stopped after the letter h.

"Hotel Blue Moon is here, isn't it?" I asked, my throat dry from reading. It seemed unlikely that the secret place would be right here in this town, but all the important buildings were around here. This was actually a good place, and if I remembered correctly, there were some old tunnels under the town. Years ago, people believed they could find gold here, so they made those tunnels, which were abandoned later since they proved to be completely useless. I thought everyone had forgotten about them at this point.

"Yeah," he said. "It's here."

"That makes sense actually."

"Really?" He raised an eyebrow.

"If you read a book sometime, maybe you'd know," I said, trying to remember anything specific from my History books. Maybe I hadn't really paid enough attention to History these last few months, but I still remembered things I'd learned in high school. Just there wasn't anything else except what had already come to my mind earlier. And exactly that made it a perfect hiding place.

"I have to tell Paula about this," I said, sitting up. Adrian painfully grabbed my arm and pulled me back down.

"No," he said.

"Let go of me!" I yelled, but his grip on my arm remained tight.

"You're going to leave a bruise on my arm, you moron!" I said, and he finally let go. I put down the journal and rubbed my arm. He observed me carefully for a moment and then reached again for my arm. I flinched, but didn't want to let him see he'd startled me, so I tried to keep still. He ran his fingers gently down my arm. Suddenly I had a flashback of the night we had spent together, and it sent chills down my spine. My body wanted him, and that scared me like hell.

I moved out of his reach, and he let his hand fall down on the bed. Damn it, what was wrong with me? That boy had used me, tricked me, manipulated me... the list was too long, but one part of me was willing to ignore it all for another night like that. Had it been like that with Michael? Had it been that good? I knew I would never know, because Adrian had taken that away from me too. No, I had actually; I should have known he wouldn't want to sleep twice with Paula.

"What are you thinking?" he asked.

"I'm thinking of an effective way to kill you." I smiled unpleasantly.

"No, you're not," he said. "I know that look on your face."

"You know nothing," I said. Maybe Paula and Michael would just believe me. Surely, I could come up with something, but that would mean lying to them again. I sighed and closed my eyes. I needed to relax first. Everything else could wait, even my inexplicable physical attraction to Adrian.

Chapter 25

Paula and Michael had already put a whole plan together by the time I came to our meeting spot. Michael thought that the park behind our university would be a perfect place to plan breaking and entering. I agreed only because we could hide behind the trees, and I wouldn't have to worry about too many elements being around me all the time. They were sitting on the grass, surrounded by papers, and I joined them.

"We'll go there this weekend," Michael said. "We don't have classes then, and the Council also has time off. Security will still be there, but we'll figure something out."

"But that's not the place!" I said. "My father's on the Council! I know that's not the right place. I think it's somewhere closer here, and I'm sure I could find out if I asked my father."

"Ria, I don't think your father has that much power in the Council," Michael said.

"Yeah, but would they be so obvious about it?" I asked.

"Everyone knows there are important files somewhere in there, but no one ever mentioned secret files, of course," Paula said. "That's why they're probably there."

"Okay, fine," I said. "But how are we going to get inside? We're not professional criminals!"

"We don't have to be," Michael said. "I already got the map of the place and all the security info."

"Where did you get that?" I frowned.

"I have a friend who works there," Michael said. I blinked. Wow. They really did believe the Council had it all in that building. There was no way to convince them the opposite. But if Michael had a friend there, then maybe it wouldn't be so dangerous to do it, and we could just go there and return. That visit would definitely prove them wrong.

"A friend?" I asked. "Great. Did you tell him what you're planning to do so he can call the police?"

"He owes me," Michael said. "Besides, we won't steal anything. Just copy the files and get the hell out of there."

"That'll take too much time." I shook my head.

"Well, we have eight hours from the moment Ted's shift starts," Michael said. "He's a guard there."

"Awesome," I said. "When exactly are we going?"

"Um, you're not coming with us," Michael said.

"Of course I am," I said, surprised. "You can't expect me to let you and Paula go there alone."

I was a little bit worried that someone could recognize me there, but I didn't want them to go alone.

"No, you're not," Paula said. "You have magic disease. We can't risk you going there and something going wrong. If we got caught, they would…"

"Michael, you can't do this to me," I said angrily. "I'll be fine. I want to come."

"Sorry, Ria," he said. "I love you too much to let you come. The decision has already been made."

"If you truly love me, then you'll trust me when I tell you I can do this," I said, looking straight into his green eyes.

"No," he said. I looked at Paula, but she just shook her head.

"Fine." I got up, smiling bitterly. "I hope you don't find anything."

With that, I turned around and headed back inside. Michael was yelling my name after me, but I was too angry to face him. I didn't want him to try to convince me how it was better for me to stay away.

I found myself going to Adrian's room even though I hadn't planned on it. But my conversation with Michael and Paula had made me angry, and I was afraid I would snap at anyone who dared to come near me. I needed a break until I calmed down, but even that had become hard with Adrian.

"Hey," I said to Adrian as I came to lie down next to him. He raised an eyebrow at me.

"You're angry," he said.

"Is it that obvious?" I sighed.

"Yes." His lips spread into a smile. "Who pissed you off? Your dear little boyfriend?"

"Michael and Paula refused to take me with them to find the files."

"So? They're going to the wrong place anyway. It's better for you not to go."

"Yeah, but that's not the point," I said. "They don't know it's the wrong place, and they don't know I've already been there. Yet they don't want to take me with them because they don't trust me enough! They think I can't control myself."

"Well, you can't."

"But they don't know that! They didn't even ask me," I said. "They simply decided for me."

"I'm not sure I see your point," he said. "But we could go find the real place."

"What do you mean?" I looked at him.

"While they're wasting their time, we could do a little investigating here. If you're willing to take a risk, of course."

"I am," I said. "But how are we going to do that?"

"Easy. We just have to ask someone to check in at the hotel for us. And then we can freely roam around."

"I don't think it's that easy to find. Maybe that secret room can't even be accessed through the hotel," I said. "The hotel may be above it, but that doesn't mean they're connected."

"We can check," he said. "It's not as if we have better things to do."

Sure, we did have better things to do, but I'd probably be worrying too much about Paula and Michael to be able to function normally. I needed something to distract me, and this was it. Besides, how dangerous could walking around an expensive hotel be? We probably wouldn't find anything anyway.

"All right," I said. I didn't feel angry anymore, and I realized that Adrian had his arm around me again. It was strange how accustomed to that I'd become that I didn't even notice it.

"Good," he said. "I'm going to pay someone to get us a room there."

"What are we going to do if we really find something?" I looked into his eyes and saw a spark of amusement.

"How can you even think we won't find anything?" He smiled.

"Okay, we'll find something," I said, not really convinced. "But what are we going to do? The security probably isn't as bad as it is in the Council's building."

"I don't think they're really expecting someone there. So I guess it's a 'less guards and more technology' kind of a place."

"Ah, great. Then we'll have to kill someone and gouge his eyes out in order to enter," I said. "Perfect."

"You watch too many movies." He was tracing circles with his finger on my arm.

"Maybe, but you watch too many movies, too, if you think we're going to break into a high tech place without special equipment."

"Who says we won't have special equipment?"

"I do." I smiled at him. "And even if we had special equipment, it wouldn't help much since we're not trained thieves, spies, or whatever we're supposed to be for this kind of thing."

"You're right," he said. "I'm actually hoping for low security since no one expects a break-in."

"Great." I rolled my eyes. "What a plan!"

"At least we can bring some color spray for the cameras."

"Huh, that's so cool," I said sarcastically. "Are we going to dress up again?"

"No, we're going as ourselves to the hotel. Later we'll need some kind of a disguise. But nothing similar to what we had worn that night."

"As ourselves?" I frowned. "No way. Then everyone will know we've been there! They'll connect it with us immediately!"

"Why? Because they know I have magic disease?" he asked.

"Yeah! Besides, it would be suspicious as hell that we appeared there, but didn't check in under our names!"

"Of course that would be suspicious, but we'd have a perfect explanation," he said. I sat up and turned to look at him. He was insane. People were going to recognize us and then we'd be in lots of trouble.

"What explanation?"

"We're having an affair, darling," he said. "We go to the hotel because they have discovered us at the university already, and you can't let your boyfriend find out. So, of course we don't check in with our own names. Besides, we'll spend all the time in our room."

I opened my mouth to say something to that, but I didn't know what. This plan was the stupidest thing I'd ever heard.

"Not going to work," I said. "Even if I agreed to something as stupid as that, they'd see us coming out on cameras, and if we don't find anything, we'll have a scandal to deal with. That's totally crazy, reckless, and stupid."

"Doesn't it make you want to do it then?" he asked, and I had a moment of realization.

I lowered myself so I could watch him carefully, my face only inches away from his. "What are you trying to achieve?"

He just looked at me, but I thought I had a good idea of what was really going on.

"You're trying to get Michael to break up with me," I said, and he actually flinched.

"Why would I want to do that?" he asked, but there was an edge to his voice.

"I don't know. But that's what you're trying to do."

I got up and went to the window. Adrian was silent. I couldn't figure out why he would try to split up Michael and me. It didn't make sense. Maybe he was envious that I had a boyfriend and he didn't have a girlfriend, but he could get one if he wanted to, so that couldn't be it. Was he jealous because Michael loved me so much that he'd actually forgiven me? Or was it all because Michael and he couldn't stand each other? My head was spinning from all the possibilities.

"We're going there, but not as ourselves," I said after a long moment of silence. "And there's nothing you can do to convince me otherwise."

"Fine," he said, but he didn't sound too happy, probably because his plan hadn't worked. I wasn't even sure what kind of a plan he'd had and I didn't want to spend any more time thinking about it.

"Are we going shopping then?" I turned to look at Adrian, and he smiled.

"Only if I can choose what you get to wear."

I eyed him suspiciously. When we'd gone shopping during our trip we hadn't had much time to choose things, so it was all done without much thinking or trying out various outfits. This time we'd have lots of time, and I was a bit curious what he'd choose for me.

"I'm not sure you'd know what to choose," I said.

"Oh, trust me, I would. Besides, we can make it even more fun."

"How's that?" I raised an eyebrow at him.

"I choose something for you, and you choose something for me."

"Okay," I said, amazed that he'd actually let me pick his clothes. "What kind of look are we going for?"

"Business look," he said. "There's some kind of a convention going on this weekend. It won't look suspicious."

"Aaah," I said. He'd known this all along but clearly chosen not to tell me while he'd been going about his little plan to make a scandal.

"Now you know what you're looking for." He got up from the bed and walked over to me.

"Yeah, but don't we look too young for business people?" I was a little bit uncomfortable because he was now standing in front of me and licking his lips. Damn, why did I immediately have to remember how good his kisses felt?

"I don't think so." He reached out with his hand and moved a lock of my hair away from my face. "I own a company, remember? And if I didn't have magic disease, I'd be definitely attending some meetings."

"Um yeah, I guess." It was still a bit hard to believe that we were technically adults now. I could actually ask my father to give me a spot on the Council, but I'd probably have no power whatsoever.

"Why don't you just leave Michael?" His sudden change of topic caught me off guard. I stared at those gray-blue eyes and didn't know what to say to that.

"It's none of your business who I'm dating," I said.

"You'd be better off without him. He only makes you worry and lose control."

"Oh, really?" I arched my eyebrows. "And why would you say that? Do you want to be my boyfriend or what?"

He didn't say anything but instead leaned in closer to me. I could smell his cologne, and my lips parted a bit. My heartbeat became irregular as I tried to concentrate on anything else but him. It didn't work. His lips were getting closer and closer to mine, and then someone knocked on the door, making me jump.

"Come in," Adrian said, taking my hand in his before I could register what type of element the person outside had. He probably knew already who it was. I heard the door open at the same time I saw a satisfied look on Adrian's face. And then it was too late to let go of Adrian's hand because Michael had walked into the room.

"Ria, I came to…" He stopped in the middle of the sentence as his eyes fell on us. I knew Adrian and I were standing too close to each other for Michael's liking, and holding hands just worsened the situation. I tried to let go of Adrian's hand, but he didn't want to let go.

"We can go to my room if you want," I said.

"No," Michael said, his brow creased. "I just… wanted to check if you were fine."

"Oh, she's great," Adrian said. "She's with me."

"You're not that good company, you know," Michael said, his anger almost palpable in the air. Now I was afraid to let go of Adrian's hand because Michael's element was probably all over the place.

"Better than you are." Adrian smirked. "She enjoys every minute she spends with me… and sometimes even more than that."

"If you say one more word, I'm going to break your neck," I said, glaring at him. I pulled my hand out of his and walked over to Michael. It seemed as if I were walking into the sea, but I tried my best to ignore that feeling.

"Michael, your element," I whispered. "Please."

"Oh, sorry," he said, taking a shaky breath. The feel of his element was weaker but still strong enough to bother me. I closed my eyes for a moment, took a deep breath, and came to stand next to him. When I was sure I wouldn't attack him, I slid my arm around him. Adrian was glaring at us from the other side of the room.

"Come on, Michael," I said, looking at Adrian. "There's nothing for us here."

Adrian crossed his arms and kept looking at me. Michael took my hand, and we went for the door. I glanced back at Adrian and saw something like anger and hurt flash through his eyes, but it could have only been a shadow. I wasn't sure, and I definitely wasn't ready to think about what he was feeling… or what I was feeling. It was much easier to let Michael take me out of there.

My phone vibrated, and I fished it out of my pocket. Of course, the message was from Adrian and it said it was time to go shopping. He gave me two hours to do it, but I knew I'd have to go earlier and faster in order to avoid problems. Being with Michael had already made me feel tired, and a mall full of people surely wasn't going to improve my control.

I gave Michael some lame excuse and only a few minutes later, I was going through things in one shop. A few people gave me strange looks because I was in the men's department, but I did my best to ignore them… and the guy who was trying to flirt with me. I picked dark gray jeans, a white shirt, and a black suit jacket. I was sure Adrian would look good in it, because there wasn't really anything he looked bad in.

I was done way before my time of two hours had run out, but so was he. We met in his room again, and he looked very pleased. That couldn't be a good sign.

"Let me guess," I said. "I'm not going to like what you chose."

"No, you're going to love it." He smiled.

"Oh, I didn't know you're turning into my best gay friend," I said, but his smile didn't falter.

"Don't be silly, Ria. I wasn't going for some bad-looking, fancy clothes. I was going for sexy."

"And that's different how?" I raised an eyebrow at him.

"Only a lover would buy you something like that."

"I'm starting to feel nervous," I said. "Can you show me what you got me or can I go straight to screaming at you for buying something obscene?"

"Why don't you try it out?" There was a wicked grin on his face. He offered me a huge, black paper bag, and I took it, eyeing him suspiciously. I went to the bathroom and locked the door behind me just in case. I could swear I heard Adrian laughing at that. Oh, well. Better safe than sorry.

I placed the bag down and slowly opened it. There was a yellow rose on top, and I picked it up to smell it out of habit. Maybe Adrian had gotten it with the clothes, but I doubted it. But why would he get me a rose? A yellow rose out of all? I placed the rose down on the sink and pushed my hand back into the bag without looking.

I pulled out a smaller bag, which contained something black, and as I inspected it, I realized it was lingerie. Really sexy, lacy lingerie, actually. I wasn't really sure if I should go out to yell at him or reach for the rest of the clothes first. I figured if I went for the rest, it would save me the trouble and I could just yell at him for both at once.

The dress I pulled out was completely black, and for a heartbeat, I thought it was quite normal. But when I put it on, I realized why it required careful underwear choosing. It was a pretty tight dress that felt like a second skin on my body, and if the panties weren't some soft, plain material, they would show underneath. The lacy bra had another purpose, of course, because the front of the dress was rather open, and I was sure that the bra would show if I bent down or something. I looked at myself in the mirror.

Well, it didn't look that bad, actually. I looked a bit older and more serious. The dress was a good mix of sexy and professional, because while it looked pretty plain, the way it hugged itself to my body made it sexy. And it came just a bit above my knees. I looked back at the bag and saw a box I hadn't even noticed before.

Opening it, I found a pair of black high heels. Great. Now I was completely ready to crash a business party. I changed back into my clothes and came out of the bathroom with the rose in one hand and the bag of clothing in the other. Adrian cocked an eyebrow at me expectantly.

"I like it," I finally said. "But I'm not quite sure what the rose is for."

"The rose's for you, Ice Queen," he said. I didn't like the smile that appeared on his face one bit, but that was nothing new.

"For me? I don't see a reason for you to give me a rose, so what's the meaning of it?" I walked over to his closet to place the bag in there. My room wasn't safe enough for things like that, and it was better to have all we needed in one place.

"Infidelity," he came behind my back and whispered into my ear, sending chills over my body. I turned around to stare at his gray-blue eyes. Why was he trying to remind me of the fact that I'd cheated on Michael?

"You're such a jerk," I said. "But you know that already, don't you?"

"I have something else for you."

I frowned. "I don't want gifts from you."

"It'll go nicely with the dress," he said and reached for something in his pocket. I gasped as he pulled out a gorgeous crystal necklace.

"I want you to have it." He took my hand and placed the necklace in it. I stared at the small round crystals, which were put together into the most beautiful piece of jewelry I had seen. It just had an unusual shine to it as the light hit the crystal. And it looked very valuable too.

"Adrian, I can't…" I said.

"Yes, you can." There was a catch in his voice, and then he turned away from me, walking toward the window. I stared at his back and bit my lip.

"Who did it belong to?" I asked after a moment of silence.

"My mother," he said. "She kept it in a safety deposit box. It's one of the rare things I have left of her."

"Adrian," I started to say, walking over to him.

He raised his hand in the air to silence me. "Don't. Like I said, I want you to have it."

"But I can't accept it. You give these things to people you care about. And damn, I'm not even sure we're friends."

I couldn't even say the word *love* in this. Was he feeling something for me? But that was impossible! He cared about no one except himself. As for what I was feeling… I didn't even want to go there. He wanted to tear me apart from Michael for who knew what reason, but I couldn't let him do that.

"Well, I don't care about anyone," he said, not looking at me. "And I never will. So I may as well give it to the girl who was the best in bed."

I glared at him. Of course, it had to be sex. Why had I thought for even a second that he could care?

"I'm flattered." I laughed. "But didn't a certain disease cloud your judgment?"

"Maybe," he said, still avoiding looking at me. I clutched the crystals painfully in my hand and realized they seemed like ice somehow… Adrian's icy heart, that is. I'd keep them as a reminder of that fact, which I often tended to forget for some reason.

"Fine, I'll take it," I said. "But when you do find a new girl, please tell me so I can give it to her."

I left the room because I was sure he didn't have anything else to say to me. As far as I knew, he could be giving these things to every girl. But then he was a bit late since we'd already slept together. As I walked down the hallway, I realized I hadn't spent enough time touching him, because people's elements were dancing in front of my eyes. Great. I stored the necklace safely in my room and then ran outside as far as I could from the building and everything.

Chapter 26

Michael and Paula were intent on going to the Council's building, and I could do nothing else but kiss them goodbye and wish them luck. If only they knew what Adrian and I were about to do. Michael would probably freak out. And not just because I was going with Adrian, but also because we were going mostly unprepared into what could turn out to be a seriously dangerous situation.

Adrian and I were already dressed and ready to go. We looked quite good in our outfits, and I couldn't help but smile that I'd managed to pick out the right thing for him. I'd bought Michael a sweater once and he'd absolutely hated it, but he still wore it sometimes and refused to admit he didn't like it. Adrian would have simply told me if he hated it. Not that I cared, but still.

We didn't do much for our disguises, except Adrian now had dark brown eyes and I had hazel. I put my hair up into a tight bun and figured I didn't look like myself at all. Not that it mattered, though, because for those who didn't know me, I probably looked like hundreds of other women. Adrian looked completely different without those breathtaking gray-blue eyes, and I was sure people wouldn't recognize him even if they'd seen his picture in the news.

There were tons of cars in front of the hotel, and Adrian's Lamborghini was just one of five or six I'd managed to see. People were walking around in expensive suits, formal dresses similar to mine, but not really, and some were wearing more casual combinations such as white shirts with jeans. Adrian and I were strangely fitting in. I had used make-up to make myself appear older than I was, but there were quite a few young girls and they didn't look out of place at all. Honestly, I had no idea why I was thinking you had to be at least thirty to be interested in some kind of business. Maybe it was just that little girl in me who didn't want to grow up and deal with anything serious.

When I came back from my thoughts, Adrian was already out of the car, and he opened the door for me. He gave me his hand and I took it, but only because it was a bit complicated to get out of his car in a dress and high heels. We walked inside as Adrian showed the guy at the door our fake invitations. Apparently, it hadn't been hard at all for Adrian to find those.

We made a circle around the huge room where people were mostly talking or drinking champagne and wine. There were lots of projects on display and people were explaining things about them. Adrian approached one girl and asked something that actually made sense to her because she went on explaining. He asked just because she was pretty. I sighed and walked away, not wanting to see him flirting with her.

"Hello there." I heard a voice behind my back and spun around. There was a tall guy in a black suit standing in front of me. He had green eyes, black hair, and he looked around fifty years old. His element was earth and the glint in his eyes told me he was interested in me, or at least he liked what he saw. Eww! That was disgusting on so many levels that I just mumbled a greeting to him and disappeared in the crowd. Why did old rich freaks usually think they could get hot young girls? Ugh.

Since I wasn't interested in any of the projects, and I couldn't keep up a conversation about anything smart, the party was becoming boring and annoying. I ended up near one of the tables, nibbling on cookies and drinking champagne. I couldn't see Adrian, but he was the one who was supposed to sneak out and go find something, and then notify me about it. If he didn't find anything, then it would be my turn to go. I really hoped he'd find something.

Just as I thought of it, the phone in my small purse vibrated. I got it out and saw Adrian's message. He wanted me to go to the elevator and press -3. Huh, three floors underground. Couldn't be good. I started for the elevator and realized my hands were shaking. Maybe I wanted Adrian to find what we were looking for, but now I was scared. Scared of being caught or something. I didn't know why I had such a bad feeling about this, but I couldn't seem to shake it off.

I slowly went through the crowd, making stops here and there to prevent any freaks from following me. A shiver ran through me as I stared at the group of four people talking. I could clearly see the faces of two women, the profile of a guy, and I could feel their elements. But from the guy who had his back to me, I could feel absolutely nothing. A magic disease carrier... who could see me any moment. I hurried to the elevator, not daring to look back.

I was flushed when I reached the elevator and finally pressed the right button. There was a sign next to the number, which indicated that it was a 'staff only' floor. I just hoped no one was there to see me, or I'd have to pretend I'd pressed the wrong button, which would make me look stupid. I didn't know why I cared about that; I just did.

It was dark and quiet as I walked down the hallway. There were many doors, but it all had an abandoned look to it. I seriously doubted that the thing we were looking for was here. It seemed as if the security were nonexistent, and why in hell would they allow everyone to get to this floor if it was so important?

I found Adrian standing in the hallway to my left.

"Is it here?" I whispered.

"I think it is," he said. "But I can't feel anyone in here, and if there are cameras, I can't see them."

I squinted and tried to find a camera in one of the corners, but I saw nothing. Maybe they were looking at us right now. But no one seemed to be coming our way and definitely no one had come while Adrian had been waiting for me. Maybe they wanted to see what we were going to do.

"I don't see anything either," I said. "Maybe it's not here."

"It has to be."

I grabbed his arm and pulled him close so I could whisper into his ear. "There's a guy with magic disease at the party."

His eyes widened in surprise. "Are you sure?" he asked, and I nodded. "Okay, forget that. He won't come here. Let's check out this place."

I followed him down the hallway, and we carefully inspected a few rooms, but they were either empty offices or storage rooms. Everything was mostly covered with dust and cobwebs. But as we went through one door, we found ourselves in another hallway, but much smaller than the one we had come from.

There were sealed metal doors at the end of the hallway. We looked for cameras or any devices that could trigger an alarm or something, but we didn't see anything. Adrian walked to the door while I waited on the other side.

"There doesn't seem to be anything here except some kind of a device to open the door," Adrian said, and I knew he was as surprised as I was. I walked over to him, carefully looking around just in case I spotted something.

"So how does it open?" I looked at the weird device that just had a screen with red, blue, and green colors flashing behind in some kind of a haze. There were no buttons to press, no keypad, or anything. I touched the screen with my finger, but nothing happened.

"Maybe we should have gouged someone's eye out," I said as Adrian tried to break in with force, but he didn't even manage to make a dent in it.

"Fuck." Adrian was rubbing his shoulder. "And there isn't even a lock to pick."

"Maybe we should break the screen."

"I don't see how that would help, except destroy our only chance of getting in."

"There just has to be a way to open the damn door," I said, observing it carefully, but nothing came to my mind. We tried to touch different parts of it, press, push, pull, but nothing worked.

"How do you open a door that doesn't seem to have a lock of any kind?" I asked.

"You don't," a voice behind our backs said. I froze, and Adrian turned around, surprise written all over his face. He was shocked because we couldn't feel the element of the man who was standing just at the end of the hallway. I, on the other hand, was shocked because I recognized the voice.

"Oliver," I said, turning around. And sure enough, there he was. He was wearing dark jeans and a black shirt, and his short dark brown hair was messy as if he'd just gotten out of bed. His brown eyes bored into mine, and then a smile appeared on his lips.

"Hello, sister," he said. Adrian gave me a questioning look, and I just bit my lip.

"What are you doing here?" I asked.

"Funny, I wanted to ask you the same question," he said, taking a step forward. I backed away because he might be my brother, but that didn't mean he wouldn't do something against me.

"I asked first." I swallowed. Even if he'd suspected it earlier, seeing me now confirmed that I had magic disease. But what I hadn't expected was that he would have it too. I should have assumed that when he'd told me not to tell our parents, but I'd thought I was somehow cursed or that it would pass.

"I saw you at the party and followed you here," he said, stopping a few inches from us. "I didn't know you'd get involved with the most famous of our kind."

He gave a meaningful look to Adrian, who just glared at him, his body tense and ready for an attack or whatever was needed. Obviously, he didn't trust my brother, and I couldn't blame him, because I didn't trust Oliver either.

"Our kind?" I scoffed. "And what would that be?"

"Oh, please," he said. "It's not time for games, Ria. You're as aware of what I am as I'm aware of what you are."

"Great," I said. "Now that we solved that, we can get out of here."

"Without what you came for?" Oliver raised an eyebrow at me. I didn't want him to know what we were doing. But I had a bad feeling he already knew.

"That's none of your business," Adrian said.

"Oh, stop the pretense." Oliver rolled his eyes. "I know you didn't come all the way here just to make out."

"And how do you know that?" I looked at him.

"Because I know what's behind these doors," he said, and I frowned.

"How?"

"I have my sources." He chuckled. "Now, do you want to go inside or not?"

Adrian gave me another look, obviously letting me decide whether we should trust Oliver or not. I considered our situation for a moment and figured we had nothing to lose.

"Well, I don't see a way to get inside," I said.

"That's because you're not looking carefully, little sister," he said.

I didn't like him patronizing me, so I crossed my arms and glared at him. "If you're so smart, why don't you tell us how to open it?"

"Do you see that screen with lights inside?" He pointed at it as if I were blind or stupid.

"No, it's too shiny to see it." I rolled my eyes.

"You don't have to be sarcastic." He smiled. "But that thing there can read your element. That's why the other forms of security aren't necessary. You can open Pandora's Box only with an element."

Huh, that kind of made sense if you wanted to keep away magic disease carriers... and who'd want more to get those files than them? Oh, wait, we fitted the profile. But both Adrian and I had an element. I wasn't sure about Oliver.

"So, anyone with an element can open it?" I asked and realized that didn't make much sense. That would be way too lame security.

"No," Adrian said, frowning. "It must be some kind of a detector. It can make a distinction between elements, can't it?"

"Bingo." Oliver clapped his hands. "It can recognize the owner of the element like we can. At the moment it opens only for four people."

I still had trouble recognizing people by the feel of their element, but Adrian could do it without a problem.

"Great," I said. "So there's no way we can enter!"

"Four people?" Adrian asked. "What happens if they die?"

"Their close relatives' elements could open it, because the genetic code is similar, but it would take a few of them," Oliver said. "But there's no way all four would die at the same time. They are kept apart all the time. Not even their closest friends always know where they are. A new element is introduced in the detector as soon as a new person takes over the duty after one of them dies."

"Like I said, no way to enter." I sighed. "Can't we just leave before someone comes?"

"They won't come so soon to change it," Oliver said. "They don't know one of their guys is dead."

I just stood there, trying to process what he'd just said. He passed me by and went for the screen. The next thing I could hear was the loud crack the door made as it parted. I started to feel dizzy. My brother had killed someone and taken his element.

"There you go." Oliver spread his hands as if he'd just performed a miracle. I thought I was going to be sick. Adrian had already used the opportunity and gone inside.

"You killed someone," I said, glaring at my brother.

"So?" He smiled. "You got the door open."

"How did you know the guy would be here?" I asked, because I knew an element couldn't stay more than a few hours inside of someone else's body.

"He wasn't here," Oliver said. "They would never keep any of them here so no one could borrow the element. But we're not just magic disease carriers, sis. We're better than that. We're element preservers."

"Better, huh?" Tears filled my eyes. "You're a murderer!"

"Are you always so judgy, sis?" He flashed me a smile.

"You're insane."

"You, too, if you dare to say that to an insane person."

"So for how long can you keep someone's element inside of you?" I asked.

"Not sure," he said. "None of them expired yet."

"How many people did you kill?" I nearly choked on the words. I didn't care anymore why we were here or what Adrian was doing inside.

"Only three. It seems like we can keep only one of each kind of element. And since I already had fire, I had to fill in other spaces. You don't know how much more quiet it feels in my head after getting the last one."

The last one. So he didn't know about ice. Oh, shit. He mustn't find out, or he'd try to kill Adrian too. I wasn't sure if that would work since they both had the disease, but the risk was simply too big. And I didn't even want to think how I felt about the fact that three people had died because of my brother.

"Isn't the police looking for you then?" I asked.

"Nah, they don't know the guy's dead. Besides, even if they do, they'll look in Italy first because the guy was there."

"What about the other two people?" I asked, and his face darkened.

"No one will ever investigate those two," he said. "Actually *they* hope no one finds out."

"Ria! I need your help here!" I heard Adrian's voice just as I was about to ask Oliver who 'they' were. I hesitated for a second and then went inside the room. This wasn't the right time and place to have serious talks with Oliver anyway.

There were just too many files to go through, and after we managed to take as many of them as we could carry, I realized Oliver was gone. It was better like that, even though I had a lot of questions for him. He'd reappear; I had no doubt about that. We sneaked out through the garage and used the stairs to reach the parking lot where Adrian's car was. Luckily, there was no one around to see us, and even if someone had seen us, they would have thought we were participating in some project.

We didn't speak at all until we were safely back in Adrian's room. The papers ended up thrown on the bed because we didn't really know where to put them. I was still shocked about what had happened. Michael and Paula still hadn't returned, but that wasn't unusual since they'd had to travel to the Council's building first and would need the same amount of time to return. That at least gave me some time to come up with a good story. I really wanted to tell them the truth, but maybe that wasn't the best option.

"You're tense," Adrian said as he came behind my back and ran his hands down my arms. I was staring through the window, motionless.

"All of this with my brother is insane," I said. "He's insane."

"So it's true that we can keep all four elements inside of us and they won't be gone?"

"According to Oliver, yes," I said. "But I don't know if it's a good or bad thing, because however you look at it, someone dies."

"Yeah, but we're trying to stop that, right?" He was clearly trying to cheer me up.

"Yeah, I guess." I definitely didn't want to kill someone, but what were the chances that we could come up with a cure? I didn't know. The government was obviously hiding so much from us. Maybe they did it with a cure too. It felt as if we were surrounded by a cloud of secrets... everyone's secrets, including my own.

"It's going to be all right," Adrian whispered into my ear and pulled my dress down a bit so he could kiss my shoulder. I closed my eyes, trying to clear my mind of all thoughts, but that seemed impossible. I badly needed something else to focus on, anything. I turned around and met Adrian's gray-blue eyes.

"I don't want..." I started to say, but Adrian placed his finger on my lips. He let his finger slide down all the way to my necklace. I gasped, feeling the desire stirring inside of me. Why was he doing this to me?

"I... can... make... you... forget..." he said, emphasizing each word with a kiss. His offer seemed so sweet and tempting, and I really wanted to have a moment of happiness in all this mess.

"No strings attached," he added with a smile. Funny he said that when we both knew it wasn't like that. If we did this now, there would be no going back. And it would only confirm we felt something for each other. Did I really want to deal with that later?

He looked at me as I ran my hand through his black hair. Then I pulled him to me in a kiss so hot that it burned through me more than my element.

Chapter 27

Michael and Paula had safely returned in the middle of the night and they were empty-handed, of course. I ignored Michael's message because there was no reason for me to be awake at that time, especially when they'd left me behind. The only reason that I was awake was that Adrian and I were going through the files we'd taken from Pandora's Box. There were some nice DNA analyses, and I was sure Paula would kill to get her hands on them. Okay, maybe not literally kill, but she wanted them pretty badly.

There was just too much text in the files, so we simply stored them safely in Adrian's closet. But we had at least found out that the first case of a magic disease carrier who could keep an element for more than a few months was more than sixty years old. How nice of the government to cover that up, and I was sure there was more of it. There had been experiments carried out on magic disease carriers just like there had been on Adrian. From what we could read, he was very lucky to have gotten out of that place alive.

"What do we do now?" I asked, running my fingers through Adrian's hair. I was sitting with my back pressed against the headboard, and Adrian was resting his head on my lap. It was one of those calm and relaxing moments we used to have sometimes.

"Wait for the dawn?" He looked up at me. That wasn't what I meant, but I guessed he wasn't ready to talk about it.

"Why?"

"I don't know," he said. "Because we have nothing else to do?"

"Actually, we have things to do." I laughed softly. "We just don't feel like doing them."

"True."

And we ended up waiting for the dawn. It was hilarious because we actually ran to the window to see the first rays of sunshine appear on the horizon. Then we went to sleep and didn't wake up until someone knocked on the door.

This time Adrian actually waited for me to get dressed and fix my hair the best I could before he opened the door. But damn, it was still early and I looked like a raccoon with those dark bags under my eyes. There was no surprise on Alan's face, but he didn't seem happy. I tried to leave, but he stopped me.

"I need you two for a moment," he said.

"We don't need to hear the same speech again," Adrian said. "Besides, we're going to be late for breakfast."

"It's not that," Alan said. "And there's plenty of food in my office."

Great. Just what we needed. But part of me wondered why Alan wanted to talk to us if it wasn't about how our romance was forbidden or something. Had someone recognized us yesterday and notified him? I hoped not.

We were sitting in Alan's office a few moments later, and really, the desk was full of food. I took a doughnut just to keep my mouth full. Maybe that way I wouldn't have to answer any questions. But damn, that doughnut was tasty.

"Would you like some tea?" Alan asked.

"Sure," I said, and Adrian just shook his head.

"Ah, yes, I forgot. You don't like tea." Alan smiled at Adrian as he poured a cup for me. I gratefully took the cup. The tea smelled good and warm, and I needed something to drink after the doughnut.

"What do you want from us?" Adrian asked suspiciously.

"I need your opinion on something," Alan said. "It's a university project, actually."

"I didn't know our opinion would be of any importance to anyone, especially not to you," Adrian said. I was happy with simply chewing on another doughnut and being quiet.

"Well, it's important," Alan said, annoyance showing in his voice. "We're planning to expand the building and maybe build the biggest university library ever. Or would you rather have a gym, a pool, or something like that? We're open to suggestions."

"How about a beauty parlor?" I grinned, knowing that he meant something educational and not stupid, but I couldn't help it. As I said it, a wave of dizziness passed over me. Maybe I shouldn't have eaten so fast.

"That's a suggestion, yeah," Alan said, then he frowned at me. "Are you feeling okay, Ria? Do you need some air?"

"No, it's just..." I started to say, but the dizziness was back.

"Maybe we should continue this conversation outside," Alan said, getting up from his chair. "The weather is nice and I could show you where we could build."

Adrian looked at me, his eyes filled with concern, and I gave him a reassuring smile. My dizziness would pass once I was out of the damn office; I was sure of it. I figured I could stand up just fine, so we started walking toward the park.

"We can do this some other time if you aren't feeling well," Adrian said to me, but I shook my head at him. We so didn't need to have a meeting with Alan some other time again. And I wanted us to be done with this so we could meet with Michael and Paula and tell them about the files.

Alan was talking about something as we walked farther and farther away from the university. I was impressed by all the beautiful colors in the park and all around us. The sky was so insanely blue and the sun caressed my skin, making me feel warm all over. But how was that possible so early in the morning? I didn't know and I didn't care. The world was beautiful... until I realized we were in the middle of nowhere. How had we gotten here?

Then I remembered we must have gone all the way to the empty fields that were behind the park. There was really nothing interesting there, except endless grass and trees and… Adrian suddenly grabbed my hand and pulled me back. Alan was still walking in front of us, and I looked at Adrian in surprise.

"Go back!" he said, his voice low and urgent. "Run! Get the fuck out of here!"

I was staring at him, not understanding what he was saying.

"I wouldn't do that if I were you," Alan said, and I looked at him. Then my eyes fell on the gun in his hand, which was pointed at us. Oh, shit.

I gasped, and Adrian stepped in front of me, shielding me with his body. What was going on?

"It's me you want," Adrian said. "Let her go."

"No," Alan said. "I need both of you."

We had to solve this somehow, and I reached for my element. I didn't care if I burned the guy alive. My life was in danger, along with Adrian's. Only there was nothing… I couldn't do it. I panicked.

"I can't feel my element," I choked out.

"Of course you can't," Alan said. "I spiked your tea."

Oh, crap. That was why I felt so dizzy and lightheaded.

"What do you want?" Adrian asked. I wasn't exactly sure it would be better if I were the one covering him, since I couldn't find a reason why Alan would want to kill me too. But madmen usually didn't have that kind of logic.

"I know it was you who stole the journal," Alan said. "And I know where you both were yesterday."

"I don't know what you're talking about," Adrian said. I just stood there in shock. How had Alan found out about all of that?

"Don't play stupid now, Adrian," Alan said. "Because I know you aren't. You wanted that journal, and I don't know how you found out about the hotel, but somehow you did. And don't try to deny it because your car was there. I know because I put a tracker on it."

Oh, nice. We were royally screwed.

"Ria wasn't with me," Adrian said.

"Ah no? But I don't know any other girl who would be willing to go with you, and you two seem to be pretty close anyway," Alan said. "Actually, I bet she's the mysterious blonde who was never seen again."

"So what? My car being there doesn't prove anything," Adrian said. "Besides, since when do you mind me taking my lovers to a hotel instead of bringing them here?"

"You're right. There's absolutely no proof against you," Alan said. "And I know your father's journal actually belongs to you, so there's no real harm. I'm suspicious about the hotel, though, so let's just try something."

"Try what?" Adrian asked. I was glad that no one had noticed we'd broken into the Pandora's Box. We'd managed to close the door, and since no one could open it, there was no way someone could find out about it so soon. Besides, there were so many papers in there that I didn't think they'd notice something was missing even if they looked. I was sure no one would risk the life of one of those remaining important people just to check.

"Stop me or I'm going to shoot you both," Alan said and he didn't look like he was joking. Adrian took a step toward him, but Alan just shook his head.

"Not like that." He smiled. "Use your head, boy."

I wasn't sure if I should do something, but nothing came to my mind. My mind actually wasn't in a good condition at all, and I wondered what kind of drugs Alan had put in my tea. I hoped Adrian knew what Alan wanted.

Adrian glanced back at me for a second, and then ice started forming rapidly all over the gun and going for Alan's arm. Alan dropped the gun and started walking toward us. Should we run? But Alan didn't have the gun anymore, and if he'd wanted to do something with his element to us, he'd have done it already. If I'd been confused before, I had no idea how I felt now.

I think Adrian still debated what to do when Alan reached us and hugged him. That was so weird that I thought I was hallucinating. Adrian seemed taken aback too and he just stood there unmoving.

"I knew you had an element!" Alan said, finally letting go of Adrian. "Your mother would be so proud."

"What the fuck?" Adrian said my thoughts exactly out loud.

"Sorry, I just knew you'd never admit it if I didn't do something extreme." Alan smiled as if nothing had happened. "The gun wasn't even loaded."

I glared at him. So he'd drugged me, threatened my life, and all for what? To get a confession from Adrian? I was so pissed I thought I could rip his head off right there. Adrian probably guessed my thoughts because he reached for my hand and squeezed it. Or maybe he was afraid like me that he would lose control and kill the guy.

"You sick son of a bitch!" I yelled. "I can come up with a million other ways to find out! This was just... fucked up!"

Adrian had to use both hands to stop me from going for Alan's throat. Even though Adrian was touching me, I could still feel the faint flickering of Alan's element, and I wanted it. And no, it had absolutely nothing to do with my disease… well, I wasn't sure. But Adrian was too strong for me and I couldn't get free. Damn! Some weird mix of an angry scream and a cry escaped my lips. I was losing it… badly.

"Ria, sorry." I heard Alan's voice as if he were somewhere far away. Things were becoming blurry in front of my eyes. I blinked, but it didn't help much.

"What's wrong with her?"

"Ria! Ria, no!"

Chapter 28

I woke up with the worst headache ever. I could feel someone's warm body pressed against mine. Someone was holding me, and we were lying on something. I wanted to open my eyes, but my eyelids were too heavy. Voices. Someone was talking, and I tried really hard to hear. But the words didn't make sense to me at first. I wanted to move my arm, but I couldn't. Oh, crap. Was I in some kind of a coma? But how the hell could I think so clearly? It must have been that drug Alan had given me. Me and drugs simply didn't go together. Maybe I should get a job as a drug tester so they could find out about the weirdest side effects.

"So you're saying I have a sub-element." I recognized Adrian's voice.

"Yes," Alan said. Ugh, why was that stupid psycho still around?

"How many of these are there?"

"A lot. But so far we know of ice, dust, smoke, mist, and whirlwind," Alan said, and I could feel Adrian's body stiffening. He'd probably thought he was the only one with a strange element, and this whole thing surprised him a lot.

"You could have told me, you know?" Adrian said bitterly. "We wouldn't be going through all of this if you had."

"Sorry, but I couldn't tell you because I'm forbidden to tell anyone who could tell someone else," Alan said. "And I'm sure that whatever I did, you wouldn't tell me the truth."

"Of course I wouldn't," Adrian scoffed. "But I could tell someone else now."

"No, you won't do that," Alan said. "Because then I would have to tell the Council about you, and they'd take you back... *there*."

Ah great, threatening Adrian with the worst thing ever. How nice. I really wanted to at least punch the guy in the face. The feeling in my fingers returned a little, but now I didn't want to move because I didn't want them to know I could hear them.

"Why did you say my mother would be proud?" Adrian asked.

"Because her family had water a long time ago, and ice is a sub-element of it," Alan said. "Your father's side of the family had earth. And I believe ice is much cooler than dust."

"Huh," Adrian said. "But my parents didn't have any element or a sub-element?"

"No."

"Why not?"

"I don't know," Alan said.

"How can I have it then?"

"I don't know," Alan repeated, probably not pleased with not having an answer. "I believe some people might know, but they're not sharing. Not with me and not with anyone."

Maybe the answer was in those papers Adrian and I had stolen but had been too lazy to go through.

"So, basically, Ria is in this condition because of your curiosity?" Adrian didn't hide the anger in his voice. Well, I wanted to know that too.

"Yeah, but I didn't know this would happen," Alan said as if that were a perfect excuse.

"That's a lame excuse," Adrian said. I opened my eyes and tried to sit up.

"Now that's an understatement," I said. "You deserve an award for the biggest idiot on the planet!"

"Glad you're awake, Ria," Alan said, but he didn't look like it. I could see relief flash through Adrian's eyes.

"Whatever," I said. "I would appreciate it if you could leave the room. Now."

"All right," Alan said, going for the door. "See you later."

Adrian waited for him to leave and then kissed my forehead.

"You don't know how glad I am to see your eyes again," he said. That was such a weird thing for him to say. I didn't have nearly as gorgeous eyes as he did. Once I'd hated his eyes, but that had been before I saw there was more to them than just coldness.

"Can't get rid of me so easily." I smiled.

"Good," he said. "Can you walk?"

"Um, I can try," I said. "Why?"

Deep inside of me something froze, because I was afraid he'd cast me away again. I didn't want to get hurt.

Not by him. Yeah, somewhere along this whole thing I had admitted to myself that I had feelings for him.

"Your brother wants to talk to you," Adrian said. "He's in your room."

It didn't matter whether I could walk or not. I had to get to my room as soon as possible. If Oliver wanted to talk to me, he wouldn't leave until that happened. I didn't want him here any longer than necessary, because I wasn't sure he was exactly safe to be around. And if Paula or Michael came to look for me in my room and found him... well, things could get ugly.

Oliver was sitting on my bed, looking as charming and dashing as usual. I wondered how many girls had gotten the disease from him, because I didn't think he cared at all about that. He smiled at me as I entered the room. I locked the door just to make sure no one would interrupt. This was something between my brother and me only.

"Hi, sis," he said. "Had a rough day?"

"You could say so," I said, walking over to him and sitting down. Maybe it was stupid, but I wasn't worried about my safety. He wouldn't kill me for no reason.

"I assumed you had questions, so I came," he said.

"Hard not to have questions when so much shit happens."

"True." He sighed. "So, where do I start?"

"I want to know why we have the disease when our family has a pure element."

"I've been trying to figure that one out for years," he said. "It's just a bad genetic code. And it all comes from our great-grandfather."

"Let me guess, it's Jonathan, right? From our mother's side? The freak who might have signed some kind of a deal to kill anyone who married a person with a different element?"

"Yeah," he said, "it's him. And guess what? The bastard had magic disease."

"What?" I frowned. "But that's impossible!"

"Impossible is nothing." He smiled. "I thought you learned that when you got the disease."

"Okay, so how did we both inherit it and not anyone else?"

"Jonathan married a woman who had a pure element. And I believe he killed only people with a pure fire element, so when he had children, they inherited fire, and somehow his wife didn't get the disease from him. It was all fine for them, but the faulty genetic code carried over even though it was too weak to show," he said. "Then it came all the way down to us and it showed, but slightly altered, so we kept our element."

"Yeah, but aren't the chances of us getting the actual disease too low?" I was not nearly as good at genetics as Paula, but I still remembered some things from high school, and the percent of genes inherited from great-grandparents wasn't exactly that significant.

"Look at it like this," he said. "Great-grandpa has the gene for the disease, grandma gets part of it, then our mother gets part from each of them, and then we get a part from all three of them. I guess that's what it takes to develop the disease."

"Huh," I said. "I've no idea."

"Well, I'm not an expert on genealogy, but it seems possible."

"Okay, so we have the disease because of stupid genetics. Got it. But I don't get why our great-grandpa would want to keep a pure element when he didn't have one."

"You sort of answered your own question."

"How?" I raised an eyebrow at him.

"He didn't have his own element, but he wanted his family to have it," Oliver said. "He obviously figured out that his idea could work. And when it actually worked, he decided to protect that, so he found an effective way to keep the family's reputation of a pure element intact. Having a family with a pure element was very important and could make you rich, if you knew how to play things out right."

"Great, he wanted power and money just as anyone else. But who was the idiot that signed the damn contract, and how can it still be in effect?"

"He had a lover. Her name was Rosalia." The corners of Oliver's lips went up. "She had magic disease, too. He had a family with her, too, and he made that deal with her. He'd give her money for killing off anyone from his family who dared to marry a wrong person, and she could also collect the element. It was a very tempting deal for her and she took it. Her children continued it and so on. As far as I could check, the money is in a bank in Las Vegas, and there are a few safes in there. Each safe opens by using an element detector similar to the one you saw on Pandora's Box. So no one can open it by killing off some random person because it opens only for family, and you can open only one safe in a week. That's to prevent the person from opening more safes with the same element. By that time the stolen element usually vanishes."

"But that happened ages ago. How did they have that kind of technology?" I asked, wondering how I hadn't even suspected that my own family would be so unusual and complicated.

"Oh, Ria. Those things have been around for a long, long time. They aren't really technology. They're normal locks enhanced with an element," he said. "You can't even imagine how many things they kept from us. It's like a whole new world."

"Great, we're related to a family of assassins," I said sarcastically. "How cute! I can't believe they're actually having no problem with killing someone related to them."

"Hey, they don't even know us. Besides, money and an element, especially a pure one, are very good reasons to off someone without remorse."

"So, why aren't they just killing us off? It's not as if our great-grandfather would know."

"There must be someone else included in the deal, but I haven't figured that one out yet," he said. "Someone who controls what happens."

"When did you realize you had the disease?" I asked.

"When I was thirteen." His face darkened.

"Did you tell anyone?" I wondered what I would have done if I had gotten it so early.

"Of course." He smiled sadly. "I told Mom and Dad."

"And?" There had been many days when I just sat there and thought how my parents would react if I told them. I would have done it actually, if Oliver hadn't stopped me. I hoped he'd had a good reason.

"They sent me to an institution," he said. His words hit me like a brick wall.

"What?"

"They didn't want me around. They said I was dangerous and let the Council decide what to do. But since Dad is on the Council, his vote saved me from being killed instantly. They sent me to one of their research centers and did all kinds of experiments on me. One of those included killing a person with an element."

I stared at him with wide eyes. No, that just couldn't be true. My parents would never do such a thing. They were kind and loving and…

"You don't believe me," he said, a spark of amusement in his dark brown eyes. "Well, it's true. If you want to check, go tell them about yourself and see what happens. They'll say you went somewhere fancy to university, just like they said I had gone to some fancy school."

"How could they have done this to you?"

"Can't ruin the family's reputation, right?" He smiled. "Besides, they didn't want me to end up killing my baby sister. That would've been tragic. They actually believe I got the disease from some girl, so that's why they told you what they know about our great-grandfather. They can't afford to lose you, too. You're the only thing they think they've got."

"Why did those people force you to kill someone?" I realized Adrian had actually been lucky.

"They wanted to see what happens." He shrugged. "I have no idea what they were doing behind that glass."

"That's horrible," I said.

"I didn't want to kill those two people. I really didn't," he said. "I fought it at first, but then they used many elements around me and I couldn't control it… I couldn't. I was too weak."

"How old were you then?" I placed my hand awkwardly on his shoulder. It felt so weird to hear all that coming from him.

"Sixteen," he said. "I escaped when they were preparing me for another experiment. I should have killed them, but I didn't. I just knocked out those who were in my way. I've been running since then. But because I could tell everything to the press, after a few years they agreed to forget what had happened and promised not to hunt me. Mom and Dad needed me because they couldn't use the school story anymore, so I had to reappear. It all went back to normal just because I promised not to talk. And I've spent the rest of my time researching and hiding, since I know the only reason they made a deal was because they couldn't catch me at a place where they could dispose of me. Guess why I'm avoiding family meetings."

"So they know you can keep an element?"

"Nah, they don't," he said. "I managed to hide that since they didn't expect it."

"But there's a file that says there was some guy who could do it, so I think they do know it's possible."

"That guy was killed, and they think it was an isolated case, so it's not something that would naturally come to their mind," he said.

"Wait, but that would mean they think you're probably killing people!"

"They don't care as long as the people I kill are anonymous," he said. "It's all about politics, power, money, greed… they don't care about us as long as they're getting all they want."

"Why are they hiding all of this from us?" I asked. "There seems to be so many magic disease carriers that it's almost impossible that no one knows about it."

"Well, some people do know," he said. "But everyone's afraid, and magic disease carriers aren't really of a trusting nature. Others prefer to turn their heads the other way."

"I don't know what to say." I sighed. I hated the world I lived in. I really did.

"There's nothing else to say." He looked deep into my eyes. "Only survival, sis. Only survival matters."

"So is there some magical cure for the disease, or are they waiting for it to mutate and become something entirely else?" If we already had magic disease carriers with their own element and those with a sub-element, maybe soon there would be no magic disease carriers. Maybe elements would just… heal back to normal.

"No cure yet," he said. "And I'm not a clairvoyant."

"Great. I wanted to know this and now I feel like ignorance was much better."

"Sorry, sis," Oliver said in a tone that clearly showed he wasn't even a tiny bit sorry, but he didn't have a reason to be. It wasn't his fault. He'd been forced to become what he was, and it wasn't strange that he was a bit insane from all of it. Except...

"Did you kill that guy just to get inside Pandora's Box or because you couldn't take it anymore?" I looked at him.

"I killed him because he was the one who approved experimenting with magic disease carriers and because he was an asshole who raped girls," he said, his voice ice cold. "The Box opening thing was a bonus. Oh, and talking about the Box, I hope you got all you needed. But you two kids are pretty reckless and... just stupid. I had to get your fingerprints off that damn screen and the door. I don't understand why you're trying to pull off movie stunts when you're clearly not ready."

"Um, thanks." Well, crap. We'd been much more careful the first time. I couldn't believe we actually hadn't thought of using gloves. I guessed we hadn't because it hadn't fitted with our outfits. How stupid indeed. I didn't even want to think what would have happened if someone had found our prints there.

"So, will you keep sitting on two chairs, or have you finally made up your mind?" Oliver gave me a wide grin. I frowned.

"I'm not..." I started to say. "That's none of your business!"

"You're right." He raised his hands up in surrender. "Just decide before they decide for you and you lose them both."

"You're pretty smart for a crazy brother."

"Nah, I'm just pretty." He laughed.

"Do you think I can live with someone even though there's a risk I could kill him?" Naturally, I wouldn't have asked him that if Paula had been available. But I couldn't talk to her about this.

"If you truly love him, then everything's possible," he said. "Even living with him. Jonathan didn't kill his wife or his kids."

"Yeah, but he killed other people and had a lover!"

"Well, if you really want something…" He smiled.

"I don't know." I ran my hands through my hair. "Will you stay here for a while or disappear again?"

"Hard to say. If someone realizes I'm here, then I'll have to disappear. But if you need anything, just call. Of course, try to say as little as possible over the phone."

"Thanks." I'd never thought there was another reason why I hadn't been seeing him a lot.

"Well, I have to go," Oliver said, getting up. "If I'm not wrong, your friends are coming here."

"Oh, great." I sighed. Just what I needed. But it was high time I'd dealt with this mess.

"Good luck, sis." Oliver smiled at me and walked out of the room.

Chapter 29

Sure enough, Paula and Michael were in my room in no time. And they spent twenty minutes yelling at me for not calling them back, not wanting to explain how I got the papers, and who knew what else. I'd stopped listening.

"Look, the important thing is that we have the papers," I said. "It doesn't matter how and where I got them. You didn't listen, so it's not my fault."

"But Ria, you could have…" Michael started to say, and I shook my head.

"Just, please, don't say I could have gotten hurt because I'm going to kick you out of here," I said. "You two did something stupid, too, so don't come to me now with stories about doing risky things."

"But you have…" Paula said.

"I'm not discussing it!" I said, reaching for my phone. "I'm going to tell Adrian to bring the papers here so you can investigate."

"Adrian, huh," Michael said, rolling his eyes. "You just can't live without him, can you?"

He was jealous and he had every right to be. I didn't say anything, and Paula looked from me to him and then back.

"I figured something out," she said, and at that moment, Adrian entered the room, carrying a backpack full of papers. He was a bit surprised to see Michael and Paula, and he walked over to us, dropping the backpack down.

"It's all here," he said. I took the backpack and gave it to Paula.

"Thanks," she said. "I'll see what I can do with it."

"I'll help, too," Michael said.

"Sit down," I said to Adrian, because he was the only one standing. The rest of us were sitting on the floor, on my awesomely soft carpet. He just shook his head and remained where he was.

"Okay, we need to talk about our plans," I said. "Summer vacation is almost here."

"You're right," Michael said. "You have two exams left, but I'm sure you can pass them. So, I have something in mind …we could spend summer vacation together somewhere, away from other people."

"Um." I hadn't expected such an offer.

"Yeah, you can do that." Paula smiled. "What I was trying to tell you before… I figured there are some pills that Michael could take so you could be together without problems."

"No, I can't make you take some pills," I said.

"But it's fine!" Michael said. "I tried them and nothing bad happened."

"You tried some weird pills?" I frowned. "Are you out of your mind?"

"I love you, Ria," he said. I glanced at Adrian and saw his expressionless face. He didn't want to give anything away. And Michael had to be the best boyfriend on the whole planet. I couldn't believe someone would be willing to do such a thing. He'd do all that for a girl who couldn't even stay true to him. Guilt was starting to eat me from inside.

"What are you going to do?" I asked Adrian. I needed to get some sign from him or anything. I wanted to know how he felt about this.

"I'm going to stay here," he said. "It's not as if I'm going to have a vacation if I want to finally pass the damn exams."

"Do you need me here then?" I asked, my pulse speeding up. It was almost as if I'd just asked him if he loved me. I needed the answer.

"No," he said. "Actually, I should go now."

And just like that, he walked out of the room. I sat there, barely breathing. He didn't need me. He could do without me. Why the hell did that hurt so much?

"Wow, the world suddenly seems like a better place," Michael said, glad that Adrian had left. I was too dumbfounded to say anything.

"Ria, don't you worry," Paula said. "Everything's going to be fine. We'll take care of you, and I won't stop until I find a cure. Then you and Michael can be happy."

It sounded so good. I could have a perfect boy, who would forgive me for all the shit I'd done no matter what. A boy who loved me so much that there was nothing he wouldn't do for me. And I knew he'd make me happy. I could be that selfish bitch Adrian had accused me once of being, and I could use Michael to have everything I'd ever wanted. Maybe even a family, because I was sure Michael would come up with something to solve that too.

"So, what do you say?" Michael asked.

"I…" I started to say, my mind in overdrive. I was feeling something for Adrian, but I wasn't sure what. Maybe it was just the disease thing. But what if it weren't? What was he feeling? Could be something. Could be nothing. What if everything he had done to me was because he didn't know how to deal with what he was feeling for me? I realized I was trying to find excuses for him. God, how sick was that? Yet I could be right.

"I love you, Michael," I said," but I can't come with you. I'm staying here."

"But why?" Michael asked, looking as shocked as Paula.

"I'm not ready to risk anything," I lied. It had become so easy to lie to them that it scared me. But I needed time to figure out what I wanted. "We can go some other time when I learn how to control myself better."

"But…" Paula said.

"No more buts!" I said. "I've made my decision."

"Well, if that's what you want…" Michael smiled. "I don't mind staying here with you."

"Hey, it's not as if I'm going to go somewhere without you two, so I'm staying, too." Paula laughed. "You just can't get rid of us!"

"No, I can't, can I?" I said. Michael reached out for me and we kissed. Everything was perfect again. I got up and they both looked at me in surprise.

"Where are you going?" Paula eyed me suspiciously.

"I'm going to tell Adrian that I'm staying," I said, wondering if they would try to stop me. Michael's face became serious, but he just nodded.

"Go, we'll be waiting for you here," he said.

I was walking down the hallway, thinking what I would say to Adrian. I figured he didn't have to know the true reason why I'd decided to stay. I wouldn't let him use my own feelings against me again. Just that was easier said than done. A wave of extremely cold air stopped me dead in my tracks. What the hell was going on?

I shivered and rubbed my hands down my arms. There was only one place from where all this freezing air could be coming. And that meant something was wrong. I ran to Adrian's room, using enough of my element to keep my body warm. The door to his room was slightly ajar, which was surprising. I couldn't feel anyone's element inside, so I swung the door open and nearly screamed as the cold air threatened to come into every pore of my skin. The room was completely covered with ice and Adrian was nowhere to be seen.

###

ELEMENT PRESERVERS SERIES

DANGEROUS
RUNAWAY
DIVIDED
NO ONE
RESTLESS
INDESTRUCTIBLE

Also by Alycia Linwood

HUMAN

TAINTED ELEMENTS SERIES

More information:
www.alycialinwood.weebly.com

Printed in Poland
by Amazon Fulfillment
Poland Sp. z o.o., Wrocław